The Telling

Also by JOHN WESTON

JOLLY

The Telling

A Novel

by

JOHN WESTON

DAVID McKAY COMPANY, Inc.

New York

THE TELLING

Library of Congress Catalog Card Number: 66-13787

MANUFACTURED IN THE UNITED STATES OF AMERICA

VAN REES PRESS • NEW YORK

for the siblings:
MARTHA, OMER, BILL, JIM

This story is fictional as are all
its characters and situations

The Telling

One

Bᴜᴛ that's just exactly the hell of it, as McCarron
would have said had he known—as indeed he did say when
it was too late to restore life and sanity. *Jesus,* he was to
say at the last, I might have known.

This day, however, the last of the unclouded ones, Peter
McCarron, balding, forty-three, with a chest that if he was
unconscious of it tended to slide rather lower on his rib
cage than it had ten years ago when he came back here to
Tigerstooth, idly flapped a cloth into the corners of the
window, knocking away the summer's collection of dust and
cobwebs. He paused, and with his knuckles on the sill,
leaned and watched the morning brighten the river and the
shadows slip down the jagged east hills as the sun rose.

From up here on the hill he could see the town, or most
of it, yellow in the sun with the railroad cutting it this side
of the green river. It would be a good day. Hot, of course,
there wasn't any way around that, but good. The summer's
rest was fine, in a way; it gave a chance to catch up on some
things—some fishing, some laziness, some thinking, it gave
a person's stomach a chance to settle—but McCarron always felt and welcomed a new shape to his shoulders when

September rolled up and it was time again to get down to the business of school.

This morning, early, before any janitor or secretary or teacher broke in to stir them up, he had walked through the halls and into some of the rooms and smiled at the smells of fresh-waxed school, returning to mind the exact odors that he had known all his life, or nearly so—all but the five years before he began going to school and the years before he came back to Tigerstooth.

And so with the whole town. Summer is a time to be got through, a bare-nerved, tight-lipped time when the hundreds and hundreds of railroad freight cars every day clank into town to be iced and switched and inspected and made up into trains and pulled out in the right directions all day, all night, when there are jobs for every male who wants one, when whatever society there might be, including churches, shuts down because the women concentrate and sleep or do not sleep according to the pattern of the men and boys, when sleep at best is a fitful, sweaty tossing because in the desert it is almost as hot at midnight as at noonday. That is why at the end of a summer Tigerstooth stretches panting like a cat lapping the river, flung down in disarray, exhausted, dusty, as from a three-month trek over the desert to this final asylum where the swift cold water cuts the land. That is why by the first of September the town that has watched the last of the fruit cars stop and go away has begun to square its shoulders, and the frenzied look in people's eyes gradually gives way as sleep catches up.

The year, as opposed to the summer, begins then as school begins, as the few college boys and girls board the passenger trains, as the mothers sew and shop for school clothes, as auxiliaries and fraternal clubs shake out their social plans for the nine-month season.

For McCarron there was one more trial to face before he would know if the year would be a good one. The settling-in, he called it. Meeting the last of the new teachers. The curse of being the school principal in a town like Tigerstooth. No one would stay but a year or two; they came and stayed awhile and went away before a person had a chance to get a grip on things. Now, thinking about it, McCarron removed one of his hands from the window sill and gently pushed it against his stomach. Coming by mail, so to speak, the way they did, you never really knew what you were getting until it was too late. Not that most of the time they didn't work out all right, but you had to face it. And things had been going pretty smoothly for the last three or four years. Nothing to really rock the boat.

There was a kind of excitement to it, of course, at least so far as the town was concerned. Something like watching someone else untie a Christmas box from a relative whose taste couldn't always be trusted, wondering if he'd be pleased or disappointed or flabbergasted by what he found in the box. Anyway, that's how McCarron saw it. The town watching him undo the red ribbon. Whatever came out would please them just fine. It was different when you were principal, when you were in charge, when you had to live for nine months with whatever came out. Well, he hoped to God.

McCarron stood awhile longer, staring down into the town, watching it fade in the piercing sun. It was his town as much as anybody's, he supposed. He had grown up there, his folks still lived over there in one of the yellow houses, and he would just as soon drift out his years there as anywhere else in the world—now that he'd seen some of it.

The thought held a certain peace but was otherwise neither bleak nor bright. With Karen gone, with brown youth passed, what matter where the stomach goes bad or

3

hair falls? What did matter was the getting through it and beyond it to where there was no watching, no caution to be expected, no public minuet to step to.

Tigerstooth, only as old as the railroad bisecting it, did not spring up, as the stories say, overnight, but instead grew slowly, every flat building, each yellow railroad house emerging painfully as if birthed from its yellow mother, the arched giantess, the depot, where once but no longer Fred Harvey dined and slept the trains' passengers who were willing, gladly, to believe any circumstance an improvement on the choking heat of the coaches. And life was like that, at least before the war when McCarron grew there. A long, taut pull upward like lifting a heavy, good weight with straining neck tendons toward something vague and green that would flash at age nineteen or twenty or twenty-one with quick brilliance brighter than the sun.

McCarron smiled to himself whenever the picture recurred. *Jesus.* It was hard to tell when the lifting up toward became suddenly a holding up against.

And maybe it was a good thing the war came when it did to chop out and fling away those years. Maybe it was better to think of it than to know. Well. Take a year at a time. This year would be here, be okay, and be gone soon. Another step. Things were organized, ready to roll. That much, anyway, they could say for him; in ten years he had done his part to roll things along up here on the hill just as much on schedule as they did down there with their goddamn railroad. And by tomorrow afternoon, by the time he had finished the interviews and orientation of the new ones, he'd know.

He straightened up from the window and put his hands to the small of his back. Some of them—the new ones— would be up this morning to talk, to settle in. The others,

4

tomorrow. They would be converging on the town now, coming across the desert from all directions, not knowing, poor bastards, that the desert is a chance even at night, a far greater one by day. That's why he couldn't really blame them for staying only a couple of years, although it didn't make his job any easier. The desert is for the end of life, the coming down, not the going up. It warms old bones but it only heats young blood hotter that is, God knows, hot enough to start with. Either that or it burns them out and that is a sad thing, too, even if it makes things easier to control, to keep track of. And when it all boils down, control, normality, team spirit is what keeps a school or a railroad or life going; it helps the getting through.

McCarron dropped his dust cloth onto the window sill. He ran the tips of his fingers over the clean desk top as he passed it. He let himself out into the other office, the actual office, the public one. There beside his desk, her red nails entwined primly on her lap, sat Miss Dunbar, Home Ec I, II, III, and IV, looking about as she had whenever she had appeared there during the last ten years, during all the time he'd known her.

"Oh," he said and stopped. The door behind him was already closed.

"Good morning," Miss Dunbar said. "And Good Year!" Her lips the color of her nails cut across her face.

McCarron stepped around her to the desk. "Hello, Patricia. Good Year." He sat at the desk and frowned, wondering if he had sent for her. He watched one of her hands lift and sweep up the loose hair from her neck toward the gray bun.

"You look fine, Peter. Did you have a good summer?" she said. "I mean, you know, restful and all?"

Get on with it. "Yes. Yes, thank you. A good summer. And you?" The secretary should have given warning.

"Oh, fine. Just fine. But I'm ready and anxious to start in again. Aren't you?" She touched the edge of her pointed glasses.

"Yes." He waited.

"Well," she said and squirmed forward in her chair. "I wanted to see you before you got too busy. It's about that refrigerator in the Home Ec room."

"Oh." McCarron sat back in his chair. "See Mr. Jaffrey. You'll have to see him."

Her red nails entwined. "But I thought maybe if you—"

"No, the vice-principal's the one to see about equipment."

"Oh."

"Is everything else all right? Your schedule?"

"Yes. Oh, yes, that's just fine."

He stood up and moved around the desk toward the door. "And the new stove?"

"Oh, lovely." She followed him to the door. "By the way, Peter, I thought maybe I'd try out the new stove today. Just test it, you know. A little lunch, I have these two little steaks like you like, and maybe a nice salad and I could make a pan of biscuits, all the supplies are checked in, and a cold dessert—"

He opened the door, the one that led directly to the outside of the building. The sun fell into the room. "No, Patricia. I will be very busy. Interviews, and things. You know."

"But you have to—"

"Maybe the vice-principal. Yes, maybe Mr. Jaffrey. And he could check that refrigerator."

He watched her walk across the narrow court into the next building. Why do the ones who teach about sewing and grooming let themselves look like someone's charwoman? he thought while he watched her pink slip flap down in back against her calves.

He closed the door and stood with his back to it. His secretary came in from the outer office. "Mr. McCarron," she said, "the Lions Club called."

"The Lions Club?" He frowned.

"Yes. You remember. They wanted you to come down today and, you know, tell them a few words about the year."

"Oh. No. No, I can't go today." He moved back to his desk. "You know I have things to do up here. Interviews today and tomorrow, Mrs. Nalor."

"But it's during lunch. You have to eat—"

"No. Get Mr. Jaffrey. Tell Mr. Jaffrey he'll have to go. I—tell them I have to be here."

"All right," the secretary said. "I'll tell him but I—"

"Thank you. Wait."

"Yes, sir?" She turned back toward him, her hand on the door knob.

"Mrs. Nalor, have any of the new teachers got here yet? Are any of them out there yet?" His voice dropped although the door was still closed.

"No," she said. "It's still early."

McCarron watched the door close behind her. Still early. That's what everyone thinks, Oh, it's early yet, There's plenty of time, take your time, it's too early, they all say. Jesus, doesn't anybody ever catch on? When you have to run things, when you have to get things started and you don't know what material you've got or where or when it will someday stop, there isn't time to say It's early. And I get an old maid at thirty-five who wants me to check her refrigerator, who gets her rocks from a new stove. And I get Jaffrey, the horn-rimmed American Idiot, for help, with

7

his goddamn stanine and IQ charts and Reading Comprehension and Verbal Expression and who knows what all. Probably a menstruation calendar for every female in this school, including Patricia Dunbar. *Jesus.* How much easier to coach a football team. Or for that matter, take a company over the top. At least then you know.

McCarron pushed down a lever on the intercom box on his desk.

"Yes sir," he heard the secretary's voice.

"Mrs. Nalor, did the Lions Club say what they wanted me to talk about?"

"Well," the voice said, "usually, the teams, you know—"

"Yes. All right. Tell them I'll be there."

While he waited for the first interview and as he rehearsed in mind what he would tell the Lions Club that they would be pleased to hear, he wandered back into the connecting room and stood again before the single window that looked out and down upon the town.

That there should have been a town there at all was against any plan of nature. Nothing was there to recommend it except the river whose beauty faded ten or twenty yards from its banks where the determined desert began. That the tribe of Mojave Indians lived by the shores beneath a wide strand of tamarack trees was nothing to speak for it either. When the first railroad surveyors arrived there years ago, led, or rather driven, by Lewis Coran, steel-limbed and steel-bearded, their number already diminished by the treachery of the black hills and the sand, they limped to the edge of the river, dropped the reins of their horses, and sank down among their gear beside the cold water. For four days they watched the Indians on the opposite bank. On the fifth day, sufficiently recovered by their rest, they concluded that no harm would meet them at the hands of the tribe on the other shore. They were right, certainly. These Indians were grown peaceful and lazy. If they had desired to do the white men harm they had nothing any longer with which to do it, nor much inclination for any movement at all beyond their twice-daily fishing.

So the surveyors passed on into the desert and a few years later the track crews arrived at the green river. They built a bridge to span it and laid their ties and steel tracks directly through the center of the tamarack grove.

When finally the first black engine howled across the bridge and into the grove, the Indians decamped to a spot a hundred yards up river where they remained until in 1938 small green-roofed white cottages were built for them by the CCC. The tribe morosely agreed to move into the cottages after first knocking out all the glass from the windows. There they raised dogs to supplement their fish, and from there they sent certain of their children to Tigerstooth schools. Despite periodic official orders, they continued to burn the bodies of their dead. Several times in a year, before sunrise, the sweet pall of smoke rose from the Mojave village and floated over the town.

Tigerstooth is a railroad town. Fred Harvey built his great yellow stucco hotel and dining room a half mile from the river. Around it, gradually spreading more south than north, the town groaned into life. Before the first generation had passed, two churches, one Methodist and one Catholic, came into being, and some said the town was ripe for a Baptist one. On Sunday mornings following services, Catholics and Protestants alike drifted into the dark coolness of Fred Harvey's dining room to eat salads and plates of fried chicken. Some returned at evening to view the trains' passengers and to comment on the fashions of the bedraggled ladies who alighted often on the point of prostration,

9

round-eyed with disbelief that they had ever in the first place agreed to venture west.

There were four saloons facing the railroad tracks before there were those two churches. The saloons stretched in a row, their solemn façades unbroken except for stairways that led to second-floor hotel rooms where crews laid over on trips. The half-dozen regular inhabitants of the hotel rooms were seen only occasionally, drifting in twos, gauzily, brazenly, some said, about the grassy Harvey Park in the afternoon. Eventually, as all things end, the professional whores' rooms were gradually taken over by yellow-bearded old men who, no longer able to work for the railroad and left without family, drifted back into the rooms to live out their days before fading blue-flowered walls where once they spent more joyous nights.

The professional women, grown old and rich themselves, moved to the salt air of Carmel or San Juan Capistrano. Visiting train crews, by glancing over the rosters of crews working out of Tigerstooth, could quickly spot which of their brothers' wives were that night sitting alone and lonesome in their yellow railroad houses. The same marvelous ingenuity that laid the first tracks over the villainous desert and spanned the wide river was passed on into the sons and grandsons.

When the trains began to pull their own dining cars the Fred Harvey closed. The once magnificently glittering dining room was stripped of its Remington prints and its carpets and chandeliers. The carved double doors were replaced with steel ones wide enough to allow the passage of baggage wagons that rolled and scraped against the red and gold papered walls until great scars of white stucco showed through. The mahogany furniture of the upstairs rooms was replaced by long rows of steel cots on which laying-over crews slept after midnight when, by law, the four saloons closed.

Over the years the town spread slowly. Streets, then paved streets, were laid out following the curve of the railroad. Trees were planted and grew reluctantly beside iron fences. Small, neat houses were built and owned, used and allowed to fall into ruin. A new and large grocery store opened, and a hardware store. J. C. Penney bolted up his yellow and black sign. A café began, then another. A movie house. A filling station. A third doctor, a lawyer, a city hall, a library, a drugstore. When the third generation was borning, a second schoolhouse was built, and the old Mexican stucco one became a high school.

There was little difference in the school or its subject matter for the first years. The obscenities in the boys' restroom encroached higher on the walls and the accompanying illustrations became more biologically accurate. A box of sanitary napkins lay open on a shelf in the girls' restroom. Old initials and hearts on the desks were superimposed with newer and deeper ones. Otherwise, much the same teachers remained diagraming much the same sentences, singing much the same songs, and rapping exactly the same multiplication tables.

The war changed all that, of course. All the boys who could legally or by lies choose the Air Corps over the schoolroom did so. The male teachers too old or sick for the army left the school for the railroad. All housewives who could, took the wives or sweethearts of the desert-training soldiers into their homes and charged them handsomely, the while keeping a bright eye cocked to their own daughters, most of whom managed to slip away with at least one soldier long enough to become impregnated either by him or by the tales he murmured of Dallas or Los Angeles or Scranton. The daughters' accomplishments attested that that pioneering ingenuity was visited upon granddaughters as well as grandsons. To find beds to lie upon in a time when all beds were rented by the two-weeks or the month, or car seats to spread upon when automobiles and their use were rationed by fathers, and entirely unowned by soldiers, or as final resort, ground to grovel on, in a part of country infested with cactus and night snakes and sand, required a deft mind. That a town the size of Tigerstooth would have at its fullest no more than fifty white girls of age and inclination to give away on bed, car seat, or sand what they had learned to call their virginity for whatever reason—call it love or patriotism or a sweet itch—to an army of thousands who had but few passes of twelve hours' duration from their brutish maneuvers, accounted for the present generation of twenty-four- and twenty-three-year-old Indians of lighter complexion and narrower hip whose children, however, were darker, already casting away their grandfathers' gift or curse as if the outer skin had been sloughed off as a snake slides from his in spring.

When the war was over, a few of the town's children returned with their own children to restore the decayed yellow houses and work on the railroad. The town had grown more prosperous through clever handling of its strategic position on the railroad by the men and its strategic position as the nearest town to the army desert corps by the women. A third elementary school was built. Additions were tacked onto the old high school in Desert Tones of rust and yellow and pale green. Teachers' salaries were made attractive enough when combined in a brochure with selected colored photographs of the river, its fish, boats, and water skiers, to attract certain new teachers for sometimes as long as three years.

Two

Today there are three routes by which Tigerstooth may be approached, not counting the railroad and the river. One highway winds from the north and west, vaguely parallel with the railroad, over a hundred miles of utterly motionless and depressing desert, bisecting at one ten-mile stretch a corner of the actual bivouac area of the desert soldiers. They left, in what must have been boredom worse than incessant actual war, their tent sites and company numerals and the dates—1942, 1943—marked out in gray volcanic rock and white sun-doomed rock, which can still be read with a shock from speeding cars. Whatever grows there now does so without sign.

From the south and from the east the other two roads converge on the town, passing through barren-hilled country only faintly less ruined than the other. The traveler from the south catches glimpses now and then of the river sliding among its own spawn of green reeds. His hope rises dimly with each sight and then numbs as the next barren hill humps beside the road. The traveler from the east actually crosses the river on a high steel bridge from which he can see straight down into the green water. The water is wide but not deep there. Even then he does not see much of the river because it curves just above and again just below the bridge. Immediately the highway ducks on into sand hills out of sight of the river but following it in a wide sweep toward the town.

It was by these ways, the three highways and the railroad and the river, that five people—four of the teachers that McCarron was waiting for and the wife of one—approached Tigerstooth this September 1st. There were others, certainly, for the town lies in the path of nearly anyone who wishes to cross from the northwestern part of one state into the middle-eastern part of the other. For the five, however, Tigerstooth was the destination and in part, at least, the destiny. If McCarron could have been forewarned this day of what he would begin to sense shortly and learn for certain in the in-rushing weeks, he would have hummed less and sweated more as he dusted and gazed out upon the town. If the town itself could have known, the excitement would have run higher than ever.

Of the five, only Baker Steinhart rode in the relative comfort of a Santa Fe chair car in a silvered train above those same blue rails over which had arrived, thirty and forty and sixty years ago, the panting, dusty ladies and the mail, and the dressed chickens, packed in ice, that Fred Harvey served in cold salads. It was from the window behind him in the club car that Baker first saw the town. Running along the edge of a long hill the train curved toward it ten miles away, and lower. He half turned toward the window in time to see the slanting sun glance over white and glass before the train itself blocked his view.

"God," he said. He faced across the car again where beyond the windows the constant sand color slid by, flicked now and then by a close-standing mesquite bush. The two cubes of ice clicked against his teeth. He set the glass in a round chrome holder on the round chrome table by his knee. He drew back from the table and pointed stiffly to the glass.

An aged porter moved from behind the bar with a fresh drink, which he exchanged for the glass of ice. Returning to the bar, he washed the glass, dried it, and set it on its shelf, making tiny adjustments of the two glasses nearest. He wiped a spot of water from the simulated mahogany bar top, folded the cloth and then leaned forward on his elbows.

"That's Tigerstooth," he said.

"Don't tell me," Baker Steinhart said. He stopped the glass before his face. He inspected his hand, then shifted the drink to his other hand and peered closely at the first. It was a thin, flat hand with long fingers, the nails clipped square on the ends. No black hairs grew between the second and third knuckles as one would expect.

"George," he said.

"John," the Negro man said.

"John, what makes blue veins on my hands, do you suppose?" He unbuttoned his shirt cuff. "And on my wrists?"

The other man said nothing but lifted one of his own hands briefly, then placed it back flat on the bar.

"Well," Baker Steinhart said, "you're smart." He buttoned the cuff of his sleeve. He took the glass in his right hand again and drank from it until the ice slid forward against his teeth.

"Why?" the Negro man said.

"What?"

"What am I so smart about?"

The man with the blue-veined white hands frowned. He closed his eyes against the sliding brown sand beyond the far windows and shifted his eyes so that when they opened they would see the glass, or the table, or the floor. He opened his

15

eyes. He pushed himself up from the chair and held on to a chrome pole and swayed with the train. He focused on the next silver pole farther along the car. He lifted his free hand and said, *"Vox et praeterea nihil,* George," and then he reached for the next pole.

From the green-dimmed upper level of the observation car he watched the town creep closer. Viewed from this last rise of desert before the tracks swung down to become not glistening lines but black rails in a setting otherwise marred and made colorless in the relentless heat, the town appeared for a moment lovely and pale against the verdant river-swath and beyond to the fierce gray hills that rose or rather hung above the sand of no color and below the deep ribbon of blue that rimmed the desert like the glazed edge of a bowl.

He slipped his thumb and two fingers up to the knot of his tie. One side of his mouth curved upward. So, as the books say, it had come to this. Fifteen years ago Professor Mackey had said it would. Only it had taken somewhat longer than the old man predicted. Since then there had been the Fulbright and the two years in Rome and the one in Paris. Then the plane back to the United States at the insistence and agreement of the two governments, one position after another, a year here, a half-year there.

"You have a fine, ah, mind," the old professor had said. "Perhaps even a brilliant one. But you haven't the faintest respect for it."

"Yes, sir." Baker sat opposite the old man in his dark and cluttered office on the second floor of the Hall of Graduate Studies. Every spring Professor Mackey called into his office certain few students whom he had watched from beneath his woolly brows if they began to spark glints of promise as undergraduates. Precisely what good the command visit did, no one ever knew, but to disregard the summons would have been considered so wide a breach of decorum that the consequences of it were beyond consideration. Each young man of the chosen, when his time came, entered the book-stacked room and coughed as gently as possible into the smoke of the old man's meerschaum.

Professor Mackey first noticed Baker Steinhart as a sophomore when the tall boy gangled into his Chaucer seminar. Although the course was reserved for seniors, the boy sat at the long table each day nevertheless, and smiling sardonically, outstripped the older students from the beginning. He spoke in Middle English in class and wrote the exams in Rime Royal—exams he was not required to write at all. Professor Mackey handed back each paper without mark or comment. But from then on he watched the boy smile lopsidedly through one class after another. Even as a senior, when the young man only rarely attended classes, he overshadowed his competitors.

As he talked, Professor Mackey shifted papers and books about on his desk searching for matches. "I wish you well, Steinhart. Maybe you will come to sense what you have and appreciate it. And what the University gave you."

Baker crossed one leg over the other. "And what is that?" he said.

"Do not be impertinent!" the professor rasped. The tufts of his white hair stood out above his ears. "That is precisely what I mean. You have neither respect for yourself nor me nor the University."

The old man gave up his shifting of papers on his desk and lapsed into a muttered tirade of the sort he ordinarily reserved for lectures on Herrick and Sucklow. He reviewed for Baker Steinhart that young man's growing reputation as a heavy drinker and trouble-maker. Baker was surprised

17

and amused that his private life was evidently less private than he thought. Since Mackey made no mention of it, he assumed that he had not received notice of his forty-eight successive hours spent in a New York City jail for throwing a martini over ice in the face of a headwaiter in one of that city's more dolorous restaurants and for screaming "Bitch!" at the bartender who called the police. However, the night he was discovered breaking into the Sigma Nu liquor cabinet at a neighboring college was known of. That incident had caused him very little more than a bruised face and certain bitter notoriety. But it caused the fraternity, of which he was not a member, three months' probation for illegal possession. Professor Mackey voiced the suspicion, unproved, that he was involved in what he termed the Infernal Orgy that had rocked the university to its Gothic foundations two years ago—an affair that caused the outright expulsion of eleven men students and the public defloration of seven town girls. That Baker had nothing to do with the balance of chastity among the girls was exactly right. However, there was one ruddy-cheeked blond boy who was less virginal after that night than he had been when he entered the university from his parents' spotlessly groomed farm in the Pennsylvania hills.

"And there is the matter of your dissertation. Another term and the degree will be completed. If you drop it now, you know, you'll never return to it."

Baker shrugged. He was counting the number of diamond-shaped panes in the window behind the old professor's head.

"The Fulbright to you will mean little else but an opportunity to carouse with foreigners," Professor Mackey grumbled on. "You have no right to accept it."

Baker Steinhart rose first, a practice not recommended during a Mackey conference. "I have accepted it, sir," he

18

said. He smiled with one side of his mouth. "Thank you for your unflagging confidence, Professor." He tightened the knot of his tie.

"I wish you well, Steinhart," the old man said. "Perhaps you will see what you have before you destroy it." He dismissed Baker with a wave of his hand and fell to searching again for matches.

Although the old professor never knew it, being five years retired and three dead, Baker Steinhart had returned to the university once, after a dozen years. Not to take up the dissertation again—that work, so far as it had progressed, had been sold years ago to a wealthy young man taking his junior year abroad—but to spend a day in cold February leaning against the iron gates or the Gothic stone walls watching his successors leap the snowbanks and slush and run through the traffic lights or pass by in twos loudly discussing Sartre or Sarah Lawrence, their striped ties flying loose back over their blue blazers, their bare ankles red from the cold in flapping loafers. In the eyes of some of them when they passed he saw and recognized the frenzied, controlled glitter.

So, Tigerstooth at last: population, four thousand. Approaching irrevocably, the train began to slow even as it passed the mound of smoldering blackened desert that was the town's refuse dump.

Along the highway from the south a metallic blue convertible piped. From the radio tuned loud to best the rush of wind and tires a monotonous and illiterate female voice collided with guitar music. "You'll come 'round to see me when she's went and left you onct again," the voice wailed before it was lifted by the wind and flung out of the car.

The man who drove the metallic blue car did so calmly, his right hand hooked over the steering wheel at the wrist, his hand and fingers hanging beyond the wheel. His left elbow rested on the edge of the door. He beat his palm against the wing window frame in time to the music. "And then we'll both be sorry for what you done," he harmonized.

The sun burned down on his shirtless shoulders, wide and meaty and thick from front to back, first from the six or seven years on the Galveston docks, then the four college football years, which had been a way to get through school but which he was happy to be shut of. He was thirty. For most of the last season he had come from the games glassy-headed and surprised. He went on to the beer kegs in the dark mountain park, nevertheless, and before long the surprise left his head among the muffled comradeship of his younger teammates and their girls.

One of those girls, too, was surprised and then indignant. Two, actually. The young one and the woman ten years his senior whom he had married three years ago for what reason he could not remember. She was indignant only that the three hundred dollars in the savings account she had built he drew out for the younger girl who wept hysterically when he gave it to her, reminding her that her father, being himself a doctor, could easily arrange for her. He had returned to the Galveston docks. For eleven weeks of the summer he had worked and written letters and signed papers. He saved enough money to have his Ford painted and to drive the fifteen hundred miles to Tigerstooth where, his contract said, the first half-month's salary would be awaiting him.

On the rear seat of the metallic blue Ford rested a black guitar case. Stenciled in white on its top were the initials B.D. embraced by quotation marks.

Five miles down the green river from Tigerstooth Angela Morton Deek laughed at the man who was loading her seven suitcases into the boat for which she had that hour traded her car.

"You sure about this?" he said.

"For the tenth time," she said, "I'll be fine."

"Don't know nothing about this here boat. Not to say the river."

"It looks like a simple, calm river to me."

"It ain't, though. It's tricky."

She ran her fingers up the back of her head and lifted her blond hair. "Don't people drive on it all the time?"

"Yeah. Fishermen, but they—"

"Well." She held to a piling with one hand and with the other reached to slip off her high-heeled sandals. "If they can, I can." She stepped into the small open boat. It tipped and she shrieked and grabbed the man. When the boat settled he stepped back from her hand.

"Which way do I go?" she asked.

"To Tigerstooth?"

"Yes."

The man shook his head. "That way," he said. "Follow the river. It's the next town, only you can't hardly see it from the river."

"I'll find it," she said. "Do I just push this?"

"Yeah. Until she starts. Then that gear lever there. There."

"Oh."

"That's forward, neutral, or back. Steer it just like a car."

Angela Deek gave the wheel a short twist one way then the other. She laughed. "Do I have to drive on the right or the left?"

The man stepped from the boat onto the weathered dock that ran fifteen feet out over the water in front of the blue and white boathouse with the words, "Boats and Bait,"

21

lettered above the door. He looked down on the blond head of the woman, who appeared more dumpy from that angle. He shook his head again, slowly. "It don't matter," he said. "Stay in the middle. They'll go round you."

She pressed the starter and the engine caught with a pop and quickly settled into a high, sustained roar. Blue exhaust rose from behind the engine. The man lifted a loop of rope off a peg on the dock and dropped it over the bow of the boat. With his foot he pointed the bow away from the dock. He put his hands into the back pockets of his pants and watched.

Angela Deek grinned, then frowned at the lever by her side. She bit her lower lip and pushed the lever. The boat started forward and headed out into the main channel. She turned the wheel sharply and let the boat slide around facing upstream as it picked up speed.

She laughed aloud as the wind caught her hair and billowed it in a mass of short, wild curls.

When she had gone far enough up river to be out of sight of the boat landing, she turned to make sure. She swung the boat across the river toward the western shore, then back again so that the rear skidded and dipped lower in the water for a moment. She held the wheel steady and gripped the side of the boat as it spun around dizzily, tilting. She laughed and pointed the boat back into the river, upstream.

Holding the boat steady with one hand, with the other she pulled up her yellow linen skirt as far as she could, then bending forward, reached to unhook her stockings. She lifted each knee, one after the other, and pointing her toes, peeled down the damp stockings. She patted them into a small mound on the leather seat beside her. She opened the buttons on her blouse and ran her thumb along the top edge of her brassiere so that the air felt cool to her wet skin.

22

Angie Deek could and would show them a thing or two. Even at forty. Give her an even chance to get her wits about her again and she'd show that pissant Fred Deek and his purse-faced attorneys that Angela Morton Deek, for all they said, would—well, she would show them a thing or two. It would be months, maybe a year, before they found her in this godforsaken country, and by then, if they'd only give her a while to catch her breath, she'd think of a way just as cleverly as she had fooled them this time.

The air above the river was both warm and fresh. A few days in this sun would restore the color to her skin, the color that the months of sanitarium had removed drop by drop and painfully. The smell of the river reminded her suddenly of a gentler time of slow-winding creeks and dogwood. She frowned to remember the time, but could not because before the picture came, a new odor on the air slipped her mind as faintly in another direction.

She spun the boat around once at full speed in the green river and laughed. The wind billowed her hair in short, wild curls.

From the east, by the road that crossed over the silver bridge, Jake Grantham, B.A., $\Delta\Sigma\Phi$, ΦBK, and his wife Anna Margaret approached Tigerstooth. He drove with one arm propping the white cloth top of the old but sixteen-coats-of-black-lacquered car. He wore white tennis shoes, dirtied, with one small hole on the outside edge of the right one. The back collar button of his madras shirt was not buttoned. Now and then with his free hand he pushed his black-rimmed glasses back up onto the bridge of his nose and touched lightly the fraternity badge over his left breast pocket and returned his hand to grip the car top in a single

23

gesture as smooth and unconscious as an aged priest making the sign of the cross.

Beside him sat the brown-haired girl, two years younger than he, twenty-three she was barely, whom he had married three months ago, two months after her pregnancy began. From the beginning he had thought of marriage with her, but as something reserved for a time when he might actually crave the corral marriage built. Theirs was to have been a *relationship* unencumbered by mores or morals that societal discipline flings around whatever young people it can ensnare. Even those, like himself, who have known for at least the last several years that they have something to say and will say it just as soon as the best medium is sorted from the rest. Perhaps, after all, a year—at most—in this wretched town would give him time to settle the direction of his thoughts.

"There's the river," he said.

From the edge of his vision he saw her lift her chin but not her body to look down into the river.

"God. Look at that green. That's pure viridian," he said.

She settled back to watch the road again. She tapped her cigarette on the frame of the open wing window three or four times. "Yes," she said.

"You crying again, for Christ sake?"

She tapped the cigarette. "Yes."

"For Christ sake."

The baby was her goddamn fault. You would think—anyone would—that a girl who wore her hair long like that and smoked like that would never allow herself to get pregnant. Of all the girls who went through college involved—well, not involved, but participating—in good, free relationships, he would pick the one who either didn't know enough not to get pregnant or didn't care enough.

24

"Look, the place can't be that bad. Sure it's small, but there'll probably be all kinds of things to do."

He exchanged hands on the steering wheel. With his right one he lifted the long hair off her neck and pulled her closer.

"You'll get to know everybody right away. That's something." He ran his hand down the inside of her blouse. "Nice," he said.

"I'm sweaty." He removed his hand. "How can anything live in this heat?" She cranked the wing window open farther and flipped her cigarette expertly with thumb and middle finger. The way she handled a cigarette had been part of the first fascination of her. Perhaps it was nothing more than the reality that she nearly always held one, or that she held one to her mouth a moment longer than anyone else would have before she said hello that night they were introduced in Emil's studio, where she sat in fluid stillness, crossed-legged on the floor much like one of Emil's elongated brass-rod figures. Then and even to the moment two months later in Emil's studio when she agreed wordlessly to his taking her, she seemed older, much older, than she seemed during the act itself when she wept some, or now that they had lived together for three months as husband and wife. But even that first afternoon when he had finished and she lay straight and brown on Emil's couch, she asked first for a cigarette. She lay there and stared at a red mobile near the ceiling and smoked, lifting her arm to her mouth and back to rest on the floor, until he grew embarrassed by his own nakedness and behind her drew on his shorts and his tight, tan trousers.

Jake Grantham wiped his palm on his thigh and changed hands on the steering wheel again. The many-coated black car rose with the road at the last cactus-spotted hill and dipped beside the Tigerstooth cemetery toward town.

25

Up on the hill, in the white, arched main building of the high school, McCarron leaned on the window sill again after a long good day and watched the sun shadow the yellow houses. In a while it would be time to drive down the hill and across town to his parents' house where his mother would be expecting him for the taglierini supper that in their house and most others marked the first of September, the beginning of the year.

Three

THE five met that night in Mrs. Hampton's dining
room, the Tea Room, she called it. The room seated no more
than ten or twelve persons at one time but that was as many
as Mrs. Hampton ever expected anyway, because although
the hotel was three stories high so few people any more, especially so few travelers, preferred the gentility of a hotel to
the splendid impersonality of the seven motels. Nevertheless,
she who undertook the Elite Inn and Tea Room upon her
husband's death could expect to feed a few each evening, a
duty she presided over with what nearly anyone could suppose to be Victorian license.

The hotel, situated decorously a long block from the
yellow depot on what was now the principal street, served
as the hub of activity for the town's older ladies and thereby
the whole town. Not that any but a few ladies dropped in for
tea after Sunday morning services. In fact, to view the visible
activity of the hotel where old men snoozed in leather chairs
beside the massive grand piano would be to think there was
no activity at all. To think so, however, would be to overlook
Mrs. Hampton's agile memory of all residence telephone
numbers and the several hours each day in which she had

27

nothing at all to do but conjure those numbers from her desk set well back in the lobby facing the wide front windows from which she would sometimes entreat, would will, the long-dead form of her husband to return and float soundlessly across the same rose-patterned carpeting he had bought new for the hotel when he married her and moved her from her parents' home across town to this that would be not only her bridal suite but her sole home from that day on. Her home through the five years of their life together while she never knew when or what to expect of him but also never tired of listening for his muffled step across that rose-patterned floor that led to their three rooms opening off the lobby.

The war touched them, too, in an especially furious way. Their hotel stood half-empty. Reba Coran Hampton saw the last of her inheritance slipping away into mortgage payments at a time when beds, much less rooms, were going at premium rates, because Charles Hampton was a moral man. He would rent no rooms to soldiers for the night, nor to soldiers' sweethearts—or wives, even, whose avowed purpose was to exhaust themselves as nearly as was possible during a twelve-hour pass beneath the sunburned bodies of their men. He would stand impervious to their entreaties, to their proffered double and triple rates, to their tears, their threats, their proffered bodies, too. He called them whores and campfollowers one and all while Reba, at his back, clutched her throat, clutched it in much the same way she did the night she watched the young corporal, desperate, tired to death of the sun and the marches and the gun practice and smell of his own sweat-whitened clothes, slowly, furiously, beat Charles Hampton to death with a copper urn in the hotel lobby while the old retired railroaders craned around the high-backed leather chairs.

After that Reba ran the hotel, doing many of the white sheets herself so that no other young soldier would be denied, for any reason she could help, the feel and smell of clean muslin beneath him whether to sleep on or fornicate in. When the last of the desert troops moved out, to Africa most believed, and the town began taking account of its labors, Reba found she had substantially regirded her finances to nearly the level at which she handed them over to Charles at their marriage. By the end of the war, at age thirty-five, she had settled into a kind of bosomy spinsterliness that belied an interior of that same purposefulness that led the first Coran in the West to return along the route of his surveying, laying claim to certain miles of seemingly worthless land on which the entire town of Tigerstooth now rested.

Adjoining the dining room, beyond a heavy drape of green velvet, was the Santa Fe Room, announced as such in Old English letters above the door. Around the corner, above the street entrance the message was stated more directly: Santa Fe Bar. Mrs. Hampton owned the Santa Fe Bar, too, because it had always been there, but she did not enter it, ever, during its hours of operation. She appreciated its contribution to her own and the community's life, however, and kept in touch through telephone calls to Ned-John, the moon-faced Mojave who operated it for her.

It was to the Santa Fe Room that Mrs. Hampton directed Baker Steinhart almost upon his arrival that afternoon. He had intended to ask for a dark room and sleep.

"I'll bet you're one of our new teachers," Mrs. Hampton had said.

"Oh, God," he had said and asked her what was beyond the green drape.

It was there just at dark that he introduced himself to

Angela Deek, who appeared through the green drape, refreshed and sunburned and flattered by the electric candle-lit room. Baker would have preferred talking with Ned-John had Ned-John anything to say. As it was, he had about decided either to face the truth of what he already knew in his mind his room would be or face the evening heat and find a movie.

He scooped his change and his glass from the bar. At the woman's table, where she sat with her back to the near sconce, he said, "Bon soir," and held out his hand.

"Oh," she said and laughed. She took his hand briefly in hers. "I'm Angie Morton Deek," she said.

He sat opposite her at the small table and methodically emptied his pockets of change, lighter, and cigarettes. "I'm Baker," he said.

She ran her fingers of one hand up her temple into her hair. "How do you do, Mr. Baker."

"Yes," he said. Then he said, "Steinhart. Baker Steinhart."

"Oh," she laughed. She reached a cigarette from his pack, then put it back and took one from her own purse. She held it just before her lips and watched him. She took up the lighter and struck it.

"Do you live here, Mr. Steinhart—Baker?"

"I am about to. Starting tomorrow. God, how can you drink that garbage?" he said.

"This? Why, I always have one. That is, my husband and I—he's Doctor Fred—Frederick—Deek of Nashville, you know. Well, we always drank one Old Fashioned every evening before dinner. Although," she laughed, "I should add that I'm not really Mrs. Frederick Deek any more. At least, I don't think I am. I haven't really seen him for I don't know how long and anyway—"

"Anyway, it's garbage."

"What?"

"The drink." He watched her hold the toothpick-impaled orange slice and maraschino cherry aside with one finger while she drank.

"I'll show him," she said.

"Who?"

"Ha. Never mind," she said. He watched her squash the cherry in her side teeth quickly, with relish, her eyes rolling up slightly. She looked toward him across the table and smiled. When she smiled, the flesh around her eyes wrinkled becomingly. Her teeth were white and straight, if too much upper gum showed.

"So you're going to live here, starting tomorrow. Well, so am I. In fact, I may begin tonight." She laughed, putting her fingertips to the low point of her peasant blouse at the spot where a suggestion of cleavage began. "What will you do here?" she asked.

Baker lifted his highball glass and turned it, watching the ice. "Drink, probably," he said. "And teach French and Latin to the Indians."

"Teach! Don't tell me you're a teacher," she laughed.

"Anywhere else in the world the idea wouldn't be so bloated with humor." He rattled the ice in his glass.

She leaned across the table conspiratorially and placed her hand on his. "So am I," she said seriously. "English."

"Well, I guess that sews up the foreign language department. I don't suppose you speak Mojave? No." He withdrew his hand from under hers.

"Isn't this wonderful?"

"What?"

"Our teaching here. I mean, here we are. I feel better

31

already. Believe me, I had all kinds of visions about coming out here."

"Visions?" he said.

"Oh, you know. Animal skeletons in the desert, positively wild Indians and horses and all that."

"I'm convinced that you have every reason to believe your visions. It is with terror that I think of going to bed tonight for fear of being flayed alive in my stupor."

She continued to smile, but her attention wavered.

"In fact," he went on, "I expect Natty Bumppo there at the bar to club me over the head with a hatchet, rob me of my riches, and sell my body to science before morning."

She was no longer listening at all. Her arms folded upward like wings for a moment. She dropped the line of her blouse an inch at the shoulders. He followed the direction of her eyes.

From the street door, his great chest and shoulders encased in a thick T-shirt, Bill Dann, lately of the Galveston docks, entered. While they watched, he bought a glass of beer from Ned-John and drank it in one sustained swallow, his head tilting slowly back until the glass was empty except for a thin white coating of foam.

He pushed the glass toward Ned-John who filled it again, then with his lips just hooked over the rim he turned on his stool and openly met the stares of Baker Steinhart and Angela Morton Deek. He wiped the foam from his mouth with the back of his hand, and lifting the glass two or three inches, he grinned and slid from the stool. Carrying the glass of beer he passed by their table, dropped his gaze down the curve of her bare shoulders, across the table and up the narrow tie to the neck of Baker. He walked in a light-footed way through the green drapes.

Baker tipped his head back to finish his drink.

32

"What were you saying?" she asked him.

One side of his mouth smiled. "Nothing. Are you hungry?"

Her eyes met his, then flicked back to the drape. "Yes," she said and began gathering her purse and cigarettes.

He held the drape aside for her as she stepped into the more brightly lighted dining room. She shaded her eyes and laughed. When she felt him run against her behind, she moved forward.

Mrs. Hampton was occupied at the other entrance to the dining room. "I'll bet you are one of our new teachers," she was saying to Jake Grantham who with his wife had entered from the lobby of the hotel.

"Yes," he said. "I guess I am. This is my wife, Anna Margaret. Mrs. Grantham."

"Grantham. Oh, you're art, aren't you? Never mind. I try to keep up with things here in town." Her voice fluted over the words.

So it happened. Doubtless it would have happened in a day or so anyway, but under Mrs. Hampton's ecstatic hostessery the five were seated together at the largest oval table and were offered the choice of Cock o' the Walk or tomato juice with lemon with which to begin their first meal in Tigerstooth.

"So you're art," Baker said.

"What? Oh, yes. Art and drama and this is Anna."

"I'm French and Latin."

"I'm English one and two."

"And I'm P.E. and head football," said Bill Dann, grinning over a spoonful of fruit cocktail.

Baker sipped his tomato juice and pushed the glass away. He ordered a bottle of red wine through Mrs. Hampton,

33

who telephoned Ned-John next door, who in turn brought it through the green drapes to their table and served it.

Angela held her glass to the light a moment and laughed a short sound. She leaned slightly over the table toward Bill Dann whose eyes followed the movement of her fingers playing nervously with the front edge of her blouse.

"Oh, yeah," he said and raised his arm holding the glass not by its stem but in his fist. "Salute," he said.

The others gestured with their own glasses. The last to lift her glass was Anna Margaret whose eyes met Baker's briefly over the red wine.

Jake Grantham relaxed somewhat before the wine bottle was empty. If these, then, were what Tigerstooth teachers were like, not that he had any prior experience from which to judge, the year might prove stimulating after all. He glanced at Anna Margaret who at that moment was grinding her newly lighted cigarette in an ashtray. With her fork she began separating parts of her salad. Probably no one had noticed her pregnancy yet. Thank god it looked as if she would never get too big. He wished she would at least take some part in the general conversation. Being a good conversationalist is important in a wife. If she would pay attention, she could learn something from that Angela person who laughed too much and was old but who knew how to keep her end of the talk.

"So you're from Texas, Bill," Angela was saying. Her fingertips touched Baker's arm, then flicked away. Her nails were the color of the wine. "I thought cowboys were somehow thinner and—well—lanky. Didn't you, Baker?"

"I hadn't thought."

"But you're certainly not." She laughed. "Lanky," she added.

Bill leaned forward, his elbows on the table, and picked

another bite of chicken from its bone. "I'm not a cowboy," he said.

"But what else does one do in Texas? Besides chase cows?" Angela said. "And shoot cattle rustlers?"

"They shoot Presidents," Baker muttered.

Bill's eyes swung to Baker and back to the blond woman. "I'm from Galveston," he said. "They have big boats there." He grinned at Anna Margaret. She's knocked up already. That kind of waist. Well.

"Boats," Angela was saying. "You'll never believe this, but I bought a boat today. You'll have to give me lessons, Bill." You may as well get over that idea, Texas dock-hand. She's six months if she's a day. A mint julep they haven't been married that long. Angela's arm folded up to her shoulder.

"Life's a terror at best without flaunting it in a boat. What happens if the damned thing tips over?" Baker wanted to know.

"You swim," Bill answered.

"That's the point. God." Baker pushed aside his nearly untouched meal. Whore. She'll have that blouse clear down to her navel if she keeps yanking on it. She's got Grantham pissing his pants now. Her skin blotched, and make-up like something in an Arabian Night.

"Don't you swim?" Anna Margaret's voice was low and brown like her eyes. She leaned over a glass-enclosed candle to light her cigarette. She held her long hair back from one side of her face.

"Anna Margaret's a fine swimmer," said Jake. "Personally, it's about all I can do to get around the bathtub," he laughed. He moved his glasses up on his nose and touched his fraternity badge.

"Speaking of bathtubs," Angela said, "guess what this

hotel doesn't have? Have you ever?" She sat back in her chair.

Baker watched her as she laughed. When she stopped, he said, "Yes, I have ever. If you mean bathtubs." He leaned toward her. "In Tigerstooth, Angela, we gather at the river to bathe. The American Ganges."

"Did they send you that brochure? Those pictures of the river?" Jake asked. "Jesus, it looks great, doesn't it. I mean if the photos are true, colorwise."

"What does color have to do with it?" Baker said.

"Well, Christ sake. If it's as good as the pictures, it'll be great. I mean, I paint some, you know, and I can visualize all kinds of great stuff around here."

Baker inspected the wine bottle. "It seems to me you could drown in any color river." He put down the bottle and turned to Anna Margaret. "And why are you smiling?"

She blew smoke down into her plate. She did not answer.

In a while the meal was over. For all but Bill Dann, at least. He inspected the chicken bones on his plate one by one and discarded them. "Is anybody going to have pie?" he asked. No one was. Baker suggested they might as well have another bottle of wine. While he and Angela and Jake discussed which would be better at that point, white or red, Anna Margaret pushed her untouched plate along the table to Bill. He grinned and traded his empty plate for hers.

"When this one's gone," Jake said, "let's all go to our house, okay, Anna? We're not moved in much—not that there is much to move in, you know, but we can have another one or two to sort of get started here in Tigerstooth, don't you think?"

At about the time the new wine was being doled into the five glasses by Ned-John, Reba Hampton floated to their table again, guiding by one arm each a man and a woman.

36

Despite her merry chatter, another man followed in her wake, his hands in his pockets, looking somehow unfairly trapped.

"Look," said Mrs. Hampton. "Here are three new friends," and she stepped aside and thrust the man up to the table. Then she began a complicated, soon mired, series of introductions ending with the proclamation, "So."

"So?" Baker said.

"So, I know you all will be just anxious to get acquainted."

But even she, for whom life was a long, banal telephone conversation, knew or felt that the meeting had come a half hour too late, that a coalescence had begun at her largest oval table that she was without wit to disjoin.

"Mr. Falmouth," she said to the odd man, "you teach social science, is that right?"

The man opened his lips thinly. "Physical science," he said. He kept his hands in his pockets.

"Oh," she said. "I knew it was a science." She touched the man's arm with one hand and Bill Dann's shoulder with the other as if to pass through her own body an electrical union. "Mr. Dann here teaches physical *education*. You two might have much in common."

"Yeah," Bill Dann said. "You want a drink?" he said to the man.

The man's heavy mustache lifted. "I never drink," he said. His gaze shifted to Angela's shoulders then away toward an empty table. He moved from Reba Hampton's grip.

"And Mr. and Mrs. Petri here are *both* teachers," Mrs. Hampton said. She touched each of them.

"Yes," the man said. "I've been brought out to do the band." He put forward a heavy arm into the midst of the five. Baker Steinhart shook the hand. "Michigan," the man

37

said. His laugh was big and automatic. "Home of the marching band, you could say. I've got the first halftime show all planned. We're going to give this town a *show*, I can say that, all right, even if I have to say it myself." His stomach moved beneath his yellow shirt when he laughed.

"That sounds worth hearing," Baker said. "I've never heard Sousa played on war drums and wooden whistles." He looked to Anna Margaret. "Have you?"

"You're overlooking the bells on the ankles," she said.

"Of *course*," Baker said to her. "The wine." He tapped his glass. "The wine has muddled my head."

"The uniforms are inexpensive, you'll have to admit," she said.

The man opened his mouth to speak.

"Not necessarily," Baker continued. "That depends on the material. Loin cloths come in some very new fabrics these days."

"True." She brushed back the long hair from her face. "Satins."

"Brocades."

"Gold braid."

The man in the yellow shirt had stopped laughing. He shuffled his feet.

Anna Margaret said, "And we are overlooking the feathers. There's an item."

"Indubitably," Baker said.

"Christ," Bill Dann said. "Would you pass the wine?"

"Well," Mr. Petri took the opportunity to say, "we'll be seeing you all around." He lifted his heavy arm. "We'll have to get together." He guided his wife away toward the table where the first man sat glumly watching them approach.

38

"Christ sake, Anna Margaret," Jake whispered.

An hour or so later Anna Margaret leaned against the kitchen doorjamb holding a coffee mug in both hands and a cigarette between two fingers. She stood watching the three of them, and listening. From time to time she bent her face to the mug. At those times her hair fell along her face covering all but the front part of it and her hands.

On the floor in the other room Bill Dann leaned against a packing case, his legs crossed at the ankles, gently fingering his guitar. The black case lay near, its lid open to red velvet. He began a new tune, but as before, after a few measures the tune went fleeting away in improvisation. His big hands, covered with heavy blond hair, seemed to move but barely while the strings sounded. Although he may have been listening to the conversation of the other two, he gave no sign. His head bent toward the guitar, which caused not only his hair but each feature of his face to appear loose and exaggerated. No single part of his face, taken alone, was unusual, but put together, the huge and broken nose, the slack-fleshed jowls, and the lower lip, the heavy eyebrows darker than his hair, and the broken front tooth created the effect of a mad collage built by an enterprising artist from leftovers.

Anna Margaret laughed. For a moment a frown creased between Bill's eyes, then he caught the direction of the sound. He looked toward her and grinned.

"More wine?" she said.

He picked up the cup from the floor beside him and looked into it. He held it toward her.

She brought the bottle, a half-gallon size, of cheap red wine and sat on the floor facing him, the bottle between her crossed legs. "I like your music," she said. "I thought you'd play cowboy stuff."

39

"I can."

"No." She lighted a fresh cigarette from his. She replaced his in the ashtray, pointing the unlighted end toward him.

"You don't talk a hell of a lot, do you," he said.

She smoothed the hair back from one side of her face with her fingertips. "Hasn't it been said?"

He frowned. His eyes watched hers for some hope of explanation. He shook his head. "Maybe it has," he said. Then he nodded toward Jake and Baker. "What in hell is that all about?"

Baker sat in one of the two chairs and leaned, weaving, toward Jake who sprawled on his back on the floor.

"That is capital Art. The gnashing of Tigerstooth's newest minds."

When Bill laughed his head tilted back showing his teeth and the red inside of his mouth.

"Don't laugh. We may be the last four people on earth."

His hands returned to play over the strings of the guitar. He stopped to adjust a white tuning peg.

"Why?" he said.

"What."

He nodded toward Jake.

She rubbed the palm of her hand across her stomach. "This," she said.

"Oh." He plucked the strings. He frowned again. "Why in the first place?"

She turned the cigarette toward the palm of the hand that held it and flicked the ashes off as a man would. "You training for District Attorney?"

"Sorry," he said.

She smiled. "That's all right." She tilted back her head

40

and blew smoke in a stream upward. She turned to watch Jake a moment. "No. I love him," she said.

"Yes," Bill said, and his eyes passed from her face down her body and on to the guitar strings. She drew her knees closer and tucked the edge of her short robe tighter to her legs. "How much longer?" he asked.

"The end of December."

Bill leaned his guitar against the wall. He picked up his cup and drained it, his head thrown back so that the muscles at the base of his neck stretched smoothly.

"Shit!" Baker was shouting. "You cannot, by any sane reasoning, call Miro a painter!"

Jake was sitting up waving his glasses toward Baker. "Not a painter of pictures, maybe, but—"

"Nor of anything!"

"Wait a minute! Not pictures—not something that looks like something, for Christ sake."

Baker laughed. "That is a pearl of wisdom."

"It's design. Who said a painting had to look like a tree, or a house, or a cow? Whoever said that?"

"There hasn't been a painter since Cézanne."

"What about Picasso?"

"Not him either. Not since 1915, anyway. You goddamn kids think—"

Bill interrupted. "Wait a minute. Neither one of you could see a picture right now if it—"

Jake turned to him. "Listen. This idiot's living in the Middle Ages. What about you? Don't you think we have painters today just as—"

"Don't ask me, Jake," Bill said. He stood up. "I don't know a goddamn thing about it." He reached down his hand to help Anna Margaret from the floor.

41

"Come on, Baker," Bill said. "I'll give you a ride to the hotel."

Baker stood from his chair and turned his head deliberately to focus on the other man. He stooped to set his wine cup on a packing box. "No," he said. "I'll walk. At the speed of light who can know what village charms one may miss?"

"You can drink at the Santa Fe." Bill laid the polished guitar in its case with the gentleness of a mother.

"I have drunk at the Santa Fe!" Baker shouted. He looked angry for a moment. He posed with one hand jammed into his pants pocket, the other pointing upward. "And I have drunk at the original Moulin Rouge and at Sardi's and," he dropped his hand and smiled, "I have drunk on the Super Chief."

Jake rolled over on his stomach on the floor and laughed.

"Well," said Bill, "don't forget we all face the principal at eight in the morning." He snapped the three catches of his guitar case. "And I oughta find some place to live besides that goddamn hotel."

Anna Margaret opened the front door for them. She clicked the switch for the porch light. It did not work.

"God!" Baker spoke. "The stars!" He stood on the edge of the top step down from the porch and rocked on the balls of his feet. In the dim light of midnight and the street lamp he appeared smaller and whiter. With his hands pushed into his pockets, his knees bent slightly, his thin back curved, and his head thrown up to the sky he might have looked like, in the proper setting, a gentle waterbird craning the air for its own kind.

The others waited for him to say more. He only repeated softly, "My God, the stars," and walked out through the gateway, onto the sidewalk, and pointed himself toward town, a brighter glow in the dark.

Anna Margaret hugged a porch pillar. The painted cement cooled her face. She watched Baker disappear. There was a familiarity to the set of his back that reminded her of someone, she couldn't think who. Then she realized that it was like watching herself walk away, transformed into neither exactly man nor woman, but person. She was conscious, too, of the wide back of Bill Dann standing one step lower. She knew he would in a moment turn to speak.

He placed one foot down on the final step and turned.

She smiled, and even in that faint light she saw his face change expression. He seemed perplexed, confused. " 'Night," he said and moved quickly to his car edged wrong-way to the curb, reflecting pieces of metallic light.

She stood a long time against the pillar after the footsteps and the car had silenced. She wept for a moment, for what reason she did not know precisely. With one palm on her stomach, already feeling full and heavy, she wondered idiotically if unborn babies cry when their mothers do. She smiled at the thought. The crinkling of her eyes caused the stars through tears to spread and waver in myriad shatters of blue and green and yellow.

She pushed herself at last from the pillar and went back into the house. There on the floor, on his back, lay the man —more boy-like and unintense in sleep—whom she had married because she loved him, not, as she believed he believed, because she was pregnant, who seemed more like a person walking away from her instead of nearer. He lay stretched straight, his lips barely parted, with one hand inside his unzipped pants cupping his genitals, the way he always slept. She sprawled on her stomach on the sofa above him. She gently removed his glasses and dangled the

43

edge of one earpiece along the side of his jaw. "Jakie?" she said.

He did not answer or make any sound. Is this, then, what it comes to, what Grandfather and Father scraped and rasped and scoured for, what they fought and married the wilderness and the Indians and the mountains for? So their progeny now focused in me, the last, can begin life and give life to a bastard in the desert, can run from those mountain pastures where no pastures were before them, where Father, old, old, in the loss of his sons to foreign guns rides his diminishing acres and sees them retaken by taxes and erosion and the wilderness that has waited a hundred years to settle the account of land raped and brown daughter taken, but raped in love, or for the purpose of love, held back with hands crooked for holding reins and tools, for branding white-faced red cattle, for holding knots of purple and yellow flowers scooped from the slopes by riders so agile they never had to leave the saddle, so that I, the daughter of old age, could not gather those blooms or have them gathered for me but could read Shakespeare and Homer, could begin womanhood here, married to an ever-boy, draining the last eighth part of that brown blood into a child of a man I did not marry?

"Jakie?" Anna Margaret propped her head on one arm and watched him sleep. So, it was true. The time for learning to love was gone before anyone had a chance at it. But you tried anyway. No matter what the older generation— and the ones before that—pointed so clearly, you found out for yourself.

Her grandfather, the one who started it, miscalculated. He believed that in the 1870's and '80's, there was still time, although he must have realized by 1890 that there was not. But when a man has sunk his whole soul into something, he does not, he cannot admit that he has miscalculated, not when the stakes are the lives of whatever seeds he has spread. He does not admit it, but he cannot live with it, either. That is why Caleb Pier gave up at forty-five and shot the Indian woman he had married twenty years before and then shot himself and left an eighteen-year-old girl to raise a sixteen-year-old sister and a fourteen- and a nine-year-old brother—Austin Pier, father of the woman who now lay drowsing and watching her young husband sleep on his back on the floor.

Caleb Pier should have done a better job of the shooting, those who knew him thought. Or he should have first tried to make it clear to that nine-year-old that it was too late for the kind of love he had set out to build in the high meadow country.

There is no one left alive who saw or knew Caleb Pier when he first came there, but there are sons among the Yavapais, who, old and bemuddled in their age, remember the telling of it from their fathers clearly (or unclearly) enough to believe sometimes they knew him then, and there are those still who remember when he died. There are yet three or four who, sitting on a warm day on wired and mended rockers before their reservation cabins, will shake their heads over the multitudinous and impossible complications of living, and as if by primeval signal glance back into a time and place now removed from them and speak of hunting elk or antelope or whitetails in the high meadows. Sometimes they speak of the white man, Cal Pier, who worked, their fathers said and they believed, so much harder and laughed so much oftener than was needed to make the trees fall and the grass grow and the deer return in autumn. Who came, from where they did not know and he never said, suddenly, with his horse and his bull and his few gloomy white-faced red cows and built a corral and then a barn and then, after five years, a house. Then he selected a wife from among the Yavapais and soon there were children. They (the old men in the wired rockers) knew those children or thought they did, could not agree if they did or not because sometime then they were themselves removed from the lush high meadows.

Austin Pier, the youngest, was born cursing, most said, but that was not true. He had not learned to curse at all until he was nine and even then, even the morning he ran into the wintry kitchen as was his habit to fling himself into the warm smells of coffee and bacon and instead flung himself down on the blood-sticky cold bodies of his mother and father and began to scream and continued to scream "God damn Jesus and God bastards!" he did not do it very well. The white people who came to fix up the bodies and build the boxes and the Yavapais who came to mourn and build fires wondered at the boy's curses, wondered that he could have known the words being the son of Caleb Pier who was never known to have need for cursing, although before the end he must have had reason.

The next time he—Austin—had most occasion for long and shattering curses was when he realized at sixteen that the last of the others, the brother five years older, was going away for certain, leaving him holding a bedraggling house and barn and ranch that the second-growth pines and the coyotes and mountain lions were already sparring for. His cursing was much improved by then and he beat them all away with the sheer fury and incineration of it, so it would seem.

The obsession that his father had was apparently concentrated in Austin, who was unable to see, as his sisters and brother had, that the time was past for such fanaticism.

46

He did know, on the other hand, that whatever the plan was, it had been set back a whole generation, but he believed that pure, hot will was sufficient to overcome the loss. That was partly why he wore out and then discarded one barren woman before he was twenty-five and then impregnated another who was but sixteen. That was partly why he returned a decorated and infuriated hero from France to marry the second woman because in his absence a son had been born. There followed two more sons who with the first helped him beat back the land and were about to have time to learn to love it when they carried his rage into another war and got themselves killed.

They were about to have time, but even then, even if they had lived, they would not have known precisely what it was they were expected to love, what it was their father had driven them toward and spoken of vaguely as they were growing up. After about age six, the brown, soft eyes of each of them began to take on the flinty glitter of their father's eyes and by the time each was fifteen or sixteen his eyes were set in a comatose, narcotic stare that reflected nothing of bewilderment or hurt or excitement. By the time they went to the war even the youngest did not any longer turn his eyes upon one or the other of his brothers. By then there was no longer any reason for words or for looks because they moved and fought and thought as one indissoluble, tenacious force. When they mended the barn or corrals, they worked together. When they worked the red cattle in the high pastures they rode together, each sitting his horse in the same loose curve. If they happened by a road and there happened to be a roadster or a pickup churning the red dust along it, they would turn their heads as one and watch the car coming and until it could not be seen any longer. At the infrequent dances in the trading post village ten miles down on the plateau, they could be seen leaning together against a wall watching from under their curled low hats. When they drank, they drank together, silently passing the unwiped bottle back and forth. When they fornicated, they fornicated together, sharing the same girl in turn from among several in the reach of their father's land who were willing or helpless under the triple stare, or sometimes, if a girl they had chosen, evidently with no word passing between them, was unwilling to be shared, two would hold her in the scent of crushed yellow poppies and blue lupine, calmly, while the third took his turn with her. In the long winters they shared each other.

Up in the tableland, on the far side of the Mogollon Rim, the three sons of Austin Pier are remembered and the tales of their fierce, silent lives are already legend among the old men and the middle-aged women, most of whom, now graceless and impenitent, once felt or wished they had felt if not the hard bodies, the hard stares of the three brothers.

Four

ANGELA MORTON DEEK sat in bed, propped up by the two hard hotel pillows, examining her hands flattened against the blue sheets by the light of a bedside lamp. The sheets were her own which she kept with her in a suitcase for times like these. It was not fear of uncleanliness that had caused her surreptitiously to change the bedding—an act she would have to reverse in the morning before she left to find a permanent place, in order that no hotel maid would find cause for exclamation—but rather that the hotel linen was white. She feared white bed linen as she feared white walls.

The examining of her hands was a concentrated exercise learned some time back. Done with one's whole mind, the scrutiny of hands, or toes, could blank the mind, she knew, of whatever whirled there. It helped to restore very ordinary perspective to life and more particularly to nights.

She had slept earlier and believed, being this tired, that the night would pass untroubled into morning. She had grown weary of the dinner banter and of trying to keep straight the names and the direction of the talk. She was happy when the last of the wine was gone and they had separated, she to her room, the others to that young couple's—the Granthams'

—house. She wondered if they now were still all there. Had they wished she had joined them? Likely not. At least not the girl whose eyes were disarming.

She lifted her hands at last to either side of her face. The hair about her temples had nearly dried, she decided. It had been wet with perspiration as had most of her body when she had awakened a half hour ago and found herself sitting bolt upright in bed, her arms stretched out before her as if to ward away the crushing heat of the night. Before she slept again, if she did at all, she would have to close the window that was now open three floors above the alley, despite the heat. She wondered if she had been screaming. Since no sound stirred in the hotel, perhaps she had not. Perhaps no one else had a room on this floor.

She listened, her head tilted toward the door and the tall, narrow hall beyond. Maybe she was alone. How far was it to the elevator? Down the hall to the right, right again—or left.

She kicked her feet from the sheets. She was about to rise and go out into the hall to settle the direction of the elevator when she heard the footsteps. They were heavy steps, those of a big person. Coming down the hall. Heavy steps. Angela's mind drew up a picture of Bill Dann, molded into a white T-shirt and Levis, stepping deliberately with a spring in his toes, as clearly as if she stood at the end of the corridor watching him come. She saw his long hair receding vaguely on either side of a shaggy-hanging forelock, his eyes watching her loosely, blue, blank like those of a man who does not see.

The footsteps passed by her door. They stopped. Her upper teeth bit into her lip. She watched the door of her room and held her breath. When the faint click of the lock sounded, Angela gasped privately, as if she expected to see her own door swing open. Of course, it would not; the door was to the room next to hers.

From the room she heard the door open and close, the footsteps again twice or three times on the wooden floor then muffled heavier on the carpeted portion. The man next door was alternately humming and whistling short parts of tunes. She heard him drop his keys and money on a dresser top. Then faint sounds like the taking off of clothes, perhaps, and the squeak of bedsprings when the man sat down to take off his shoes. And the dull sound, twice, of the shoes.

Sitting on her knees atop the pillows, she flattened her hands and arms and the side of her face and as much of her upper body as she could extend over the headboard against the wall that separated them and listened with tight-closed eyes until the sounds of the man went away at last.

Or so it seemed. Bill Dann, in the next room, did not sleep immediately either, although it was not his habit to have the clustered thoughts of the insomniac that refuse to separate and melt. Life was ordinarily a noncomplication where one event led naturally to another, the first being a sort of cast-off skin from which the new event slithered. This night, however, he lay stretched on his back, and scratching the wide expanse of hair on chest and belly, he watched the dim-changing town lights reflect on the ceiling.

As a boy who holds off till last the best chocolate in order to live the excitement of anticipating it, Bill Dann shifted to the deeper part of his mind the image that he would in time allow precedence, and instead, thought of Caroline. Not as the woman so much too old for a man in his twenties, the woman who believed him at 28 or 29 too old to continue playing football—even for a college degree—the woman whose face and mouth and indeed whole relationship with him became one capitalized Bitch, but as Caroline the woman

51

who had the decade of life enough beyond his to develop purpose of intercourse and fullness of breast. In fact, to his mind the name Caroline forever after conjured up the twin image of her round, great, brown-tipped breasts that had from the beginning reminded him of something you ought to be able to order at a soda fountain if you could only think of what to ask for.

The first time he had seen those breasts they were in pale contrast to the dark brown blanket of Coach Talimski's bachelor bed with the coach himself—his deep-tanned back yet another tone among the browns—sitting, slightly slump-shouldered, on the far edge of the bed luxuriously contemplating a cigarette.

Coach Talimski had turned and grinned. "Okay, Big Bill, you're on," he said. "This is Caroline." Then the coach of the favored Chaparrals scooped his pants and shirt from off his own bedroom floor and stumped into the other room, feeling somewhat fatherly and depleted, to join the two or three other guards or tackles or fullbacks who had risen in that night's game sufficiently, in the coach's estimation, to take the bait. The waiting young men grew excessively less able to control their direction of thought when confronted with the naked form of their coach who, as he slowly dressed, seemed preoccupied and a bit dew-lappy about the jowls. The one who by decree according to his merits was next in line of ascent after Bill Dann divined the nervous problems of whether or not another whisky would help or hinder his prowess, and whether with his newly bandaged right ankle he could in fact achieve any degree of dignity with Caroline.

The young man would have had less reason to worry had he known what Bill Dann and Caroline knew from almost the first instant their brown thighs touched. From that moment Caroline swore—and Bill came deliriously close to doing the same—that her thighs would never touch any but his.

Finally, Coach Talimski, disgruntled, asked the other waiting Chaparrals—grown progressively more drowsy from too extensive thoughts of eroticism—would they mind going home since he for one needed sleep and they were sitting on the only other piece of furniture in the apartment that could be used as a bed.

Bill Dann's favorite retrospective view of Caroline was a panoramic montage formed from the events of that first night with her, and the following early morning. Well, he was out of it now. Here in Tigerstooth, already he found he could snip away the rest of the picture of his and Caroline's connubial existence leaving for lonesome nights' sake not much more than the two great brown breasts.

He ceased rubbing the hair on his belly. He considered whether or not he was too sleepy to build a projective series of scenes with Angela Deek, or, better, with Anna Margaret Grantham. It was hard, he decided, to fit pieces into either picture on such short acquaintance with the subjects. There really wasn't any hurry. They'd all be there tomorrow. They'd all be there for the whole goddamn year.

He turned over on his side. He adjusted his scrotum and went to sleep.

As for Peter McCarron, his night's sleep was not any better or much worse than what he had grown to expect in these last years.

The taglierini supper with his mother and father had been fine, at least until later when the old man had swung open and left standing the door to his—Peter's—youth-cluttered room. The food itself was predictably good, exactly the

53

same as it had ever been on September 1st since whenever in his memory he first saw his mother, tiny in her white apron, carry with woven potholders the big black pan of taglierini to the dining-room table. Then she would stand back, as tonight, and tilt her head to the side and ruffle her hands in the apron and watch the cheese puff and bubble, and they knew she was mentally clicking off the steps of the recipe. The black pan was as old, probably, as the recipe itself. She would use the fancy pottery or glass dishes that he and his sister had later given her for other casseroles—never for the taglierini. There is something about the black pan, she would say, for taglierini.

From the glass of port to the thimble of brandy, the supper was right, a pleasant enough time with the old folks, predictable like the food itself. McCarron knew before he went what they would talk about, how she would bring up the subject of his returning home to live with them, how he would sidestep it, when his father would push back from the table and rest his splintered, horny fingertips on the crocheted cloth and belch and say, A good one, Irene, sticks to the ribs. And then the old man would dig out the gold watch from his vest pocket and click open its round lid. He would seem to be listening for something that neither of the others could hear even as all talk stopped and they held their breaths. Then he would nod and snap shut the watch.

"You men just pass me your plates and then run on in the parlor out of my way while I clean up," she would say and reach for the plates to stack on her own.

And finally they, too, would hear it coming and she would stop her stacking and the old man would pause where he stood and listen until the train came abreast, rattling the miniature teacups in the secretary, slowing down for the yards.

54

"Four units," his father would say, or, "Not but forty cars. Things is slowing down," and then, satisfied, he would walk on into the living room—the parlor—and they, he and his mother, could expel their breaths.

While he poured the two glasses of brandy and set up the checkerboard his father would say, "I'll just step in here and get out of some of these clothes." When he came back out of the bedroom, Peter knew, he would be stripped down to the elbow- and knee-length cotton underwear he wore summer or year with the baggy, codpiece crotch, with his black stockings gartered still to his calves, in the maroon, shuffling slippers.

When he came back out, they would begin the first game and the brandy, the single small glass of brandy, never more. Santa Fe regulation number something—the old man could have quoted it. And in a while she would come in from the kitchen, still with the white apron, and sit in her black rocker and get the right squeak going in it and crochet and chat.

So the evening went this time, until in the middle of the third game, the one that decided, his father did an unexpected thing that upset Peter enough to send him scurrying to his own house on the other side of the hill. His father got up to get something from his bedroom—a pipe or a pipe cleaner or a handkerchief. Peter, watching the board, listened to the shuff of the slippers and to the sound of the bedroom door opening.

It was a simple enough mistake. Except that his father never had made that kind of mistake. Peter's eyes met his mother's and saw the worried lines push up into the natural wrinkles around her eyes. Then he saw what his father was doing. He had opened the wrong door and gone, not into his own bedroom, but the one next, into Peter's old room, the one his mother was fond of reminding him awaited as he left it twenty-four years ago, ready for him to come back to.

From where he sat Peter could see straight into the room where he had not looked once in ten years. In the center of it the old man stood bending his white head this way and that, bewildered, lost, with his arms at his sides and the rear of his underwear bagging down, and behind and above him on the wall the boy things, the faded, blue felt pennants, the deflated football, the raccoon hide, the shelf of tarnished trophies, the calendar with the monkeys and chimpanzees for every month, and on the desk the tilted lampshade and the track shoes and the tattered books and above his head hanging from the light by wires the bi-wing, balsa airplanes faintly stirring.

Peter wanted to shout at him, to yell, Get out of there, Father, don't you know? but he could neither shout nor laugh nor move until his mother hissed "Hush!" beside him and he turned his head back down to the checkerboard before the old man, the moment over, came out again, his slippers whispering, and closed the door and went to and opened and through the right door.

"How much longer?" he said to his mother.

"Only three weeks. I pray to God," she said.

Three weeks until the old man would retire. Three weeks until he would bring in the El Capitan for the last time and then he could sit back and click open and shut his gold watch forever until he grew too old to remember to do even that.

McCarron was gone before his father returned to the checkerboard. When he stopped his car before his own house he rested his forehead for a minute between his hands on the steering wheel. It was not the simple error that caught at him—anyone that old could be expected to do something like that. No, it was the picture of the old man, not so much older than himself, *only twenty-two years* older, standing in his drawers with his thin white hair like down on his head among the faded, curled remnants of young sweat and joy that brought McCarron's forehead knocking against the wheel.

Five

THE following morning dawned hot and typical for September. The sun rose full of light from the jagged east mountains. With its coming the birds in the tamaracks stopped their singing, wilting into the purposeful business of finding beetles and yellow grasshoppers. From the back yards of the Indians' white cabins pale smoke drowsed below and around and above kettles and battered pots of carp and mesquite beans. In and out of the windows the blue, fat flies flew with indecision. In the mountains the coyotes ceased their yapping and went searching, yellow-eyed, home. The cold river brightened.

In his hotel room Baker Steinhart, sitting in the center of his bed, contemplated the mouth of a black cannon pointing directly to his window from the Harvey Park. It was the first thing, beyond his trousers on a chair back, that had caught his attention upon rising. When he first noticed it he could have sworn it swung an inch eastward to mouth at him directly. At any rate, it certainly was not facing straight on its block. The black cannon had not moved, however; it had not moved at all since 1917 when in a fit of night patriotism seven or eight boys, feeling the frustration of a war in which they had not been called to participate, stuffed it with several varieties of gunpowder and lead pipe and set it off. The explosion, while not lethal to the gun or the boys, was sufficient to send the lead pipe, or pieces of it, over the hotel roof and clanging into the bell tower of the Catholic church in such a way as would have caused the Baptists, had the pipe dropped into their tower—and had there been a Baptist church in Tigerstooth then and had prayer meeting been under way—to believe the Ghost himself, eavesdropping in the belfry, had fallen down among the chimes. As it was, the sound was enough to raise the citizens to the temporary belief that their town had somehow fallen prey to a new German assault. That was the night the railroad superintendent was seen running down from the blue-flowered rooms above the saloons without so much as his underwear. That was also the night the cannon shifted on its block. It no longer aimed directly ahead down the center path of the half-dozen paths radiating from its base.

But to Baker Steinhart the oblique angle of the cannon, and the accusing direction of its mouth, could well be connected to the severity of his jaw ache this morning. Holding the tip of his chin in his fingers, he gently worked his lower jaw back and forth. It hurt still as it had all night, or rather for the last half of the night after he had run into the cannon while sprinting across the park from the River Street Saloon.

For a time, passing from bar to bar along River Street, Baker had enjoyed himself in the esteem of being a new hue to the local color. It was not until he had progressed the whole span of saloons and was working his way back up the row that he made the error that cost him most of a half-night's sleep and left him a spinning head and sore jaw.

He had learned long ago through a dozen years of acquaintance with new neighborhoods in cities and towns on this and the other side of the ocean that with a certain amount of histrionics he could gain access to the generosity of other people also set about the business of drinking in café, pub, bar, or saloon. This night—last night—he had chosen as a night compatible to poetry recitation, a form of expression rising naturally from such an earlier declamation as "My God, the stars!" and a form of entertainment he rightly calculated to be far enough removed from the general trainman's experience to be unique. "To His Coy Mistress" and "La Belle Dame Sans Merci" shouted the length of the polished bar had served to put him in touch with three or four drinks in each of the four saloons.

As he began working back up the row it happened. In the second one, the Kutkilya, he wedged himself at the bar between two tired brakemen in blue and gray striped overalls. One of the men was ordinary-sized, if not smallish; the other was a good deal larger than most men. Baker bought a drink for himself and before long had interested the brakemen in poetry, or so he could have imagined. At least he had their attention.

After "La Belle Dame" the big one asked him did he know "The Cremation of Sam McGee." Baker snorted before he thought and in a flash of ill-conceived pride said that he was not interested in reciting shit, but poetry. Baker felt, in the next few moments, what would have been under sober conditions a kind of tongue-tied panic and rage and resignation—panic because he had spoken metaphorically to one who was unlikely ever to have accepted the truth that metaphor, by nature, belongs to the poet, especially when one axis of the metaphor turned on so unpoetic a word as shit; rage at himself for having once again pitched headlong into the well wherein he believed all the world loved a fool; resignation because he knew that however unsullied

60

his intentions, he was about to be cracked in the face. He watched the area of white thicken around the trainman's eyes. The man's ears seemed to fold back and in doing so stretched the skin on the brows and along the cheekbones so tightly that the lips had to part and draw back too in order that the contracting skin would not by excess pressure pop the eyes.

The first slam against the wall cleared his head momentarily. But it left him breathless and water-kneed. The passage from the bar to the wall had been swift. He found himself staring along the length of a hairy arm that ran straight out from his bunched shirt front to the shoulder of the big man. The big man brought his round, unshaven face close and through meticulously drawn-back lips said, "How do you like this, you bastard?

> I think that I shall never see
> A poem lovely as a tree.
>
> A tree whose hungry mouth is prest
> Against the earth's sweet flowing breast;
>
> A tree that looks at God all day,
> And lifts her leafy arms to pray;
>
> A tree that may in Summer wear
> A nest of robins in her hair;
>
> Upon whose bosom snow has lain;
> Who intimately lives with rain.
>
> Poems are made by fools like me,
> But only God can make a tree."

On each of the last three beats—on "God" and "make" and "tree"—the brakeman-aesthete thumped his captive's head against the wall. "Tree" was an especially numbing crack.

"Well?" the man said. *"That's* poetry. How do you like it, prick?"

"Christ, that my love were in my arms and I in my bed again," said Baker.

"Hemingway," said the little man.

It was at that moment that Baker chose to break and run. It was not many moments later that he ran full tilt into the black cannon.

He stood to examine his face in the mirror above the dresser. He had to hunch down his shoulders to see into it. By moving his head he was able to get a clear view of most of his face between the wavy panels of glass. He waggled his jaw. He dreaded having to shave it.

In the hall, on the way to the bathroom, he met Bill Dann just emerging, shirtless and heavy-headed, from his room. They eyed each other. At the door Bill said, "Shower or shave first?"

"I don't care. I'll shave," said Baker and touched his face.

"Jesus, you always look so rocky in the morning?"

"I had an altercation with a Civil War monument," said Baker.

Bill looked sorry to hear that. But before he had said anything beyond "Yeah? Jesus," he had opened the bathroom door and come face to rear with Angela Deek swathed in great white towels. She turned. She stopped toweling her head and smiled. Her face was flushed and warm looking, fresh from the hot shower. The lines at the outer edges of her eyes crinkled when she smiled. The small room was crowded with steam that had clouded the mirror and was running down it in minute rivulets. The opened door caused the steam to swirl about her damp body, momentarily creating the illusion of a floating torso, deus ex machina. "Oh, my goodness," said the torso, "good morning!" Baker said, "Bonjour, Madame—" "—oiselle" added the torso and giggled. "Jesus," said Bill Dann.

With one hand she tucked in the ends of the towel about her head. With the other she held closed the one that ran sari-like over the top of her body. She licked the tip of one finger and ran it quickly over the eyebrows and over the corners of her lips where flecks of toothpaste clung. Baker wondered why she hadn't locked the door, although he knew why, although his head still rang too much to face the realization, although the realization had been clear the night before. And he wondered how much make-up it took each morning to disguise that complexion. Bill Dann wondered if her breasts were brown-tipped.

The torso spoke again, only it wasn't so much a torso any more because most of the lower part of the body and the legs had cleared into view through the thinning steam. "You boys want to shower?" She turned back to face the mirror and began toweling her hair.

"Not necessarily right now," said Baker and stepped into the hall.

"Not right now," said Bill and closed the door from the inside.

Angela wiped a clean circle on the mirror with an edge of towel. Behind her own reflection she caught Bill's eyes watching her from under his yet uncombed, shaggy hair. He grinned. She could handle this one if she could keep her eyes and more important her hands off his wide chest. If he had had sense enough to find her last night, well, the story might be at another chapter by now, but here it was seven-thirty in the morning of the first day she—and he, too—had to become a schoolteacher in Tigerstooth, and she feeling

63

good and fresh from her shower and with at least another half-hour's work ahead of her before she could feel right about a public appearance, to say nothing of a tiring day ahead, meeting the principal and Lord knew what-all in the way of other teachers all eyeing her into mental pigeon-holes, and the afternoon to find an apartment. And no car. A lot of good that boat would do, searching for an apartment, or better, more private, a little house. She could handle this one. She had had enough practice, she figured, more than most women have in a lifetime, but then most women did not have a twin brother to grow up with and learn with on the banks of Green's Creek, Mississippi, learn things like where the first blue flowers would appear in spring or where mud cat would likely be waiting to be caught or where the best moss grew for making nests for stolen birds' eggs that never hatched but looked snug against the moss, especially if they were blue and spotted, and learn other things at night in bed between whispers of the day's gains, even after they were fifteen and sixteen and had to cross the moon-cold floor under the crazy quilt that hung between their cots.

Angela turned and leaned her hips against the sink. "Aren't you going to shower?"

"I thought that could wait," Bill answered. His loose-hanging hands clinched and opened. He stepped closer.

She lifted her hands. Don't touch that chest. "No," she said. "Take your shower."

He grinned again and watched her face. "Okay," he said. "Good. I won't be long, five minutes." He turned his back to her and unzipped his pants.

She leaned back against the sink until the shower curtain was closed and the steam had begun to rise again. She turned, silently gathered up her toothbrush and toothpaste

64

and comb and small case and as silently let herself out into the hall. In six minutes he would probably be rutting and snuffing at her door if he could discover which was hers, but he wouldn't raise much of a noise in the hotel, not if he stopped to think of his reason for being in Tigerstooth. In her room Angela laughed and let the towels fall. She ran her fingers into her damp curly hair.

At three in the afternoon Peter McCarron, Principal, sat at his desk in the small room he called his cell—a room dark except for one window, untouched because of its inaccessibility to either teacher or parent by paint or more than cursory dusting—that was the outcome of architectural lack of planning resulting in a surprise chamber or alcove at one corner of the principal's office, a space for which no one could for years find a use, it being too large for a coat closet in a climate where coats were rarely necessary by day and too out of the way of things to interest a secretary, until ten years ago when McCarron realized that by having a door hung there he could be out of reach of virtually anybody including Samuel the Mojave janitor who never saw any reason for disturbing whatever gathered behind a closed door.

McCarron found himself, over these past few years, becoming more addicted to the ante-office. But never before this day had he felt the urgency of seeking out its solace so soon in the school year. Here it was, the first day of school and not regular school at that, only Preschool Teachers' Orientation and since noon he could think of little else beyond the hour when the teachers would have drifted away from their fruitless arranging and decorating and rearranging of classrooms and he could retire to the arms of his cell.

He sat for a long time, first, just watching the shadows

lengthening over and beyond the river. The small window gave onto what was possibly the only unbesmirched view of the river as seen from the town, certainly it was the best from any window in the school, which might be taken as a clue to what it was the architect was getting at before his mind and pencil wandered. Most of the other windows faced the dirt practice field and the barren desert, doubtless to underline the original board of education's belief that to have the windows of a school (costly, at best, but probably necessary considering, in the long run, the cost of electric light) look out upon anything but utter dejection would in some way be undermining the very heart of democracy, to say nothing of inciting truancy. It was crass enough, in the minds of most Tigerstoothians (or Tigersteeth, as some maintained), that the school occupied the top of the highest hill thus thrusting the children into a type of overlordship up toward which they—the parents—must look from their houses or stores or railroad. Those with more liberal imaginations, however, saw in the red-roofed, white stucco structure and its porticos of high Mexican arches a kind of Southwestern Parthenon benignly gazing out over the town, protectoress-fashion; in fact, the school was as often as not called the Acropolis, thus merging together the building and the hill it stood on.

McCarron watched the green river over the rooftops of the town. He saw the banks and the hills beyond take on dark, sharp shadows like the strokes from an indomitable brush. From such a distance he could not see the water move. But he knew it did: swift and deep and cold. As swift as it had when he himself, a boy, son of a Santa Fe engineer, had paddled its backwaters (in the days before loud motors ripped and tore it), or swam naked with naked friends across it diagonally, letting the current carry them a hundred yards downstream from where they began, to rise shivering and shouting up its far bank, laughing, pointing to, grabbing one another's shrunken manliness until the enkindling sun restored their blood and their adolescence, sometimes further than they intended which necessitated another plunge into the icy water. As silent as the dawns when he crouched with his father and Alf and Alf's father behind natural reed blinds, in clammy hip boots, waiting for the sounds of geese against the red east, taking the bottle from Alf, drinking with clenched teeth, passing the bottle back to Alf. As deep as the dark itself the night of his nineteenth birthday when Alf's sister lay with him on its bank on a Navajo blanket and confessed that she would not have given herself so to him, not three times at least, were it not that tomorrow he would leave to join the faceless, mindless ranks of men and this she gave but made him more a man, more so, certainly, than did the knitted socks and cans of date-nut bread she gave Alf who would have enjoyed, had he been any distance further removed than brother, the same gifts, warmer than socks, sweeter than sun-ripened dates.

She had not waited for them, could not have been expected to in a town overrun with young men, milling, milling, watching, wanting, sweeping before themselves and into themselves the town boys not yet enlisted or drafted and the other girls and then moving on to Africa or wherever. McCarron himself had not returned for fourteen years and only then because the world he had grown accustomed to elsewhere was jerked out from beneath his feet the way children jerk rugs from under brothers and send them cracking down on their behinds, enraged and helpless.

He was a long time thus in thought before turning his mind in on that which had sent him here to his cell in the first place. The premonition of something indefinable and unpleasant had been growing since late morning in his brain. No, more in the bottom of his stomach it was. He wondered before lunch if the infant gnawing, skirting, was caused by something he had eaten for breakfast. He wondered after lunch if the growing tremors were caused by something he had eaten for lunch. He wondered those two thoughts as people do, as anybody does, as first defensive measures before facing the more serious implications of gut ache. Because anyone can have an upset stomach and live through it with comparative peace of mind knowing that there is no phenomenon attached, but a very ordinary, very temporary malfunction. This was not that same kind of sensation. McCarron knew that. He knew he had known that all along but hoped by believing it to be rooted in something else, something like an overripe egg or too much peppersauce, it would become that. He had known the feeling before but not for nearly ten years, almost from the time he had come back here to Tigerstooth as principal of a school for which there was not or never had been any lineup of administrators, come here to remove himself from the death of his young wife and the horrors that surrounded her death, come here to the searing desert town where the sun in time burns away all but what is immediate.

He looked down at the fingers fumbling in his shirt pocket. He had stared so long at the bright horizon that he at first seemed not to recognize the fingers. He frowned and slid open the center drawer of his desk. When would that absent-minded habit leave? Of course a principal does not carry cigarettes in his shirt pocket, not in a climate where jackets are so seldom worn. He took a cigarette from the pack in the drawer. When it was lighted he sat back in his chair and blew the first smoke toward the window. His

68

stomach hurt more when he stretched back that way. With his elbows on the desk he finished the cigarette.

There had been new teachers come to his school before. Every year some one, if not a dozen—a third—of the teachers moved on and were replaced the next fall with new ones who would in their turn stay two or three or four years vascillating between the urge to return to Michigan or Ohio or New Hampshire and the urge to continue west to the Coast. They had always adjusted sufficiently, if not expertly, to Tigerstooth and it to them. That was it, no mistaking it. He had known that was it since morning when he had interviewed, briefly, singly, the four last new teachers to arrive. He had felt no such intestinal flutterings the day before after meeting the other six or seven new ones. Nor had he this morning, at least not so he noticed it, until he had reached the third and then the fourth interviews. But he had had—had been glad—to put the embryonic fears aside in order to see to the orientation meetings, the assignment of rooms and keys and paraphernalia. So the embryo had grown until now it would no longer be still but must be dealt with.

The first one of the four had been easy enough, had seemed ordinary enough, malleable, adjustable—in other words a teacher of the sort a principal likes to have. So had the second. And the third and even the fourth, taken singly signaled no distress, caused no waves. Ay, there you have it. Taken singly. Taken singly, McCarron, a resolute man, could bring all sharp edges to the round.

The first was Bill Dann. Not overly—nor under—bright, no quiz kid, certainly, but wide-grinning, respectfully nervous, and big enough through the chest and arms to gain the respect of a team of boys and their fathers. He—Dann—

had answered questions directly and clearly, if monosyllabically, and had himself asked the standard ones.

"What is your philosophy of education?" A rotten question.

"Well—my philosophy, sir?" Bill Dann scowled.

If it weren't for the damned Board—a really shitty question. "You know, why we have P.E., for instance. Or football."

"Well, Jes— Well, to teach them the games, to let them play. Everybody's got to know how to play ball *some*time."

"Yes. Do you think physical education ought to be required for everyone?"

Bill Dann frowned. "Is it? Here, I mean?"

"Yes."

"Well, sure. Especially for the real athletic guys. The ones that are, you know, handy with sports and stuff like that. They ought to have to take P.E. and go out for varsity sports. Sure, I'm all for it."

"But what about the others, the ones that really aren't very good. What about them? What would you do with them? In P.E. classes, I mean."

"Oh, there's things they can do. Games, you know, while I'm working out with the guys that have a interest, that really want to learn."

And so went the interview. Standard. McCarron could tell that the new coach had kept his head about him through the university, through the interminable garbage of education college, through the bits about "teaching the whole child" and "meeting the child where he is" and "meeting the needs of every child." Impossible goals that sound fine in textbooks, fine for college professors to talk about, but they didn't win games. McCarron knew that. It hadn't taken him long to learn that. He had coached football, and basketball, too, enough, God knew, to figure out how to get your school on top, to have people notice you, remember your name so that when you were tired there was an administrative job waiting for you somewhere. When the interview ended McCarron was satisfied with the Board's mail-order purchase. God, he's big, he thought again as he watched Dann stand, grin, and adjust his crotch.

The next was Jake Grantham. Nothing wrong there that age wouldn't settle. Age and with it the flattening of thought that experience renders. He would have to learn to focus his eyes on the person he was talking to and keep his hands still, that is, if he ever expected a class of sweaty kids to pay attention to what he said. They would have one or two altercations—not altercations, really, discussions—during the first few months about methodology, about the way things were done here and had been done here and would be done here. The standard, the accepted ways by which one accomplished the goals of a public school—then he would come round. McCarron would have to remind him sooner or later that things like art and dramatics were at best only peripheral to the main stream, frills they were called by the townspeople whenever the school budget was aired or whenever someone new was campaigning for a position on the Board. And, for Tigerstooth, McCarron had to agree. Such courses were best for shunting in the malcontents or the uneducables who could not be expected, after all, to progress very far in the solid subjects. Art, especially. Dramatics was safe enough. The people did like to see three or four plays a year with maybe *Why The Chimes Rang* at Christmas. So long as the teacher kept out that Broadway language (and come to think of it, there'd be some watching, some checking up, to do there this year) and used good things, things like *Arsenic and Old Lace* or *The Thirteenth*

71

Chair or *Little Women,* have at it, and welcome. It was art that bore scrutiny, it was art that tended to get out of hand, tended to overrun the boundaries, that gave rise sometimes to long-haired boys and boy-haired girls. But Grantham was male, anyway, which reduced to less than half the problem at the beginning. Tigerstooth hadn't forgotten Isabelle. Neither had McCarron. She was here when he came, in her third year, the last female art teacher Tigerstooth had tolerated. McCarron knew that near his right foot in the bottom drawer under layers of later accretion lay a folder of those pictures yet. Nine and eight years ago those pictures that he kept from destruction had solaced him in this secret place while he still kept himself away from actual, flesh women because the death of his wife hung close. Isabelle would have, in fact did, offer herself during the months before the scandal, but he had steadfastly declined. If he had not had to refuse her, if he could have wrapped himself into those long arms and legs, perhaps he could have helped her more when she needed help, or when he believed she needed it because any woman must be fragile and vulnerable under such attack. But he had not been able to, therefore he had said and done little when the town turned on her and she held them at bay alone.

So all that remained of Isabelle were those pictures—ink sketches, pencil drawings, charcoals, pastels—in his folder. He seldom looked through them any more, did not need to, and when he did it was with the detachment seen on the faces of men lined up at the back rack of a magazine store. He still knew some of the boys and girls—men and women now, twenty-seven or twenty-six years old with their own children in first or second grade—who had made those sketches, these the best of dozens, probably hundreds, that had been made of Isabelle who believed that advanced art students had a right to learn, indeed must learn, anatomical drawing from real anatomy. McCarron, at the time beside himself with rage that seventeen- and eighteen-year-old boys had seen with impunity that which he refused himself, later could chuckle. He would still give anything to have heard the original conversation between Mr. and Mrs. Marspack when they, fanning through their son's sketch books, began to realize the awful truth—that progressively, as the boy's talent improved through the books, the nude studies more and more resembled his art teacher.

But, McCarron rethought to himself, Grantham—any man—being male, struck out most of that problem. Except he knew, too, that such things, like lightning, never repeated themselves so that all you really knew was that someday the lightning would strike again ten, twenty, a hundred feet to the right or left. It was enough to hope that the damage would be slight or, better, would go unnoticed. It was more than enough to hope that in the twenty-two years remaining to him before retirement, the coruscation set up any time boys and girls and male teachers and female teachers gathered for nine months under one roof, so to speak, would not burst into holocaust.

"Could you state your philosophy of education? That is, how—"

"To bring to the most students the best experiences of learning, and particularly in my case, a knowledge of the humane and the good," chanted Grantham. "Through the expression of the arts, that is, the *fine* arts—music, painting, drama, you know—to release them into the full stream of life, to awaken them to what—"

"Yes," interrupted McCarron. "Fine." God spare me. After all I've lived through and have yet to live through, spare me that. "Are you—how do you feel about modern

73

art?" Yes, perhaps the question was wide. "You know, this wild stuff, this paint-throwing?" Now, with all your enthusiasm, answer me that.

Jake began several times to formulate an answer but gave up in despair. Palms up he answered, weakly, frowning. "There won't be any paint-throwing in my classes."

And so with the other two interviews with Mrs. Deek and with Steinhart. There was a disarming vagueness about their answers, as there was a certain ambiguity about their manila-foldered files, doubtless accountable to their older age—and he did not believe Steinhart was actually only thirty-eight—as he, himself, were he in their spot, could sympathize with. Age taught you to cover up some, taught you—discretion, that's the word—taught you not to spill your guts (even your pedagogical guts) all at once or ever if you could help it. She was on the make. It didn't take a Ph.D. to figure that out. But who isn't? On the make, that is; what woman slipping past forty, without a husband (why?), isn't? Nothing ever comes of it. Steinhart would get on his nerves a little, probably. The kind that's hard to talk to when you're principal. Too cool. Sure of himself and looking a little like he has just smelled shit in the corner. He'd been around. Might have some good stories. One of these nights he might ask him over to the place for a pizza and a can of beer.

Sitting at his desk now in the bright, late afternoon, McCarron knew the pain in his stomach had risen sharply during those last two interviews. There was nothing he could put a finger on. That was the trouble. It was as if the pieces of a great, four-part puzzle had appeared to visit him singly, each unrelated to the other, each with its own distinct jags and curves and edges, but each in some way connectible, cut from the same board by an intrepid sawman

74

too devious and illusive to match. He believed that if he could match the sawman in time, if he could fit the pieces into one recognizable square before they discovered their kinship, before they flew together like bits of iron to a magnet, all which way out of order, he could win.

It was Angela who suggested the picnic in the first place sometime during the afternoon of that first day of orientation meetings when the four of them converged at the teachers' mailboxes in the outer office. The last of the gatherings they were expected to attend as new teachers was over, so far as they could tell from the dittoed agenda. Like the last step of a treasure hunt they each took a large manila envelope from their boxes and leaning side by side along the counter that separated them from the two secretaries, they mulled the envelopes' contents.

"This, I assume," said Baker, "is the authorized version of our bible." He flipped the pages of a spiral-bound booklet: *Teachers' Handbook, Tigerstooth Union High School,* it read on the cover.

" 'To be kept at all times in the teacher's desk for handy reference,' " Angela read. She was idly slipping her fingertips along the collar of her blouse. "My, it's hot, isn't it," she added.

" 'In case of fire, this book and the charred remains of the teacher had damn well better be found in the desk,' " Baker said, holding the book up close to his face, fanning the leaves.

Bill Dann stepped closer and spoke over his shoulder. "Where does it say that?" He looked at his own copy. "Mine doesn't say that."

Angela slapped him on the arm and laughed. "Oh, Bill," she said.

"Oh," Bill said.

"Jake," Baker said, "what the hell was he talking about in that session after lunch?"

"What? You mean the whole child and all that? The moral and the educated?"

"Yes."

Jake shrugged. "How should I know?"

"Well, I thought you had the degree in education."

"Art education," Jake corrected. "I consider art a discipline, you know. Distinct from educational theory and philosophy, as such. The fact that esthetic appreciation and talent are innate qualities makes them fall beyond the realm, as it were, of the standard—"

"Oh, my God," Baker interrupted.

"Well, you asked."

"Yes, but I've changed my mind." He poked the brown envelope back into its box. "Besides, I'm going to have an attack."

"Of what?" Angela asked. She moved her fingertips from her blouse top to Baker's arm.

He smiled. The silver fillings of his teeth showed on one side. "Of sobriety," he said.

It was then that Angela suggested the picnic. She had been thinking of it all day, she said, and had it all planned. Before the others had much time to consider, she dictated to them a list of the things each could buy at the store.

"We'll meet at the Granthams' at about six o'clock. Is that all right, Jake?" she said. He said sure it was. Then she turned to Bill and said, "That is, Bill, if Baker and I can ride with you from the hotel? No car," she laughed.

"I thought you were going to look for a house."

"Tomorrow."

"I hate picnics," Baker said, just as Angela imagined all was settled.

"Oh, you couldn't! I have always loved them." She looked past him out the glass doors to where the sun was brilliant and relentless. "We used to have these wonderful picnics when . . . oh, a long time ago. Didn't you?" Her eyes came back to his.

"No. I could never imagine why anyone would choose voluntarily to go out in the woods and sit in the cow dung to eat food that isn't any good in the first place but is worse eaten in the company of bugs and wild beasts. Can't we just sit in someone's place and drink?"

"Balls, Baker—" Bill stopped as the two secretaries' heads rose up from their typewriters like puppets. He lowered his voice and moved toward the doors. "Christ," he modified, "it won't hurt you none." He opened the doors and went out. The others followed.

So the picnic was held, despite Baker's protesting—assuaged somewhat by Anna Margaret's pronouncement when they stopped by for her. "I hate picnics," she had said. But she had gone, too, happy to be shut of the house whose furnishings had grown worse, it seemed, at second inspection and which would not, with any amount of moving and rearranging, improve themselves. "You moved the furniture," Jake said when he entered. "You shouldn't do that. Just leave it be."

"If I had the strength, I'd throw it all in the alley. Orange crates would be better," she had answered.

"Do you have an alley?" Baker said, incidentally. He was inspecting one of the chairs. "God, I haven't seen lion claws on chair legs for a hundred years." He straightened. "What period would you call this, Mrs. Grantham?"

"Early attic, I think it is."

77

The others had gone on into the kitchen where Jake was pretty sure there was something to drink. Anna Margaret and Baker stood for a moment laughing at the motley collection of horsehair furniture that bulged in shiny lumps in the center of each chair and sofa seat. Then they went into the kitchen, too. When they came to the doorway he stood aside. He touched her elbow as they passed through.

Angela had directed the picnic with more verve than the heat, even at evening, would warrant for most circumstances. The food was got through, although Baker ate nothing, having made the mistake of placing his sandwich momentarily on its waxed paper on the ground and then discovering a bug of unrecognized species but of disheartening size and color, on it. He would not be persuaded even after Bill's suggestion that that sort of bug doesn't eat sandwiches but was just walking somewhere.

When the food was gone Angela said it was time to swim before it got too dark. She stood and by untying the belt of her wrapper emerged from it like a black and white butterfly from its cocoon. She fiddled with the folding of the wrapper for as long as it took for the four other pairs of eyes to glance and appraise. She had chosen her black bathing suit wisely of a material that pushed and held the parts of her body in a flattering arrangement, even if in so doing it bulged out the meat of her thighs too much and too white below the elastic.

"Come on!" she called and ran down from the bank of willows toward the water, fluttering her arms the way women do who are beyond the age of running naturally in public or who dread having to turn their backs, however briefly, to inspection. At the edge of the river where the water cut back into a sandy inlet, she turned to wait for Jake who ran after her. At that distance, against the water

78

that yet caught some of the receding yellow sky, she appeared younger and slimmer and her skin less pale.

Bill stood slowly. He brushed idly at the dirt on his trunks. He looked down at Anna Margaret. He frowned. "Aren't you coming?" he said.

"No. If I'm going through with this," she patted her stomach, "it's time I gave it a rest."

Bill watched Jake and Angela splashing out into the water. He turned back. "Baker?"

Baker shook his head. He held a can of beer between his knees, muttering at it. "Automatic openers be damned." He yanked at the thin metal tab. "It's all part of a diabolical scheme," he said. "People who design cereal boxes and frozen-food containers and automatic beer cans must hate their jobs. And other people," he added, giving the partly lifted tab another jerk. "I can see the glee on their faces. 'That'll fix them bastards' they say every time they come up with a new box nobody can open."

"Christ," Bill said. He reached across and took the can from Baker. He wrenched off the tab. "Here."

"Thanks." He watched the foam edge up around the opening. "I'd hate to be a poor peasant depending on American Care packages. God, think of the frustration." He drank from the can.

Bill moved restlessly on his bare feet. "You coming?" he said to Anna Margaret.

"No, really."

He hesitated again. Then he walked down toward the water where now Jake and Angela were splashing each other.

"What a specimen," Baker said, watching him go. "He would've given Darwin fits."

Anna Margaret laughed.

"What a gentle laugh you have," he said.

"And what a caustic one you have."

"Have I? I'll change it. Here, do you want some of this?" He offered her the can. "We'll have to share it, you know," he said.

She took the can. "Well, how was your day? No one has said."

Baker snorted. "Beautiful beyond all dreams, as you can imagine. We have reached the true Utopia."

"Seriously."

"How can you be serious about such a place?"

"But how about the school. How about Mr. McCarron."

"I don't know." He took the can back. "Standard, I think. Up from the locker room. I could have said his speeches for him. In anybody but a school administrator, you'd blame the sun. I don't know."

Angela shrieked, down in the water. They looked up in time to see Bill lifting her above his head. The strain of the lifting bulged his arms. He tossed her out into deeper water where she disappeared for a moment, her white legs churning the water white.

"McCarron's point this afternoon had something to do with morals and teaching, so far as I could tell," Baker said. He dug in the dirt between his arched knees with a stick.

"Was he for them or against them?"

He lifted his head. "Morals?" He smiled. "It's the same line—no better than the kids themselves. They all think the word moral derives somehow from the word sex."

"And?"

"Me? They don't pay me enough to teach morality and French both."

"You don't mean that."

He looked at her again. He stopped talking to watch

80

her light her cigarette, leaning toward the match so that her hair swung forward beside her face. "Morality is honesty. That's enough. That's enough for any of us to carry."

She blew on the match. "How nice it would all be, then, if you were right."

"I am right."

"No. Then every person's honesty would become his private ethic. Just for himself."

"That's exactly the way it has to be. We're just jacking off, otherwise. Pardon the analogy."

"I follow." She stood up and they laughed when her joints crackled. "I've got to walk for a while."

They walked along the bank parallel with the river that below them had turned darker, caught now by flecks of orange reflecting from the bare rock peaks on the far side. To their left the sun, gone from sight, lit the sky with a swath of orange. The tamaracks and willows and mesquite turned to silhouettes between the orange and them. She walked a little ahead of him. She shook her head.

"No," she said. "But I wish that were so. You have to be something for someone else, not just you."

"In God's name, why? And slow down. I'm not from the provinces."

She fell back in step with him. "Then why bother with any of it? You sound like Polonius. To thine own self and so forth."

"Laugh at the old fool. He was right after all. But what you say is, too. Why bother. You can never mean as much to anyone else as you do to yourself."

"What a sad, sad thing to say."

"It's the root of all sad things."

Caught by the change in his voice she turned half back to him. He was watching the ground as he walked, for a

81

moment lost to consciousness. His cynical mouth was relaxed, his thin lips parted. He looked older. Anna Margaret walked on. "How can you teach, then? And be any good, anything but a fake?"

Baker laughed. "My lovely, there you have it. Precisely that. I am a good teacher—and I mean that—exactly because in that case I am a fake. A grand, dishonest, moral charlatan. That's the secret in civilization, you know, to what we call maturity. Teach them a set of fake truths so when they grow older they can discover for themselves that all that was crap. That way everyone feels smug and marvelous."

They came then to a place where the shore curved and mesquite scrub brush came down to the river bank and blocked their way. They looked out onto a small sand bar set like an opal in the water. On the sand bar a single waterbird—a killdeer, or perhaps a sandpiper—stood on his still, black stick-legs and looked across the river at nothing but the other side. He held his pose a long moment, as they watched, then waded a step or two into the water.

Near her shoulder Baker spoke quietly. "God, it's enough to make you lose your mind."

Then the bird, the color of the sand, cried a tiny, two-note sound and flew up from the water toward the far bank and was lost from sight. The orange beyond the misshapen trees had burned out. The colors of the east hills and the river and the desert faded quickly without the sun—the source at once of both whatever torture and beauty the Mojave Desert gives.

Each had, like the day colors, drawn back into himself as if knowing separately that the nervous moment of the bird and the water and the last sun had passed seductively close.

As they walked back they could hear Angela's fluid voice rising, falling, and Jake's laughter. At the picnic site Bill knelt before a pile of sticks, watching them catch fire. He looked up at her. "Where have you been?" She smiled at him. The creases smoothed on his forehead. He looked down into the fire that was more smoke than flame. He sat back on his heels and said, "I've built a fire."

By full dark Angela and Jake had quieted, drawn back up the bank to the fire. She huddled into her wrapper and stood watching the fire. The mesquite limbs did not flame much, but along them orange and red squares and rectangles formed like stained glass and reflected in the blue metallic paint of Bill's car. Her head lifted, her eyes circled in white, when suddenly the first coyote experimented with the night from across the river where the rocky peaks began. His yap and mourning sounded close and far away. From somewhere he was answered.

"It's all right, Angie," Bill said. He was leaning against the side of his car fleeting with his guitar.

Angela looked back toward the river. She moved around the fire and sat next to Bill.

"That's a werewolf, Angela," Baker said. "It's that damned guitar. He thinks he hears his mate. Or a victim."

"What the hell's the difference?" Jake said. He pulled the tab of a beer can with a snap. He laughed. "I mean, between a mate and—"

"Sit down, Jakie," Anna Margaret said. She pushed away some sticks from the ground beside her.

Jake looked at the spot she had cleared. He sat there. He did not see her raised hand about to rest on his shoulder as he leaned forward clasping his knees to stare at the burning limbs. "Look at those colors and shapes!" he said.

"That's true encaustic. I wish I'd brought my sketch pad, at least. Why didn't we think to bring it, Anna?" He looked at her briefly, then turned back toward the fire.

Baker said, "Wouldn't it be easier just to build a fire in your studio every night? The whole house in flames ought to be a hell of a painting."

Jake sighed. "No, there wouldn't be time. Look. Already the forms on that log have changed. It was just a moment there, when they were perfect. It's gone now."

Peter McCarron had a rotten night. He went to bed early, calmly, deliberately, bathed, but unrelaxed. He ate carefully, or rather he sipped a bowl of beef broth and a whisky. He stretched himself out on his bed, under the sheet, and leisurely willed sleep. He lay listening to the night come on from the desert that stretched away from his small house, the outermost one of the five streets of new concrete block houses past the school on the farther slope of the Acropolis. Nights, rather than days, in the Mojave Desert are more full of sounds. The going of the sun gives rise to small creature noises and later, in the full dark, the sounds of the coyotes skirting the hills and the maniacal answers of the town dogs.

In the early dark morning, long before time to be up, he awoke. He lay straight under the sheet and waited until at last the ceiling turned gray and then white. His stomach did not hurt any longer, but it was not satisfied, was not normal, either. He awoke frightened still by he knew not what, unless of course, it was the dream. The dream, that particular one, he had not dreamed for nine—nearly ten—years. He wondered why it returned now, why after he had so long forgotten it it should come back. A station wagon full of nuns. That's what it amounted to. He always was shorter than the station wagon as if he were lying or sitting on the ground as he watched it appear close at hand and pass by. Always the white-framed faces beneath black cowls, smiling altruistically into distance with only the head robes of the driving nun gently flapping and fluttering, presumably from the air of the open window. Then round and round, with him in the center still looking up, the nuns drove, their faces gradually changing from benevolence to joy then to mirth then to gaiety. Round and round, the station wagon and its passengers growing smaller as he sank deeper into the vortex looking up at them—he surrounded by swirling black, they silhouetted against blue—until he awoke vomiting. This morning, by lying still, he avoided the vomiting. This time, unlike ten years ago, the nuns drove a Volkswagen bus.

As he dressed and drank coffee with his poached egg, as he drove to the high school, he felt again the rising beat in his stomach, something connected to the events of yesterday. In the parking lot he saw them. His premonitions, unidentifiable, were nevertheless confirmed. This was the first time he had seen them together, the four of them, five now. There they stood, talking, until he walked by, then turning together to watch him, impassively, he thought, and there in the car—he only glimpsed her—that must be Grantham's wife. Long, straight hair, a cigarette (should not smoke on the school grounds) in the hand dangling out the car window, long eyes. Like a scene from a pageant they seemed to look out upon him from an invisible niche.

McCarron whirled toward them again. The puzzle. There were the pieces together against the black car. Could he match the sawman? He wondered. Steinhart raised his hand then. It was as if an electric switch had been thrown. Their voices chimed in scattered tones. "Good morning, Mr. McCarron," they said.

All but the girl with the long hair. She did not say anything.

Six

IDIOT," Anna Margaret laughed. "If you know it's going to hurt so much, why do you do it?"

Baker was holding his head in his hands gently, as if without support it would shatter like a glass ornament dropped. He turned his whole torso partly toward her. It was a doleful look. He faced the athletic field again. "It's the goddamn heat," he said. "Anywhere in the civilized world this wouldn't happen. Jesus," he said. He rubbed his temples, ruffling his long hair there where the gray was picked out by the sun.

"If you had gone home like the rest of us."

"Aren't you going to add 'at a decent hour'? You sound like a parent already."

"I'm practicing."

"Yes." He looked at her again. "You shouldn't be smoking on the school grounds, you know. You'll bring the ten plagues down on the land, selah."

"Maybe we could burn down this stadium. For diversion." She tossed her cigarette out onto the cinder track that circled the ball field.

"You're bent on cardinal sin, aren't you?" He rubbed his forehead.

"Is pyromania a sin now?"

"When it threatens the people's temples, it is. Can't we go now?"

"I promised Jakie we'd wait for him," she said.

Baker looked toward the school buildings that edged the south side of the ball field. "What in hell's he doing, painting the Sistine Ceiling?"

"I don't know."

"We could have had an even dozen martinis by now. And be, if not cool, at least in the shade." He flapped the front of his shirt. "If I weren't at death's door, I'd walk downtown."

"Think of something pleasant."

"I've tried."

"How about your students? Any good first impressions?"

He groaned. "I'd rather think of the heat." Then he shrugged. "They don't look any different. No smarter or dumber than anywhere else in the world. Only McCarron's got such a routine to get through it'll be a month before I get to the first lesson."

"Where else in the world have you taught? You never say."

"I forget." He nodded toward the ball field. "Here comes Mr. Physical Condition."

Bill had left his teams sweating and pounding in the center of the field. As he came toward them he peeled off his T-shirt and wiped his face and arms. His shaggy hair splayed down over his eyes. His face looked tired and red. He flopped down on one of the wooden risers, a step lower. "Hi," he said. He mopped his hair back from his eyes.

"Hi," Anna Margaret said. She watched the light shift on the wet skin of his back.

He turned, shielding his eyes with one hand. "It's hotter than hell, isn't it."

"Impossible," Baker said. "This is hell."

"Jesus, you look dead," Bill said.

"Thank you."

"Here," Anna Margaret said, reaching her hand over Bill's arm, "give me your shirt a minute." She wiped the perspiration from his neck and shoulders. His back arched under the touch.

"Good," he said when she had finished. He took the damp shirt and idly rubbed his chest, watching the boys moving listlessly in their white jerseys on the field.

"Well, what do you think of them?"

"The team?" Bill lifted his shoulders. He wiped under his arms with the shirt. "Okay. They'll be okay." He leaned back with his elbows on the plank above. "You shouldn't be out here in the sun, should you?" he said to Anna Margaret.

"She wants it to be born with a suntan," Baker said.

Bill tipped back his head so that he saw her upside down. He waited for her answer.

"I feel fine," she said. She moved her leg away from Bill's arm where the contact made it hotter.

A football came arching and tumbling out of the field and bounced onto the cinders before them and once against the wooden risers. After it came the boy for whom the pass was intended, his cleats noisy in the cinders. They watched the light sweep of his torso and arms, belied by the knotty pads under his shirt, as he bent to the ball still spinning. When he straightened with it in his two hands, he faced them for a moment and each saw variously a kind of smile

89

flash, and black-lashed wide eyes pass over them from his brown face the color of the football.

Then he turned and was gone as if he had not been at all, fading back into the identical figures in white on the field.

"What was that?" said Anna Margaret.

"That is the difference between winning or losing this season," Bill said.

"Does all your team look at people that way?" She rubbed her upper arms with her crossed hands. "I feel like I've just been stripped."

Bill laughed. "No. That's Rudy."

"He's Indian, isn't he," she said.

Baker answered. "Yes. He's in one of my classes, too."

Bill sat forward again. "What time is it?"

"Nearly six-thirty," Baker said. "When are you going to halt this sadism so we can all go home and drink? PTA tonight, in case you've forgotten."

"That late?" He squinted at the sun. "Christ, it feels like noon." He got up. "Okay. I'll call it off." He walked out onto the field.

"Let's go roust out Michelangelo." Baker stood and held to her hand while they walked down the stadium levels.

They found Jake in the art room confronting a large canvas that rested on two easels placed side by side. "Look what I found," he said, tapping the canvas with a brush handle. "Back there in the storeroom, abandoned." He grinned. "I couldn't resist it."

Baker peered closely at the partly finished painting. "Don't you have it upside down?" he said. He shook his head sadly.

"It's late, Jakie," Anna Margaret said. "You have that meeting tonight, remember."

"I know, but Christ sake, I'm excited about this painting

right now. It's really *moving*, don't you think?" He stood away from the canvas and tilted his head.

"Yes."

"You and Baker take the car. I'll walk home after while, okay? I've got to work out something here." He stepped back to the painting.

"You could come with Bill. He'll be through soon. You could ride—"

"Okay. Look at this area right here, Anna. Isn't that color great?"

"Yes."

"I still think it's upside down," said Baker.

Jake turned. "Christ sake, how can a *color* be upside down?"

Baker smiled. "Anna?" he said.

"Come home before long, Jakie," she said. "Will you?"

"Okay. I said yes." He faced the canvas again and idly sloshed a paintbrush in a can of turpentine.

They left the art room and walked across the asphalt campus toward the parking lot. "You see?" Baker said.

"Nevermind. Just nevermind," she said.

"Does he have talent?"

She stopped with her hand on the fender of the car. She looked back toward the school buildings. "Yes," she said.

"But not as much as you hoped."

"Why do you say that?"

He wiped a streak along the fender with his finger. "I'm just looking for a reason."

"A reason for what? For marrying him? Talent isn't everything."

Baker smiled. "That hardly becomes you," he said.

"He has enthusiasm and . . . and energy. He will be successful." She opened the car door. "Come on, if you're going to work on that hangover again before PTA."

McCarron moved back a step from his cell window in case they could see him if they looked up. But they went on past. Two more of them gone. With Angela Deek, that made three. He didn't mind teachers hanging around for a reasonable time after school—that showed a certain esprit, and of course, Dann had to if that team was ever going to shape up, but Jesus, he didn't feel too great this afternoon. He could do with some rest. He scraped his desk chair over near the window. He propped his elbows on the sill and watched the shadows of the buildings grow longer and beyond them, across the river, the shadows blacken in the jagged hills. He wondered if chiaroscuro applied to real-life views. Karen would have known.

Karen McCarron. How the name had lilted when she said it. But enough of that. She was dead and he had wrenched out the new roots they had put down on their hilltop and brought all that was back here to the desert where no root ever holds deep. Enough.

Back to where having been a child at least makes things, some things, predictable. Where you know and do not need to think. Where you are too far away from the green hill above the green bay ever to be tempted to fall on your knees and hug the gravestone. But enough.

McCarron still sat at the cell window after the last of the football boys had streamed from the gymnasium, fresh and loud, horsing in half-dozens toward the student parking lot or down off the edge of the hill. He watched Dann and Grantham cross toward the lot, Grantham talking, moving his hands in big gestures, Dann walking heavily, tiredly.

It would be nearly another hour before the meeting.

Before the teachers began returning, before Patricia Dunbar and her refreshments committee began puttering, pecking over their goddamn platters of cookies and their doilies and their punch and their ten-gallon coffee pot.

The PTA. Jesus, deliver me, McCarron mused. Where in the world do they leave you alone? Where is the fairyland where no one hangs on fences to give advice, where they've all learned that it's the getting through that matters, that Treasurers' Reports and Minutes of the Previous Meeting and New Business and doilies only heap the manure pile you have to climb over before it's all wrapped up.

McCarron smiled. Madam President I wish to make a motion. Screw you, Madam President.

The five drew together outside the door of the glass-walled cafeteria, the Multi-Purpose Room, at eight o'clock.

"Well," Jake said. "We might as well go on in. We're here."

"Your logic eludes me," Baker said. He stood unevenly, staring into the big room. "God, look at them. I know now how Daniel felt."

"Oh, Baker," Angela said. Her fingertips touched his forearm.

"Or Prometheus' liver. Behold the vultures," Baker said. He turned. "Anna?"

"Here."

"Oh. Behold, I say."

"I behold."

"This," he pointed toward the room, "is the pinnacle of matronhood. The true attainment, the apex of life up toward which you must strive."

"Christ," Bill said.

"Let us not mix our images," Baker said.

93

"You're drunk," Bill said.

"I bow to your superior observation. But remember what Our Lord said about casting stones."

He flung open the door and led the way into the cafeteria where the high-strung sounds of renewed acquaintance, of inspection and anticipation floated now that the year was surely begun, now that the summer was surely past, now that McCarron's new acquisitions were in the corral ready to be sized up.

Bill held open the door for Anna Margaret, the last to enter. When she smiled his eyes darkened. "Hi," he said.

"Name tags!" a lady said. She officiated at a small table near the door. "Everyone must get a name tag." She pushed five cards forward and extended a pen. "We all like to know who we are," she said. Her smile was bright, cheery, practiced.

Baker took the first card. "Madam," he said. "Do you know who you are?" He drew a wavy-lined X on his card and pinned it to his shirt. The woman did not lose her smile.

Past the name-tag table the five found themselves in the center of a deep circle with the other new ones. "Michigan," the big man in the yellow shirt was saying, "the birthplace, you could say, of America's marching bands," and another voice, "Physical science," and another, "I consider Tigerstooth a challenge, don't you?" and "I always begin by laying down the rules." The voices rose and drifted in the center gathering. On the fringes the town people circled and talked of railroads and Eastern Stars. Each group appraised. The older teachers, the accepted ones, held to the fringes and their own conclusions.

"Pardon me," Baker said. "I would introduce myself, but I don't see your name tag."

"They gave me a blank," Anna Margaret answered.

"Ah. Well." Baker shook his head. "Perhaps if you could remember?"

"Not the faintest notion."

"Terrible. Could it be Grantham?"

"How do you spell that?" she said.

"Oh, for Christ sake, Anna Margaret," Jake whispered.

From his chair at the speaker's table set on the low dais, McCarron drew football-play X's and O's in the margins of his notes and watched the people gather and separate. Like yearlings at a cattle auction. And there they are, those five, off by themselves already. Match the sawman.

McCarron poured himself a glass of water from the pitcher. It was too cold to ease his stomach much.

All tagged and ready for the pens. Give everybody a tag so we know. Tag the whole goddamn world, Madam President; all the better to know who's screwing who—whom. X takes the ball and runs between O and O. Give that man a name tag. Do good, Sonny, and you will be a four-name-tag man.

"Why do you smile, Mr. McCarron?"

"Oh." He half rose in his chair. "Madam—Mrs. Roslo." He touched the chair back next to his. "Nothing. Nothing."

Mrs. Roslo continued to stand. The peonies on her hat bobbed when she talked. "Isn't this lovely," she said. She surveyed the crowd.

"Yes. Very lovely." What, in God's name?

"All so lovely," she said. She breathed as if standing in crushed flowers. "Do you like the blue name tags? Better than the white ones we used last year, I mean?"

"Oh, yes," McCarron said. "They are—well, they go good with the walls. Or don't you think so?" Jesus hope in time of need—however it goes.

95

"But the walls are green, Mr. McCarron." The peonies bobbed and shook.

"Yes." Of course they're green.

"The refreshments are lovely. Just lovely."

"Yes."

"Isn't this lovely?"

McCarron's glass was nearly empty when it dropped from his fingers onto the table and tipped over. There wasn't much water to sop up with his handkerchief.

"My, he's big, isn't he," she said.

"Who?" McCarron squeezed the handkerchief over the righted glass.

"That one." She pointed. "That new one."

"Oh. That's Dann."

"Football?"

"Yes."

"My." The peonies bobbed.

All balls, Madam President. That's the way you might put it.

"She's dark, isn't she?"

"Who?"

"His wife."

"That's not his wife."

"Oh?" The peonies stopped. Mrs. Roslo waited. Then, "And the other one? The blond one?"

"Mrs. Deek. English."

"*Mrs.* Deek? Where is her husband?"

"I have no idea."

"Oh? My."

Angela Morton Deek, Madam President. On the make. And I don't know where her husband is and I don't know if she dyes her hair and I don't know if her boobs are really that big or whether that blouse will still hide them five minutes from now.

Mrs. Roslo sat in her chair and prepared to rap the people to their seats and the meeting to order. One more question: "Mr. McCarron?"

"Yes, Mrs. Roslo."

"Why do you suppose those five hang back like that? I mean, they don't seem to be mixing."

"I don't know, Mrs. Roslo," McCarron said.

"Well, it makes one wonder, doesn't it."

"It certainly does."

"And I don't see but one of them wearing their name tag." She lifted somewhat in her chair. "Do you?" The peonies shook vividly. "It makes a person wonder."

Wonder away, Madam President. I once saw a French whore with an ass the size of yours with her name tattoed across it. It was a long name. The crack made an accent. How do you like that name tag, Madam President? Do you think that would up the percentage? Your name tattoed with every life membership? Rap your goddamn gavel, Mme.

"Secrets again, Mr. McCarron?"

"No, Mrs. Roslo. Shall we get started? My stomach hurts."

Seven

ANNA MARGARET lay far over on the edge of the bed staring up, her eyes following the rumples and cracks and circles. The ceiling, a piteous gray, had once been papered. Under god knew how many later coats of paint the paper had pulled loose. It bagged and pouted, and in a few places tiny ferns of the paper had broken through and hung downward, beginning a patient recoil that would in a few years leave gaping, jagged pores. She watched the breaths of her cigarette prowl upward. Sometimes the smoke reached the ceiling and fanned out flat against the timeworn paper.

It was an old house set a block back from the street that faced the railroad, which meant that originally it had not been built for a railroad worker. The house was too big for that, anyway. Whatever had been its early conceit, it now would have been long collapsed into dust had it not been built of stone—painted a brilliant red-trimmed turquoise—instead of clapboard. Outside, the house seemed, despite its size, to shudder back in terror from the five or six giant tamaracks that surrounded it, treacherous, brittle trees that fly apart in a high wind. It seemed to be held up in defiance by the majesty of its paint rather than its stone. Inside it was rambling and purposeless and dark.

Anna Margaret could tell from the light that shadowed through the curtains that it was time to be up and doing something about dinner. Jake would be hungry when he awoke.

She tugged her right leg from under his where he had flung it in a last spasm of wakefulness. Her leg was numbed by his weight. It was sticky. He would probably catch cold lying that way in his perspiration, even on such a stifling day. She turned her head to watch him sleep. He sprawled flat out on the bed, his head turned toward her, his face calm and if not handsome, more handsome than at any other time. His body was long and slender-hipped, the kind of body that without consciousness carried about it an insolence centered in those forward-thrust hips. It was the kind of body on which clothes—no matter how much too big and how sloppy—seem only a veneer. And he would probably always remain that way, driven to slenderness and hardness by the sheer force of his nerves. So unlike Emil who had been gentle and quiet and whom she had hurt. With Emil there had been hours of peace in his studio, she sitting on the floor or making coffee in the electric pot they had joined funds to buy, while he painted or made lovely, long things with his hands. And when he was tired he would come to her on the floor where she sat watching or reading, or on the slender cot, and they would make love and talk and share a cigarette.

Emil would have loved the idea of the baby. And again she wondered, was that something she should tell Jake. Probably. Probably not.

Funny. She had not loved Emil, just the solitude and beauty of being with him in the studio. Of watching him

99

work the grace of his own person into what he was painting or sculpting. Of sometimes not talking for a half day when he was absorbed, when his last sentence had stopped in mid-flight and she knew that he had forgotten her. Nor had he really loved her because in the life of a person like Emil there is nothing that is permanent beyond the creation. That is why he would have delighted in knowing the baby was his. That is why he would have forgotten all about the child in time.

She stood up to dress, then she pulled the sheet from the end of the bed where he had kicked it and covered Jake. She watched his sleeping face as she closed the door of the bedroom.

"Don't you know better than to back into a room?"

She gasped and whirled. "Baker!" He sat on the sofa, his legs fastidiously crossed, a glass in his hand. "Where in the world—"

"I repeat, don't you know better than to back into a room? What if you had been naked, as I gather you have just been, and there was a perfect stranger—a burglar, say, or a rapist—sitting here?"

She sat down abruptly. "God, you scared me!"

"Sitting here," he repeated. "What would he see first?"

"What are you talking about?"

"At least if you face the room you are entering, you have a chance to make a decision before he attacks. Whether you'll run to him or away from him. Drink?" He lifted his glass and shook it.

"I don't know whether to be mad or laugh." She pulled the hair back from the edges of her face. "You've got a monumental nerve, I know that."

He shook the glass again.

She smiled. "Yes," she said. "I need one." She followed him to the kitchen and watched him mix the drinks.

"Water?"

"Yes."

He turned to her with the finished drink and with a lopsided smile clicked his heels. "To the phenomenon and wonder of two weeks' life lived in Tigerstooth."

Anna Margaret laughed. "Two weeks. How many does that leave?" She took the glass from him.

"Until what?"

"I don't know," she shrugged. She held the glass in both hands. When she tipped her face, the long hair swept forward to hide it. Then she said, "But it should be until something. Shouldn't it?"

He watched her eyes for a moment and his own seemed to soften, then glint again. "Idiot child," he said. "Don't you know? It's always a week until the next week starts. That's enough."

"Give me a cigarette?" She took one from the pack and reached a kitchen match from above the stove. "So shall I roust the sleeping prince for our celebration? From what I learn of art teachers here, he's gone the limit."

Baker sat at the kitchen table. He pulled out another chair. "I prefer to let sleeping princes—and artists—lie. And, I presume from your rose-flushed cheeks, he is at the moment exhausted."

"So it would seem." She took a saucer from among the dishes in the drying rack. She sat at the table. "Well, what's your judgment of Tigerstooth Union High now? Are you sorry you came?"

"Am I sorry? No. That gets you nowhere—which is, you might say, where we've got. My first judgment holds; McCarron is a fool."

"He's in the right place."

"Yes. But the philosophy is wrong. You should either have a wise, or at least a sane, man leading fools. Or the other way around. It's when all levels are the same that the boat rocks. And I think McCarron's boat is rocking."

"I'd say it has reason."

"Would you now?" Baker drank until the ice cubes slid forward. He lowered the glass. "So would I. More?"

"I'm fine."

He brought the bottle back to the table with him. "More than anybody, I think Angela's got him on his knees praying every night."

Anna Margaret smiled. "Meaning?"

"She kicked a kid out of her class already, for a starter. Although," he held up his hand, "I am totally in favor of as much of that as possible, it is a bit early. Next week should have been soon enough."

"Has she kept her blouse on?"

Baker laughed. "I didn't think other women were supposed to see such things among their kind. Yes, that is also cause for a drink. But give her time. Bitch."

"Angela? Jakie seems to think she made the world."

"No, I mean you. And Jakie doesn't know it, but he's probably nearer right than not. Don't forget, I have seen her sans Revlon. She looks as if she has made the world— or is working her way."

"Now who's a bitch?"

"You're beautiful," he said.

"You've changed the subject."

Baker went to the sink for more water. With the full glass in hand he leaned forward to look through the window above the sink. There was nothing to be seen but the side yard littered with the constantly dropping tamarack needles, and at the back edge of the yard the odd little two-storied cottage. "That place for rent?" he asked.

She put out her cigarette in the saucer. She came to stand beside him at the window. "Yes."

"Good. Tomorrow I'll move in there."

"You haven't even seen it inside. It might be worse than this place."

Baker turned. "It could not possibly be worse than this place," he said.

"As a young Tigerstooth matron, I should be insulted."

"What does it matter? I can't go on living in that hotel. And one place is about as horrid to live as another. Besides, if I live next door, we can drink every afternoon. That way, my beauty, you and I may survive more weeks than you've dreamed."

She swept back the hair from her face. She held out her empty glass. "What about Sleeping Prince? Don't you think he'll mind? Any second now he may come foaming out of that bed and tear us limb from limb."

"Do you think he'll notice?"

"That hurt."

"Sorry. Do you love him?"

She watched him and frowned. "Why is everyone so worried about that?"

"I didn't know everyone was."

"It's as if the idea is out of style."

"Well?"

"Yes. Yes! Do you think I'd be here? Do you think I'd be in this god-forsaken, stinking town if I didn't? And pregnant as a toad?"

"My beauty, that has nothing to do with love. Mere biology has never——" He stopped. She was crying, her face let down into her hands, the long hair shielding her like a veil. He watched her for a moment, then stood looking out the kitchen window.

"Does he want the baby?" he asked.

She blew her nose on a paper napkin. "Why should he?"

"Well, my God. What kind of question is that?"

She faced him, her eyes red-rimmed and fierce. She spoke in a brittle whisper. "Because it's not his. And because he doesn't know that and if he did there'd be reason for his not wanting it, but he doesn't know and—and—why in hell am I telling you?"

"Jesus," he said. From the window he watched the last glaring edge of the sun go down behind the red-roofed white school atop the hill. It was six o'clock.

When the knock sounded, Baker turned to her again. "Who will that be pecking at our chamber?"

Anna Margaret snuffed and smiled. "It couldn't be the Welcome Wagon, I've been through that, so it must be Bill and Angela." She stood and straightened her blouse.

"Shall I?"

"Yes. I'll go repair this face. And kiss the sleeping prince," she added.

At the door stood, indeed, Angela Deek looking freshly showered in a full skirt and low-shouldered peasant blouse, and behind her, his eyes blue and distant, Bill Dann.

"Well. Mr. and Mrs. Tigerstooth," said Baker. "Come in."

Angela's fingers danced across the top lace of her blouse. "Hello, Baker." She came into the room. She turned to him with arched brows.

"They're here," Baker said. "She's doing something to her face. He is lying, I understand, prostrate and doubtless naked in his bed."

Bill Dann aimed toward the kitchen, his heavy steps

104

booming against the house's age, rattling the window frames. "I'll have some of that I smell. Angie?"

"What? Oh, yes. Small, with water." She sat on the sofa and arranged her skirt over her legs. Her face beamed. "Well," she said, giggled, "it has been two weeks, hasn't it."

Baker, standing before her, beginning to sway faintly, said, "That, Mrs. Deek, is a bit of profundity. I hear you have already lowered the class count?"

"What?" Her eyes roved the room and came back to his.

"That you already kicked a kid out."

Her smile left. "Yes," she said. "Baker, I had to, I—had to." She was sitting up on the edge of the sofa suddenly, her hand plucking his sleeve.

He pulled back, frowned. "God, Angela, don't panic. It's normal. I say kick them all out and talk to yourself. You get better attention." He sat in the chair facing her. "But why Rudy Yhazi? In beginning French he seems brighter than most, which in itself says little. Besides," Baker added quietly, "his eyes."

"His eyes? Yes," Angela said, "I know."

Exactly that. His eyes. She knew from the first day she saw him sitting in her classroom that she could not face those eyes day after day for a whole school year. Not and keep her mind on verbs and nouns and Charles Dickens. The most beautiful eyes, heavy-lashed, innocent-looking but you knew they were not innocent. But warm, too; eyes that drew you into corners where—and who would know better than she?—you did not mean to go. Where it was ruination and disaster and horror to go. She knew she must act quickly, more than a couple of weeks would be too late. In three weeks or four she knew she would be fighting and clawing to keep him. McCarron had not believed her flighty story of his insolence, of the lies she invented to convince him that the boy would do better with another teacher. At last he agreed, more because she had so intensely confused the issue than convinced him, and because when she accosted him with the problem in the hall outside her room, she unconsciously rubbed her breasts on his arm. Backed against a row of lockers, perspiring, he said yes, he would make the transfer. He knew her reasons were not truth, but as he pondered in his cell that afternoon, late, he could discover no cause why anyone would not prefer Rudy Yhazi to any other boy in Tigerstooth. The boy caused no trouble, as far as he knew, was courteous, if stoic solemnity could be considered courteousness, and a graceful athlete. There was nothing more to expect, then. No, he could not imagine the origin of Angela Deek's concern. But he was not overly surprised, although he had not expected insensitivity to be part of her.

McCarron shared the communal warm glow of most of the town where Rudy Yhazi was concerned. Because of the half-explained mystery of his birth (attributed, most said, to a white father by a Mojave mother, a mother who was never seen after the birth—dealt with, doubtless, by the tribe who either kept her in constant subjection within the village, which was unlikely after all this time, or who ended her earthly form summarily atop the pyre) the people felt from the time the three- or four-year-old began to walk into town alone, hanging around corners, flitting in alleys, scavenging, that he was their child of dark. Given to them to raise—not love, precisely, because he was half Mojave—they found pleasure in leaving beribboned (to catch his eye—such beautiful eyes) sacks of clean scraps and mended clothes for him to find in the alleys behind their gardens. More than once when Rudy was five or six or seven a quartet of ladies, ay, even twice a whole auxiliary, lay down their canasta hands and took their Cokes on the patio in order to watch the boy's brown head bobbing along the alley, they waiting breathlessly until he came to their special bag or box, dumped it into the giant pasteboard carton (contributed by Roslo's Furniture Store, the rope by Marspack Hardware) he dragged everywhere with him. When his head had bobbed on to other fences, they smiled with misty warmth and squeezed the hostess' hand for being so generous—to say nothing of being so clever.

Because such warmth must be shared, when someone at last thought of sending the boy to school, the Lions Club voted itself perpetual books-and-supplies furnishers for the number of years he would remain in school; the Rotarians elected shoes twice a year at Penney's; the Elks chose an outfit of jeans, underwear, and two shirts; the Eagles a Christmas basket sent to the village chieftain in Rudy's name each winter.

Although fraternal orders dedicated to the discussion and perpetuation of good works did not, in Tigerstooth, give official voice to such considerations, a certain amount of scoffing went on informally in each organization regarding the contributions (by comparison with their own) of each of the other orders. Some felt, for instance, that the Lions' contribution was less than estimable because school books and supplies were furnished gratis by the state until high school; Rudy had, possibly, hundreds of pairs of cast-off shoes, thus rendering the Rotarians' two pairs annually superfluous; likewise with jeans, underwear (and who knew if he wore it at all?) and shirts. As for the Christmas baskets, it was highly unlikely Rudy ever saw so much as a pecan from them.

Lemuel Oatman, the barber, contributed, independent of any organization, three haircuts a year after closing time.

It was not until he was eleven or twelve (no one was

certain any longer, some dating his birth from the year the geese landed by the thousands in the backwaters, some from the following—or was it two?—year when the Bureau of Reclamation built the recreation lagoon) that someone discovered that Rudy lived in a mud and wattle hovel tucked in among the dense reed undergrowth near Indian Neck Bend, a half-mile beyond the village. How long he had lived there alone, the ladies shuddered to think. The Masons were able at last to make retribution by paying Mr. Roslo three dollars a month to let Rudy move into an unused garret of his warehouse from which time many commented on how much happier and healthier the boy looked, whether or not they had actually seen him. No one thought to ask the boy his preference. Not even those who walked out the following Sunday after the discovery to view the hovel and eat picnic lunches in the willow shade and who further discovered that the grass-banked view of the river from that point was beyond description in its beauty. They commented on the quaintness with which the shelter had been built and added on to, and with only two Sundays of judicious poking about with long sticks, they succeeded in collapsing it into the river.

From his new quarters in the warehouse Rudy continued to forage in town and dump, accepting with a glow of his deep brown eyes whatever came to him. At thirteen he was sweeping the furniture store for Mr. Roslo for a quarter a night and at fourteen he added the smaller grocery store and the drugstore. He did indeed seem healthy and happy— if not quite so clean as he had been while living near the river.

And so here he was, a sophomore in high school, big for his class—either seventeen or eighteen, intelligent as most, no trouble, courteous, a graceful athlete. Some of the older members of the men's clubs more or less settled back in their worn leather chairs and sighed with satisfaction. A year or two more and the fruition of their labors would ripen. Too bad the boy did not seem to make friends so far as anyone knew. Outside of school, that is. During the school hours and on the ball field or court he was well liked, naturally. And plenty of the mothers (who had themselves been taken in by those eyes—when the boy was younger, of course) had to take a firm hand sometimes with their dewy daughters (My! One could so easily forget he was Indian.) who came home from school muttering about him. Too bad, his five hundred parents lamented, that he couldn't seem to find any nice boys and girls of his own kind to chum with.

No, McCarron concluded again, he could not fathom what could have turned Mrs. Deek against the boy. He hoped she had the—discretion—to say nothing derogatory about Rudy Yhazi in town.

When he discarded the thoughts about Angela's treatment of the boy, he allowed his mind to consider whether or not she rubbed her starched blouse against him purposely. She sure must know they are there. He opened the bottom right drawer of his desk and fished out a manila folder.

"Then you understand?" Angela said.

"Yes. Yes, I'm afraid so," said Baker.

"I'm afraid McCarron didn't. But how could I tell him? How could I tell him—?" She wiped her hand over her eyes and brushed back her hair. Her glance darted.

"You couldn't have. But I understand." Yes, he understood, but he did not understand why he should be called on to say so, why he, who had never wanted to take on the confessions of anyone, had never himself confessed, twice in an hour should be allowed to see a bare portion of the souls of two women. It had ever been so. Instead of the chatter of love, the litany of the unhappy whose own marrow and heart were insufficient to hold their own grief.

Bill returned, then, from the kitchen, cradling in one crooked arm a pitcher of water and a bottle of whisky. In the other he held four glasses of ice. His teeth overlapped his lower lip in concentration. "Here," he said, extending the glasses to Angela. He lowered himself onto the floor with the bottle and pitcher.

In the bedroom Jake had awakened and was at the moment watching Anna Margaret brush her hair, pulling it over one shoulder, tilting her head so that the brush swept from crown to ends in a straight stroke. That was the way his mother had, still did, brush her hair in the mornings and at night, had in fact, as long as he could remember when as a small boy he had sat in the middle of her bed and watched her at her dressing table until his father, either rising from or retiring to the bed, removed him from the sight. He watched Anna Margaret and felt himself grow again.

"You up?" he said.

She turned to him and smiled. Then she turned back to the mirror. "Yes. For ages. Feel better?"

He yawned. "Have I been asleep?"

She laughed. She came to sit on the edge of the bed. "It's after six," she said. "And we have company."

"Shit." He flung back the sheet. "Like?"

"At a time like this?" She smoothed back the hair from his forehead. "Do you love me?" she asked.

"Didn't I prove that an hour ago? And I'm ready to prove it again right now." He tried to pull her over him.

"No." She stood up and smoothed her skirt. "Do you love me?"

"What the hell?"

"I just want to know, do you love me."

"Christ sake." He rolled onto his stomach and leaning over the bedside searched for his shorts. "Why do you ask that all the time?"

"Why? Why else. I want to know."

He pulled on his shorts and pants. "Christ sake, Anna. I married you, didn't I? And I still give you all you want, don't I? Isn't that love, as you call it?"

"Okay. Don't shout." She opened the door into the bathroom that led in turn to the dining room. "Don't be long."

When she was gone Jake sat back on the bed and began putting on his socks and shoes. Jesus. That's just what he had tried to straighten out with her a dozen times before, starting the first night she told him she was pregnant, their fifth or sixth time together, still in Emil's studio on his narrow cot because there was nowhere else to meet, not in his fraternity house, certainly, nor in her dormitory, and she would not go to a motel. He had tried to explain then and two or three godknowshow many times since, that for sensitive and talented people the word was beyond use, that it was the . . . the relationship that mattered. He thought no less of her, in fact more, that she had met him on free and adult terms, in what in another age was called an enlightened way. She should not have got pregnant, that was really pretty crude, what with pills and contraceptives practically given away with meals at the university, but he supposed there was enough of the gentleman left in his old Grantham blood to righten things, it was just that this meant, as she could well see, that his work, his real work— his painting—would have to suffer for a time while he taught or something until she was over this business of the baby.

He walked into the living room, tucking in the ends of his shirt.

"Here's a vote for our side," said Bill. "Listen, Jakie, had you rather drink?"

"Rather than what?" He took a drink from those set on either side of Bill.

"No," Angela giggled and slid from the sofa down on her knees close to Bill. "We're going to this potluck."

"No!" Baker shouted. "We're going to drink," and as if to prove it he sat on the floor, too.

Anna Margaret spoke. "I'd forgotten, but we have to go to that new teachers' thing at the church."

"Ah, shit—shoot, Anna Margaret," Bill said. "What church? We don't even know what church."

"Assuming there's more than one," said Baker.

"The Methodist," said Anna Margaret.

Baker sneered his half-sided laugh. "They'll shut up the doors so loud, when they smell us coming, the crash will reverberate in John Wesley's very tomb."

"I've got Sen-Sen," offered Angela. Her hands fluttered as if the Sen-Sen might be cached in her bosom.

"Good," said Anna Margaret. "Everybody take some."

"Jesus, Anna Margaret," said Bill. He took the Sen-Sen. She has been crying. She caught him watching her eyes and smiled. He turned away and began chewing.

Jake wondered why Anna Margaret never thought of things like Sen-Sen.

Baker stood, one hand jammed in his pocket, one with a drink, in the center of the room. "Do any of you know the background of the potluck in Tigerstooth?"

Bill watched him, curious. "No," he said. "Do you?"

"Of course. And so should you if you're going to partake

of the ritual. In Tigerstooth it comes, I understand, closer to pagan rite than anywhere else in the world."

"Where else in the goddamn world do they still have them?" asked Jake.

"Don't be obtuse. Do you ever want to know anything at all?" Baker's voice had taken on its histrionic lace, the same edge that caused people in classrooms or bars anywhere to pause and listen despite themselves.

"What are your sources?" said Anna Margaret.

Baker looked at her and laughed. "Oh, you're lovely. If you'd leave this dreary house at night and wander the world with me, you'd know these things, too. Don't forget, these past weeks while you four slept—singly or in pairs—I have been out merging. I am about to tell you of the history of the Tigerstooth Potluck, which, Mrs. Grantham," he bowed to her, she returned the bow, "I have on excellent local authority."

"Baker," Angela giggled. He turned to her but she said nothing more. She moved closer to Bill on the floor, being careful that a little of her skirt caught over his knee.

Baker rocked on his heels. "In Tigerstooth, since before anyone's memory, the call to fraternity has been the potluck. Whenever, as I understand it, in the estimation—especially, but not exclusively—of the ladies, there is reason for more than four people to gather, the call goes out. Sometimes the reason, evidently, is only that there is no reason; therefore, by gathering a crowd over potluck a reason for the next materializes. Do you follow that?"

No one answered.

Baker shook his head, as if the lack of desire for knowledge was beyond belief. He went on. "Some ladies, through serious attention and talent, are considered, at least by my River Street sources, to have risen to what could only be called dynastic heights as potluck givers and are called upon as professionals, without pay, of course—it is the least one can do, much as you imagine their counterpart in Perle Mesta might be called on in Washington. Mrs. Hampton, for reasons you all can imagine, enjoys the reputation as empress, although she never attends a potluck except by phone. We, of course, can sympathize, remembering the myriad responsibilities which are hers operating that fine hotel in which, until tomorrow, I still reside."

"Where are you going to *reside* after tomorrow?" Jake asked.

"Sh," said Anna Margaret.

"Well, I want to—"

"To go on," said Baker, "if we may?"

"You're my guest."

"That's so. Well, as in all guilds or professions, discounting our own, naturally, there are from time to time outbursts of jealousy among those who have strived—striven—their way up and those who are climbing. The more Christian way of eliminating such recontres is—"

"Such whats?" said Bill.

"—*affaires d'honneur*—"

"—?"

"—is the sort employed by the Methodist group, Methodism in Tigerstooth being more an organization than a doctrine; that is, the position of Potluck Mistress was created to which a candidate can be elected for two-year terms and to which office, it is always understood, she must devote her total attention and a certain portion of her prayers, and must never splinter her trust by giving aid to other organizations—videlicet, the Eastern Star or the Ladies Auxiliary of the Brotherhood of Railroad Trainmen—beyond the menial scullery chores. The Potluck Mistress is entitled to appoint Vice-Mistresses who operate in subordinate positions, ready to take over in case the Mistress becomes inefficacious through pregnancy, melancholia, menopause, or general fatigue."

"Baker," Angela twitted. She touched Bill's knee with hers.

"Please. Among these lesser votaries is one who will, in time, be elected to replace the incumbent. Past Mistresses usually serve in ex-officio capacity, and in their full senility become the Mary and Martha Circle.

"Just why the potluck has become so entrenched in this we now call our home, is problematical. One of my sources said, although he had reason to be confused, that it all harks back to the time dining cars first appeared in trains—trains that now and then jerked to starts and stops, to say nothing of outright collisions, in such a fashion as to send the pots of food flying about the train resulting in nothing to which anyone could properly put a name. Others say it goes back still further, to The Drought when the few families hereabouts would have perished had not their kindly brown brothers let them share their kettles. A few, I surmise, believe it didn't begin, really, until the depression when the churches and clubs demanded tithes of everyone, in the form of leftovers to be cast in the communal poor pot."

Baker slumped from his lecture height. "At any rate, whatever its generic origins, I am given to understand that the most glittering, the one that actually begins the season, is the one we are about to attend in our gradations of sobriety."

"After that," Bill said, "I'm damned sure I ain't going."

"Oh, Bill," said Angela. She slapped him on the thigh.

Anna Margaret stood up. "Of course we're going. I wouldn't stay away for the world."

Indeed, the New Teachers Annual was the most glittering of the potlucks. This year it would again be directed by Adelaide Marspack, Mistress in her fourth term, who had dedicated her summer, along with those of her Vice-Mistresses, to making this the most splendorous of potlucks, an occasion not only and not the least to welcome Tigerstooth's new teachers, but to make an announcement of her own, the nature of which her aides could but guess at, judging from the nectareous, therefore foreign, smile that etched the corners of her mouth through most of July and all of August. The ladies had searched their attic boxes and those of friends who could be trusted to divulge propitious tidbits in search of dried, preserved desert flora : arrow weed, ocotillo, yucca. Many hot days were happily spent scouring the face of the desert itself for more specimens which were washed, allowed to dry in sunny places, and sprayed with multiple coats of clear varnish. It was Adelaide Marspack's idea to use a desert theme this year—and who but she would have thought of it, would have thought to bring the natural surroundings in?—instead of importing cartons and cartons of fresh gladiolas and greenery from the Coast. A week before the event, these guarded objects were driven to the church basement. The window blinds were drawn. For six days the ladies entered there by morning and returned by dusk, tired, wan, but emitting an inner glow. On the seventh day they rested under facials and hair dryers.

At the bottom of the stairs leading into the basement the new teachers were met and passed along a reception line which bloomed at last upon Adelaide Marspack looking round and Rubenesque in Grecian gown. She endured, apart from the rest of the line, backed by a kind of mesquite mosque devised by interlacing branches into a garden trellis.

Near her ankles ranged red and black Indian pottery, great and small. Beneath her sandaled feet, a Navajo rug.

"Oh ho, ha, ha," she sounded, "you are Anna Margaret Grantham—you don't mind if I call you Anna Margaret, do you?—aren't you."

"Why, yes, no."

"I'm Adelaide." She pronounced it A-dell-aïda. "So nice of you," she said and passed Anna Margaret on to a void in the room. "Oh ho, ha, ha, you're Jake Grantham—you don't mind if I call you Jake, do you?—aren't you."

Jake caught up with Anna Margaret smiling wistfully back at him from the void while the voice said "Oh ho, ha, ha, you're Angela Deek—you don't mind if—"

"What now?"

"Eat?" Jake whispered.

"No one else is."

"They're all in that goddamn reception line."

When at last the five had filled their plates from the long buffet table (and Baker had whispered to Bill to put back the yucca blossoms that he had taken from the centerpiece mistaking them for some kind of culinary craftsmanship) they were ushered to spaces at another long white-clothed table. Onto the center of each plate had been ladled a mound of what was the main dish, judging from the silver bowl from which it was served to them—a footed, elaborately crusted bowl of gigantic beauty, presided over by blue-draped Vice-Mistresses.

"What's this?" Bill asked.

"God knows. Angela, in your opinion—now, take your time," Baker said.

Angela clipped the fingertips of both hands to her blouse top. She looked down into the plate. She shook her head.

"I'll ask," whispered Anna Margaret, pulling apart a

fragment of the mound. She turned to a friendly face. She smiled. "Pardon me," she said. "What is this?" She dabbed her fork into the mound.

The lady to whom the question was pointed gasped audibly, mannerly. Then she relaxed and smiled. She got the joke.

Anna Margaret looked across the table to Baker. Her eyebrows shrugged.

"She's serious," Baker said to the lady. "We don't know what it is."

The lady looked from one to another of them. She looked into her own plate and back to them. "Why, that is taglierini!"

Angela leaned toward her and pursed her lips in the manner of women about to solicit recipes. "This—this—how did you call it?"

"Taglierini. T-a-silent g and so on."

"Italian?" asked Baker.

"Why, no," said the lady. Her black eyes, honestly concerned, looked into her plate again. She drew her hands away into her lap. "I don't think so," she said.

"This taglierini," continued Angela, "and my, it looks good, how is it made? That is, you know, what goes into it?"

The lady, still unsure but that she was being unfairly put upon, said, "Why, it's made with—well, it's—it's complicated to say. Well, everyone knows how to make taglierini," she finished lamely.

"Noodles," said Bill.

They all looked to see if that was true. It was.

"Hamburger," said Anna Margaret.

"Tomato sauce," said Baker.

"Whole kernel white corn," said the lady.

"Peppers."

"Yes. You see? Everyone knows how to make taglierini. A mixture, you might say." The lady relaxed against her stiffened corset. "Like people," she added.

"Better," said Bill, chewing.

Again the lady sat forward. The tips of her fingers touched her lips. Conspiratorially, and the five heads leaned like Medusa's toward hers, she whispered, "But it hasn't been *blessed* yet!"

The heads swung toward Bill. He stopped chewing, and from under his shagged brows he looked belligerently from one to the other. He swallowed.

All this time, more people were passed by the white glove of Adelaide Marspack into the big room to be given, each in his turn, his plate of taglierini. From the ladies floated subdued sweet sounds of admiration. Possibly, never since the birth of time, had prickly pear and mesquite and palo verde and shellacked, dry arrow weed caught the attention of so many admiring glances, had wafted among their branches so many centrifugal scents of cologne and talcum, had juxtaposed to them such cottons and silks and shantungs of such colors, had their bodies pierced by so many nails and wires and frogs, had snagged so many stockings. Adelaide Marspack heard the awed voices drift back to her in her niche and was complete.

"I feel like Hansel and Gretel," whispered Baker to Anna Margaret. "You don't suppose these things——" he waved his fork at the false wall of bushes and cacti, "are still growing, do you? We'll be overcome."

"The desert forms are interesting," Jake was saying to the lady, "because, despite their rather monochromatic palette, as it were, the lines, shapes, are—ah—*clean*, almost *primitive*."

"Oh, yes," said the lady.

"It seems to me that we have here the chance to rediscover in art, forms that by their very datelessness are really, in a way, entirely new. Don't you think so?"

"Oh, definitely," said the lady. She chanced a quick look about the crowded room. Then she added vacantly, "Do you paint? Are you an artist?"

Jake tipped his head to one side. "Yes," he said. "I have just had a one-man show in Phoenix. Went pretty well. Sold nine pieces. You know, my things go for two hundred and fifty dollars now?"

"My," said the lady.

"Yes. That's fifteen hundred dollars I cleared after commission. Thirty-three percent they took. Isn't that criminal? That's why art's so high now, the galleries take off the top third. But, anyway, my things hang in lots of important homes around there."

"My, you must be good." The lady smiled and slipped her eyes over the crowd again.

"Well," Jake said, "my stuff sells."

"Yes."

"And that's the important thing, don't you think so?" Then she was able to say, "Oh, look! The minister is about to give thanks."

A man, small, dismally enough dressed to be obscured in the gay colors, looking in fact more like the mesquite background, separated himself, and stepping onto a platform appeared to grow in stature and command. With a grand crucifix-extension of his arms, he silenced the people. "Shall we bow?" he asked. None answered, but all heads dipped and the five watched one another from under scowling brows. "Lord," the minister addressed an enshrubbed hanging lamp, "we gather together—"

Bill twisted his mouth toward Anna Margaret. She smiled.

120

Angela saw the look pass between them. Her hand went up to the shoulder of her blouse. Baker watched the triangle of glances bounce and fade. Jake wondered whether a knife or a hog bristle brush would better capture the weedy texture of the centerpiece.

"—how blessed are we, amongst briar and thorn—"

Anna Margaret felt Bill's ankle ease against hers. He coughed. Angela smoothed the edge of her skirt. She rested the back of her hand on Bill's thigh. The pose was awkward to hold without quivering.

"—and fitting to give thanks for; remembering the thorns that crowned—"

Anna Margaret shifted. She drew her feet back under her chair. The spot at which his ankle touched remained warm. Bill dropped his gaze back to his plate. He frowned. With the tips of his fingers he shifted his spoon forward an inch on the cloth and back again. Then he turned his leg so that Angela's hand slipped easily over to the inside of his thigh.

From the table behind them, his face propped on his hands, McCarron watched the uneasy rustling of the five. He saw Dann's leg shift forward in reaction to the girl's smile, then her slight movement away. He watched, incredulous, Angela's hand accepted into Dann's lap. Their backs— Dann, Steinhart, Deek—were to him but there was no mistaking the rising color on the back of her neck or the warm discomfort of Dann's body.

"—in this season when summer's growth, however spare, gives way to death—"

Perhaps it was only that he had really never noticed before. His years as principal had moved him automatically to a place of reserve, to a distance from people "administrative-wise" as he put it, but still and all, he was in contact with them, was literally surrounded by them each day. Why should he feel so suddenly this year that the view had altered drastically? Had the aging of a summer wrought in him some subtle realization not there before? Had he in fact so habitually looked over the heads of people—a habit incumbent to any administrator who must encompass in his sights a panoramic view of his responsibilities, especially when the raw materials were in constant flux, apt to explode in God knew what directions—that he had completely failed to see what the human forms were doing? He shuddered to think what might have been going on beneath his notice these past years while he trained his mind to the larger perspective.

"—and when the desert, beauty of thy beauty, at last reclaims its own—"

McCarron resolved to lower his gaze this year. And, he smirked to himself, he meant that literally, as his present lowered gaze watched Dann's tight-clothed thigh swing in and back slightly, enough only that Angela's hand rubbed in and out on the inside, causing the tips of her red nails to flick into the warm light then disappear. McCarron felt his own leg twitch and thrill as Dann's must that moment be. The pleasure that came with the youthful warmth in his groin left him staring over his propped hands a long moment after the mellifluent voice of the minister ceased.

"—and for these as well, thy ageless treasures, we give thanks. Amen."

Angela's hands returned to her fork and glass, Bill enjoyed without censor his second mouthful, Anna Margaret smiled toward Jake who had resolved, he was certain, the esthetic problem of the desert weeds and did not notice her smile. Baker, turning to view the room, met the staring eyes of Peter McCarron and nodded wisely. A warm fall of voices filled the room, pitched softly across the spell of the minister's poesy and the succulent, if cooled, mixture, taglierini.

At a certain learned moment, as forks clicked against empty plates and coffee saucers, Adelaide Marspack nodded to the minister on her right and arose. From the forested small stage whence she was aided by two ladies lifting delicately on her elbow tips, she faced the congregated heads beneath her with a faint expression of surprise and alarm like Susanna caught at her bath.

"Ladies and gentlemen," she began, "and teachers, that is, especially teachers, we are warmed to see you all here, each and every one of you, on this special occasion so dear to you, I am sure, as it is to mine—to me, particularly dear friends old and, I hope, new, because this night I step down from a position I have held only to serve these years—to give my blessings—I—" She stopped in the stillness of the room and dabbled with a tiny handkerchief at her eyes. There were audible gasps of "No!" among the crowd.

So it came to be that Adelaide Marspack retired from Potluck Mistress amid the damp eyes of her Vice-Mistresses each of whom in her own mind totted up her chances for accession.

Baker whispered, "Lord, what staging. Can't we get out of this now?"

"No, not yet. There's more." And there was more, beginning with the songs of a tiny, powdered Japanese woman, "war bride," the lady beside Anna Margaret whispered, "bride" of a Tigerstooth son who chose to absolve his part in the war or to vindicate himself upon the girl who had preferred what was near rather than distant, brought not only from a delicate country to a new one but to the very part of that new one most incongruous to her plaintive,

123

bird-like songs and twittered fingers, used, called upon time after time to entertain at potlucks, at inaugurations of Job's Daughters, at Elks Benefits. She who in her own country would never have appeared, much less sung, before crowds of diners or drinkers or dancers, still called "bride" after eighteen years of marriage and life in this town having never in all that time seen another Oriental face or heard her native speech save from the lips of her own children to whom she had taught some of the words, listening most nights from her yellow stucco house, like dozens of other women, for the sound of the seven-forty or the nine-thirty or the midnight that brought her husband home, tired, who had for his part never regained in his own country the white-toothed grin she first knew in Japan.

McCarron was not listening, sitting yet with his face propped in his hands, staring over the littered cloth toward the five people, now turned at wider angles from their table in order to see the stage. He did not need to listen to the eccentric misplaced voice. It was the same voice he had heard at these pompous, pitiable gatherings since childhood, whether from the Japanese bride or the Indian girl trios or some staunch defeated woman warbling away the final notes of her dream career here in this living anachronism. The words and the notes were all the same. They had always been the same only he had not realized that until he left it for fourteen years and returned. But notes and voices from brides or girls or ladies or birds do not matter. Those are the shards that batter the ear sometimes, deranging the order of things, until you learn to shut them out, to let them drift overhead. It is the discipline of things, the ordering, that will keep things going until you are ready to pass them on to others. When that time comes, let me have, God, ten years to sit by the cold river and fish, then take me and welcome.

He had watched them for two weeks. Watched them as the school got under way, somehow, as it always did at the appointed time. He watched them from his office window, from his cell window, from wherever he could find something—a wall or door or flagpole or fence—to lean his back against, singly, in pairs, sometimes all five together as they still appeared in the parking lot before school or after school.

He watched them now and was suddenly furious, for no reason any more than there had been reason at any time these past weeks. What was Steinhart saying to the girl? A strange one, that one. The kind of impervious face that might do some places; he had seen that face in a dozen cities over three or four countries of the world. It might do some places. But not in Tigerstooth. The hair, too long, too straight, like her fingers. Her eyes that never seemed to widen in recognition or alarm or friendliness but only slid from side to side as if independent of her. But at that, despite that, she was the obvious—to him, if not to the others yet—center which drew to herself and round herself the other four. There was no reason, though. There wasn't any reason.

No one, at least he could not see how anyone, could call her beautiful, what with that too-long hair and those too-long fingers and, yes, those too-long, sliding eyes. And that knocked-up belly just at the stage where it spoiled the waistline and not yet big enough to be voluptuous, to be warmlooking, thrilling in the way a child-bearing woman gets when her burden is heavy, when you think of her lying down and you laying your head in the valley just between the belly and the spreading breasts, or in the valley just below it. She will look like a pear with four toothpicks stuck in it when her time comes. McCarron bet to himself that that was sure as hell no immaculate conception.

Then he was furious again at the sight of that other-world man, the man she was married to, that abstraction of a man, Jake Grantham, who with his close hips and tapered torso had, and did not know it, the body that he and a thousand thousand other men, he supposed, like himself, would have sacrificed anything for, including any part of their present body, if they could be given, at the same time, the knowing. Grantham did not realize his body. That was what caused the rage to rise up in McCarron's throat. He had seen that ideal body a few times before across the world, in the army for instance, dressed or nude—it makes no difference with that kind of body—and always with the same rage because when God (or whatever) gave the body He did not also give the knowing.

And so it has always been, evidently, as he began to realize when he saw the Greek statues with Karen, or before Karen, with the embarrassed, joking army buddies in Europe. They did not know their bodies, either, if the sculptures could be believed—not the same as the Romans did, but then the Romans did not have the same bodies. The Greeks, or anyway the Greek statues, and the Jake Granthams had the skin and muscle and shape that would be beautiful to watch at hard, fierce games—not boys' games like football or baseball or hockey with ugly pads and helmets and shoes—but man games, death games. Yes; how magnificent war would be if both bands of enemies had bodies like that and killed with their naked hands naked foes.

Instead, there he—Grantham—sat next to his insuperable

wife, his eyes half-squinting behind horn-rimmed glasses at who knew what, the table centerpiece, the idiotic cactus and mesquite branches and weeds that never should be brought inside where any human lives, at whoever it is that now is singing or playing the piano or reciting a piece. *Jesus,* McCarron thought. *Jesus.*

"He's leaving, why can't we?" Bill leaned and whispered across the table.

"He looks sick. No. It will be over soon."

"It will have to be," whispered Baker. "There couldn't be many more singers or piano players left in town."

Lying in his bed in the corner of the room against the wall, outside which he could hear the sandy, lizard and rodent sounds of the desert night, McCarron knew he was going to be sick, not yet, but sometime in the night or in the early morning. It could wait, could be held back until he was ready for the wracking vomiting that would exhaust him and put him into sound sleep. In the meantime he knew he could do it, although how long had it been? ten eleven twelve thirteen years? because he had used to do it so often at night at eighteen or twenty or twenty-four on the beds bunks pallets berths ground.

He slid back the sheet to his thighs then kicked it with his feet out of the way over the end of the bed. He felt of himself and smiled straight up in the dark. This much he could still do. Then he began, first to float the heads into the darkness above his vision like cupids, at first, or seraphim without bodies. It had been so long. He wondered which heads would appear; that was the first exciting part. The first to fade in and then burn out like a projected image gone out of focus was the head and face of his sister. The others stayed as they appeared, sometimes shifting, trading positions in the zodiac-circle. The girls, Alf's sister smiling patriotically; another, dark-haired one, who was she? France? Italy? the great blond Los Angeles one, the one he paid the first time; Karen, almost clear, but fading, fading. On they came until there was a full wide circle of them gently rotating clockwise. He could reverse that. He could make them stop, then circle the other way.

The face he did not expect, one that should not have been, had no right to be there at all, came into the center of the galaxy and he was powerless to stop it. He ignored the head and began the second part, the attaching of bodies, the part that once was the greatest fun because as master over all these he could interchange bodies and heads as he was moved to do so. Or he could make up entirely new bodies, fat white grub-like bodies he had seen in art books as a child and in galleries where Karen had taken him, the kind always seen bathing in threes or fours or better, being seen almost-raped or after-raped by great ugly muscled horsemen, or round brown tubular bodies like Indian girls have, or skinny bodies or ones with four breasts.

The game was spoiling because of the face that persisted, that thrust itself into the center, growing larger until he had to notice it. A face that was no face but eyes balanced on the tips of long slender fingers. Anna Margaret Grantham. He quickly put the body of Angela Deek beneath that head and laughed. It was a monstrous marvelous trick, the short lumpy body beneath the eyes-head, like the bodies McCarron had known and used a hundred times, pale almost to white, square low breasts and square wide hips. He laughed. Then he saw it. He should have known it would happen. The faces, the adored ones that had girdled his visionary zodiac were gone, all gone, vanished, and in their places slowly circled the four new heads around the new composite in the center. They, the four, all smiled benignly. The one in the center watched but did not smile.

McCarron was sick on the floor beside his bed.

Eight

SEPTEMBER 23. So here we are, my beauty. Three weeks." Baker lay on his back on the floor holding his glass with both hands on his chest. In the tiny room his long body stretched nearly from one wall to the other. From time to time he raised himself enough on one elbow to drink from the glass. "How do you like my charming web, now that, with your inimitable decorating, it might be called livable?"

She sat above him in the one big chair, her legs tucked up under her, her own glass balanced on the chair arm. She laughed. "It's the ugliest place I've ever seen."

"You cut."

"Look at that ceiling. Those spots. You know, some day when you're up there on the pot, the whole bathroom is going to come crashing down."

"If it fell now, it would kill us both."

"Yes."

"Glory be to God for dappled things."

"Idiot."

Then they did not talk again for a long while, as they had not for most of this evening. Baker had moved, as he said he would, into the tiny two-storied house that stood like a forlorn, abandoned waif back among the tamarack trees behind the larger house, the one Anna Margaret and Jake lived in. Together, Anna Margaret and Baker had cajoled and coerced and confused the landlord into putting up fifty dollars cash at Roslo's Furniture for redecorating. After three afternoons spent arguing and laughing, the results of the fifty dollars hung at the windows, on the chair and sofa, and covered most of the center of the downstairs floor. The upstairs—bedroom and bath—reached by a staircase that shot up nearly perpendicularly from the kitchen, could not be revived, they decided, with anything less than a fortune. "It's still too bad something can't be done with that bedroom," she had said. He had shrugged. "I don't expect to entertain there much."

Finally she stirred from the big chair. "I hear the traffic," she said. "The game must be over."

"Yes. Doubtless Beowulf has ripped off Grendel's arm at the shoulder by now." He got up from the floor and took his glass and hers and the bottle to the sink, hidden, more or less, in a narrow alcove at one end of the room. "Why the hell did Jake go? There's nothing he can paint at a football game, is there?"

She opened the door and waited for him. "Because Bill wanted him to."

"Yes."

"It's the first game and, well—"

"Yes."

They crossed the soft, dusty yard to the back door of the larger house. "He'll do anything Bill wants him to."

"Yes."

In a while, after the sounds of the homebound traffic had died away from the street, after the yelling and showering and towel-snapping was over and the gymnasium locked, Bill and Jake came in. Anna Margaret came from the kitchen to meet them at the front door.

"Jesus," Jake said. "I'm thirsty." He passed through the living room toward the kitchen. Bill stopped at the door.

"Well?" she said.

"Dirty bastards," said Bill. He was smiling.

"You lost?"

He closed the door behind him. "Screw it. It don't matter," he said. He came on into the room and stood looking down at Baker who was again stretched out on the floor holding a fresh glass. "On your ass again?" He prodded him with his toe.

"Yes. Join me?"

When Bill laughed the sound was huge, like himself, larger than the room. It seemed to shake the house violently, but gently, as a boy might shake a coin bank—enough to cause the nickels to fall out but not enough to shatter the bank.

"Where's Angela?" Baker asked.

Bill took the glass that Jake offered him and drank from it in a long draught, his head bending back, his throat moving. When he stopped he said, "I don't know. Something changed her mind. She wouldn't come out tonight."

"Pity."

"Hey, didn't she have a scrap with that half-breed kid last week?" Jake asked.

"The Indian kid?"

"Yes."

Baker snorted. "She kicked him out of class, as a beginning, if that's what you mean."

"Why?"

Jake said, "The one with the eyes? You know."

"Yes, that's the one."

"Well, I saw her talking to him in the hall today right after school."

"So?"

Jake shrugged. "So, nothing. I just thought it was funny, her talking with him like that, quiet and all, after she'd booted him out."

The four of them were seated now, Anna Margaret in a chair, Baker lying on the floor, Jake and Bill propped against a wall. They drank and no one said anything for a time. Then Jake began talking again.

"Dumb bastards. You can't get them to say three words in a row. I tried to talk to a couple of them again today, a couple of guys just leaning on the wall outside the cafeteria, and I didn't get anywhere. Dumb bastards."

"You talking about the Indian kids?" Bill asked.

"Yes. I don't see how they even think they can raise themselves up to our standards if they won't even communicate, for Christ sake."

"Jesus," Baker said. "What standards."

"Well, the standards the rest of us have reached. That's something. That's what I mean. And they've been here a hell of a lot longer than we have. They had the chance to make something out of this country before we came."

"Before 'we,' as you say, took it away from them."

"That's just what I mean. They should never have lost it. If they'd advanced themselves, they'd never have lost it. Look at them now. They won't work, half of them, except as janitors or railroad gangs."

"Balls," Bill said. "You sound like some Southerners I've known."

"No," Jake said. "Those people back there deliberately set out to screw the Negroes. This is different, the Indians were never slaves, were they? They were never bought and sold and forced to do anything like the Negroes in the South, were they?"

"You don't know much American history, then," Baker said. He rolled on his side to reach the bottle that stood beside Anna Margaret's chair.

"Take these Mojaves right here in Tigerstooth. They were just sitting by the river when the white people came a hundred years ago and they'd still be sitting there not doing a goddamn thing but fishing if the white man hadn't made them get up off their asses. Look, I'm just trying to be objective." He was talking fast. "We've given them schools to go to, the same school as everybody else, and they don't even come half the time and don't say three goddamn words in a day when they do come."

"There should be more like them," Bill said.

"Look. You may think I'm prejudiced or something. But that's not right. That's not it at all. I've had friends all my life who were of—of other nationalities and races, who—"

"God," said Baker, "don't tell me, please, that some of your best friends are Negroes."

"Well, it so happens it's true. Anna Margaret knows. She can tell you. Why, we have one very good friend, both of us, who's Negro."

"It doesn't matter, Jakie. Never mind," she said.

"No. Wait. The guy that introduced us—Anna Margaret and me, he's an artist too—I've known him all through college." Jake grinned. "Anna Margaret did some modeling or something for him. We met in his studio, didn't we, Anna Margaret? Of course, he's only part Negro, I don't know how much, but he is just the same."

"Never mind," Baker said. "Get on to your point about the Indians."

"Well, that is my point, don't you see. Here's this guy, a Negro or mostly, part, Negro, and he's risen up to where he's in the same position, the same stratum, you could say, as white people. The Indians could do that except they don't want to, and then what're you going to do? Christ sake, I don't know. I don't know." Jake lapsed back against the wall in silence.

Baker turned to look at Anna Margaret. She watched him. There was no need for either of them to say it. They both rose.

"Where are you going?" Bill asked.

"Some air," Anna Margaret said. She opened the front door and stepped out onto the narrow porch leaving Baker to close the door behind them. She leaned her face against a cold pillar.

"Walk?" he said.

"Yes."

They began walking away from the direction of town toward the desert, toward where before very far the last house on that street stood where the pavement curved away to join another street nearer the railroad tracks. Past the house, a small yellow house with a single light burning in it and from where the loud sounds of radio racketed, the desert began as if no man had ever disturbed it. The desert does not look so flat, so much of one hue or surface at night as it does in the daytime. Nor is it as dark on moonless nights as most land is, not as completely, deeply black as mountainous or forested land can be. There are always stars that light the desert, enough at least, as on this night, to individualize the mesquite bushes and the taller cacti and gentle ravines that show as darker strokes on the sand. As

135

they walked, she leading slightly with a stride that was both undetermined and natural, they said nothing until she sensed that he was about to speak. "Not yet," she said.

When they had walked past the last sounds of the town, she stopped abruptly so that he stumbled a little trying to avoid her whose silence it seemed to him would shatter into irretrievable pieces if touched. She sat on the sand, on a small updrift of rock. When he sat by her, her silhouette was no more against the sky. He could not see her at all, whose eyes had never learned to read the darkness.

After a while she asked for a cigarette and Baker spoke. "So the father of your child is a Negro." He watched her face in the light from the match. It told him nothing. "What are you going to do?" he asked.

He saw the coal on her cigarette burn up, then dull. "I don't know," she said.

"Can you tell him?"

"No. You heard him. You heard what he said."

"Yes," Baker said.

Then she was laughing, or so it seemed, but he was not sure. He waited until she stopped. He watched her fingers in the light from her cigarette when she pulled on it. It was going to happen again. Why must I listen? There is no sympathy left in me to give. A long time ago I gave up pity and commiseration and condolence. I do not ask it, not any more, and I do not have it left to give.

"You wonder how I could have so messed up my life and his and God knows how many others?"

"No," he said. "I do not wonder." And I do not want to know. I should not have to listen because whatever you can say or whatever you have done I have done worse.

"You know, the really funny part," she said, "the funniest thing of all? I am as much Indian as Emil is Negro.

How do you suppose he will take that news if he ever knows? Do I have the right, now, to tell him?"

"What can I say? There is nothing to say."

"I can't say I did not know. About screwed-up lives, I mean. I have lived with the phantoms of screwed-up lives all of mine." She sounded old, older than twenty-three years, older than fifty years.

Baker scraped his shoe in the sand making a long furrow that he could not see. "You don't have to tell me," he said. "And I do not want to know."

"It was too fast. It all began and happened and was over too fast. There wasn't enough time," she said. He thought she must mean the affair with Emil or with Jake, but she did not. She was talking of something larger than that. "A country needs more than fifty or sixty years. And that's all we had, you know. Only about fifty years and that was not enough time."

He did not know what she was talking about. *I do not want to know.* "Do you mean America? or what?"

"Yes," she said. Her fingers showed faintly in the cigarette light. Baker watched the coal of fire swing down in an arc. She would be resting her arms on her knees, leaning forward. "No, I mean the West. We just got started too late and it was all over before anybody had a chance to catch his breath. It takes a long time to learn to love. That kind of love, I mean."

"I don't know what you're talking about," he said. There had been a time, he thought, when he would have known, when the pieces would have locked together. But it was too hard to do now, it took too much effort, too much control, too much frowning of the mind. The time when he could have anticipated her was past, left flake at a time in dark or raucous places the names of which, the locations of which he could not remember even if he had wanted to, and he did not.

"A country—any more than a house or a barn—is not made with love. It's made with labor and muscle and sometimes frenzy and hate and fornication. But not love. That comes later. And that's why there has to be time after the finishing to walk in that country or live in that house or let the smells grow in that barn."

Should I know what she means? Has there ever been a time when I would have known? I do not want to know now.

"My father at seventy-five or seventy-six still doesn't know. That's why he brought me wild flowers every day in summer. Or provoked a neighbor boy to ride miles to do it."

Baker was no longer trying. He heard the sounds of the words but he did not know their meaning, knew only that chopped, blunted that way, they should be coming from the throat of a man.

"Ever since I was nine or ten until I went away." Her voice grew softer for a time. "He believed he still had time, or rather that the West still had the time to love in the old way. The way his father thought it could."

Baker heard her rise abruptly from the rock beside him. Her feet scuffed loudly in the sand.

"Can you just imagine the desperation after his three sons were killed? The rage that sent him back to my mother again after God knows how many years and she not even sure she could conceive? Can you imagine how he watched and waited to see if it—if I—took? Can you?"

"What can I say?" Baker reached his hand toward her voice in the dark but did not find her. Then he felt her sit beside him on the rock again.

"No wonder he brought me flowers," she said. "No

wonder he does nothing now but ride around and around in the meadows cursing and snatching handfuls of poppies."

Baker watched her cigarette skitter, over-ending in the air, until it hit and splashed fire in the sand ten feet away. She had not tossed it, as a woman would be expected to do, but had flicked it away with her thumb and finger.

"It was too late fifty years before I was born," she said.

He still did not know what she meant nor what it had to do with anything. What it had to do with the fact of her part-Indian part-Negro part-whatever (Pier. Pierpont? Pierson? Pierchoski? Pieragostini?) baby and Jake Grantham, artist, who was God knew beautiful to look at. Because he believed he should say something, he spoke. "You can always leave and go back to your mother, can't you? They'll not mind, will they?"

"Mother?" she said as if the word were new to her. "There have never been any women in my family."

Angela Morton Deek had heard the after-game traffic, too. Most of it wracked and shouted along the street before her house. It was a tiny, neat house gathered back from the street in the dark. From the outside, at the end of a long cactus-bordered cement walk, it was simply a white asbestos box with a door in the center of two four-pane windows under a gray asbestos roof that came to a courteous peak exactly above the door. Inside, scattered in studied dispensation, were three chairs of wrought iron in very new shapes covered with orange and blue and black Naugahyde. One was slung with furry animal skin. With these was a variety of small, round or oblong tables ranging in height from six to twenty-six inches, all standing like flatheaded mushrooms on a rich hand-hooked rug of abstract ambition. In the odd places there were Indian and Mexican pots and primitive, obscene carved figures. On the one wall without a window there hung a Navajo rug and two Mexican serapes.

That was at ten o'clock. When she heard the traffic. Two hours ago. She wasn't as nervous in the stomach now as she had been then. At first, when she heard it, she flicked off her reading lamp, throwing the room into a glow of mystery, and turned on the outside light. After fifteen minutes she turned off the outside light. She went into her bedroom and exchanged the low peasant blouse and full skirt for a light sweater and pants. Later she changed that for a white negligee and peignoir, after moving the source of light from one corner to a seven-spired Menorah on one round, low table. After perhaps an hour, and all the traffic, had passed, she poured herself a Scotch over ice in the kitchen. She carried the glass with her into the bedroom where she turned back the blue sheets another four or five inches and then exchanged the negligee for a plain white shirt and plaid skirt and loafers.

At eleven-thirty she turned on the outside light again. At eleven-forty-five she turned it off. At twelve, wrapped exclusively in an Indian shawl, she polished her nails and cried.

That always made her feel better.

At one o'clock she flung off the shawl. Standing naked in the kitchen she wrapped the sandwiches in waxed paper and put them in the refrigerator next to the beer. It was then, leaning against the cool refrigerator door, that she realized that she no longer knew and had not known for more than the last hour who it was she was expecting. That was funny. Really hysterical. She looked at the refrigerator. She jerked open the door and unwrapped one of the sandwiches. Ham and cheese. No. He had never eaten ham and cheese that she knew of, and she ought to know, after nearly twenty years of marriage to him. Well, no wonder he hadn't shown up. She snatched out the sandwiches and flung them into the sink away from her with both hands. She leaned over the sink and with a fork poked them toward the hole and watched, smiling, as the electric disposal teeth ground and masticated and munched the waxed paper and the ham and the cheese and rye bread into itself through its black rubber lips. She pressed her fingertips over her cheeks. Frederick? Of course not. How could he know, two thousand and something miles away. Or care. McCarron? Peter. Peterpeterpeter. No. She smiled. He hasn't really spoken since the day the Indian boy— Ah, God. The boy. Silly. How could she have heard him knock, and it would be a gentle knock, with her in here and that gadget eating? She ran her fingers up the back of her neck, tossing the curls, and snatching up the discarded shawl, ran to the front door.

There was no one there. She stepped out onto the straight walk. The night was dark beyond the porch light. Up on the hill, the Acropolis, she saw a single light burning in a small window. It must be the janitor. Then she went back into the house and turned off all the lights. Then she slept between the blue sheets.

The light she saw in the school was not, of course, the janitor. He had gone away hours ago, and besides, he would not have had business in the room from which the light shone. Peter McCarron had seen her light, too, the outside light, and paused to wonder at its frequent changes. He knew whose light it was, that was part of his business to know who lived in each of the few houses that could be seen from his window between where the sharp-dropping edge of the hill cut off his view and the river which he could not now see but would in another hour or so when the moon rose. If he was still up.

141

He had finished counting the money long ago. It checked the first time and the second time and the third. It always did. It had for the last three years, every game. He had fired a young man teacher three years before because the football ticket sales were almost always off four or five or once, the last time, fifteen dollars. He had done it himself after that, locking himself in the booth outside the gate or in the booth inside the gymnasium for basketball games. It was really simple, he learned, to make the numbers on the tickets at the end of selling match at seventy-five cents per ticket (twenty-five for children, punch the activity card for students) the ticket numbers with which he began the selling (everybody free after halftime), which continued to stand him firm in his original conviction, despite the levity with which at least one board member took his decision. He had counted and locked away the money in the vault long ago. Nearly five hundred dollars, four hundred and ninety-three dollars and seventy-five cents. Not bad. But then it was good cheap entertain.nent.

He went to the window again and cupped his hands on either side of his face. Well, she's gone to bed, finally. He changed his view to the right somewhat. But the others haven't. The lights are still on there. McCarron's spine thrilled. It had been two afternoons and then evenings ago that he had discovered with delicious Machiavellianism that he could see from his cell window not only Angela Deek's house but by laying his cheek against the glass could also see the Granthams' house and thereby Steinhart's precarious roost. He could even see the top two floors of the hotel standing higher than the other buildings, if he wanted to. But that didn't matter so much because Bill Dann would be at one of the other three places. It was part of his job to know these things. Certainly it was. Friday night. Well, no harm on weekends. The one house was the only one lighted over the whole part of the town that he could see. What was there to do at midnight and after?

He turned back from the window. He knelt in a corner of the room and turned on the hot plate under his glass coffee pot. He watched as the red rings of heat glowed brighter through the glass and the bubbles began to rise up through the water. He mixed a spoonful of instant coffee and one of powdered cream in a cup. When the water boiled he turned off the electric plate and poured the water over the mess in his cup.

Seated at his desk he mused over the past week: week three.

Well, things were going. Since he had followed his resolve to lower his sights he had discovered a number of things. It was the mark of a quick-witted administrator not only to see what was going on but be able to anticipate what might go on later. Take, for instance, the hour spent in the library. He had already begun a note to Miss Keerbaum about what he learned there. In the first place, there were too many kids using it after school. That meant one of three things; they were either gathering there to pass notes and formulate plans for disrupting the school mechanism, or they were being given too much homework, or they were plainly lazy, staying indoors when they ought to be out for a team or a club—something to work off the steam and wear them down a little before night.

That was part of this juvenile delinquency problem that, thank God, hadn't hit Tigerstooth much yet, but would seep in from the big cities if others, like himself, didn't wake up and nip the bud. Kids ought to be worn out from some Educational Opportunity like football or hiking or bad-

143

minton before they went down the hill, and then they'd be too damned tired to get into trouble.

And if they have to stay after school in the library to get their homework done, then there's too much. A few problems or a chapter after dinner wouldn't hurt them, might, in fact, be good for them, but other things are important. All work and no play, you know. He made a note on his pad to assign someone, possibly a committee, to run a check on just what the kids were up to in the library. Catherine Keerbaum won't like it much, but she probably needs and is going to get some stirring up. Anybody who has lived so long with books could stand some stirring up. My God, she's been here since before I started high school. And she's not going to like it a bit when I complete the rest of my investigation. Here we've been spending more than a thousand dollars a year on books for God knows how long and she must have run out of space five years ago. Got them stacked all over the place. Jesus, there must be ten thousand books in there. She must think we're trying to be a goddamn university.

Well, the number had already been reduced a dozen or so. McCarron looked at the short row of books on the shelf beneath his window. And those in not more than ten or fifteen minutes. The old girl must really be cracking up. Faulkner, Hemingway, Steinbeck, Caldwell. Jesus. No wonder the kids stay in the library after school. You can't take that sort of thing home, at least not in my day. My father would have numbed my ass good. And that *Scarlet Letter*. It was dull as hell, but Jesus. McCarron smiled. If he had not seen that scribbled note on the bulletin board he might have missed that one. Another thing a good administrator does that they don't tell you in any education course is to always pay attention to hand-scribbled notes. They're always

144

obscene. He picked up the note from his desk top. It was written on a hastily torn sheet of lined paper. *COME TO ENG. 6 AND HEAR HOW HESTER EARNED HER LETTER*, it said. *Jesus.*

McCarron did not look forward to the meeting over that one. English six. That was Mrs. Walpole. Well, he guessed he could still run things around here. There must be some other seventeenth-century novel she could use besides that one. That proved another thing. The parents these days don't pay any attention to what their kids are reading. He'd think of something. The PTA ought to be able to handle this. Bring the parents in maybe two nights a month and have reports from the teachers on just exactly what was being done. McCarron sipped the last of his coffee. No. On second thought, that wouldn't be a very good idea. At least not until he'd had a chance to look around a little more.

Not a good idea at all, considering some other things he'd seen that week. The worst of it, probably, was past, had happened. That was the Monday morning after last Friday night's sickness and the long, lonely weekend lying hot and flat, waiting. But by Monday morning, the sickness had subsided enough that he felt only a small soreness in his belly when he moved certain ways too suddenly. And that was to be expected.

He was there, at his cell window, early, before even the first yellow light came over the jagged hills to spill onto the desert, to glint the river. So he may have been the first white man in the town that morning who caught the sweet whiff, who turned his gaze automatically to the north, who was not surprised at all to see the lazy, greasy-brown smoke rising from the Indian village and then flatten and float, whitening some before it disappeared. With his window open, in that clear-aired hour, he could hear, or believed

145

he could hear, coming from the village, the far tap of the funeral drum. And if he could not hear the wailing of the gray-haired women, he knew it still in his mind's ear. The dogs' barking and the coyotes' last morning answers were clear enough.

He heard and he saw because he had not nor ever would forget. It had just happened that way—that he and Alf had been near enough at hand one morning at age fifteen or sixteen to crawl through the greasewood and mesquite to a point on the bluff above the river when the drum began and the smoke first hit their nostrils. Near enough, and brave enough together, to see the smoke roil below and around and over the pyre, and sometimes through a parting of the smoke, orange, licking flames. Near enough to see the cross-legged drummer pound it, to see and hear the old women with their hair flowing mourning and moving, to see boys their own age standing back, sullen, outraged, watching, also, the licking flames, smelling, also, the sweet burning. To see the mad young dogs bark.

What a way to do it. When the herbs and the roots no longer spirit the heart, when the wine no longer numbs the pain, what a way to go. The women mourning, the men shuffling, drunk, pounding a drum, the young ones awed and angry. Up in sweet smoke.

It was over, all signs of its having happened gone, when McCarron first stepped back from his window last Monday morning and shifted his thoughts to the students and the teachers then passing outside, gathering for another day, another week. So move the years.

He watched the four of them pass by together and was reminded that this was the week when he must invite himself for a time into each of the new ones' rooms. You have to know what they're doing if you're principal. When the phone

146

rings, you can't be taken by surprise. And Jaffrey, the Horn-Rimmed Fool, is about as much help as that poor heap of ashes in the Mojave village.

McCarron felt a little of the soreness when he pressed his hand over his stomach.

A half-hour later, when he left Grantham's painting class and leaned for a minute or two against the warm side of the building, his stomach felt no better. *Jesus.*

When he had first entered the art room it was the gliding stillness that should have warned. The soundlessness. The moving, working, colored absence of normal noise.

And then he had his first shock.

"Grantham!" he whispered. He cleared his throat and spoke. "Mr. Grantham."

"Yes sir?"

"What in God's name is that boy doing up there?" He pointed. The heads of the nearer students turned, annoyed.

There, if he could be believed, his head near the ceiling hanging loose on his shoulders as if dead, a boy hung, his hands tied with cloths to the water pipes. His crossed feet rested on a desk top. Beneath him, students were painting on canvases, seeming to McCarron to be moving in some secret, silent dance.

"Sh," Jake Grantham answered. "This is a happening, Mr. McCarron."

"A what?" Lord, Lord.

"A *happening.*"

McCarron sat on a high stool.

Jake went on. "This morning we are doing the Crucifixion. You see," he explained, "with happenings like this, I am able to bring about an esthetic spontaneity from my students, an undeliberated unity of mind and energy impossible to achieve until they become emotionally involved, until they believe in the improvisational power of the creative spirit. As it were."

Jesus. How much is one expected to bear? "But the boy," McCarron said.

Grantham looked up to the hanging boy. "It is his turn, Mr. McCarron. It's his day to happen. Don't worry, he is safe."

"Why are his arms and chest and face so white?"

"Oh, that," Grantham said. "Flour. You see, he has chosen to be bloodless. Of course."

"Then what are *they* doing?" McCarron pointed to another small group clustered intently.

Jake led the way to the group and pointed into their midst. He dropped his voice. "This is a different happening, but one which is symbolically and intrinsically related in the larger frame, so to speak, to the other." He edged McCarron closer. "You see?"

In the center of the group, its body furiously flinging and coiling in on itself, a brown snake writhed, impaled by a large nail onto a board. Its mouth gaped white like the underside of its belly when it twisted.

McCarron's legs weakened. "Why are they kneeling?" he whispered. "Why aren't they painting, like those others?"

"They are getting ready," Jake answered.

McCarron moved away from the snake. "Do you think this—this sort of thing is best? I mean—" He opened his hands.

"See for yourself." Jake indicated the pictures being painted. Before each canvas a student moved rhythmically, now closer, now back, in, out, dipping into his paints, onto the canvas. McCarron watched the swaying silent bodies juxtaposed to the rectangles of colors until he grew dizzy. Beside him, he saw Grantham's body moving faintly to the rhythm of the painters.

"This is perhaps the culmination of the arts," Jake was saying. "The high copulation, as it were, of drama and dance and pictorial expression all moving together toward ultimate creation."

"But high school kids, Mr. Grantham?" McCarron said. He studied the nearer paintings. "And, Mr. Grantham, none of these *look* like the—the boy up there." Do not rub your temples, young man. Give me an answer.

"Christ sake, Mr. McCarron. Excuse me. Listen, you must understand, the act of creation is a matter of interpretive illusion. We are having the Crucifixion today. If this girl sees it as squares of blue, or that boy as all black, then that is what must be. The outcome is art, Mr. McCarron."

"That one," McCarron said, pointing, "is all white."

"Bloodless, you see. To him the happening signifies the total draining away of life into purity; into nothingness."

But for the warmth of the building as he leaned against it after leaving the art room, McCarron would have wept. Or come as near to doing it as he had at any time yet in these last years. Karen, be happy. Be glad. Be bloodless.

Speaking of happening, what happened to pictures that were sure? What went with the stirring in the groin? Jesus, can he really believe that shit, can the world so have turned? Well. McCarron pushed himself from the warm wall. If it were anything important to the school, it would be stopped. A goddamn screeching halt. Let Grantham make madmen of them all. Just keep them in that cage until it's over, until it passes.

As he walked away from the building, before he could cross to his office, the bell rang and spewed out from every door loud, bright, hurried students. He regained the wall at his back and clenched his teeth as they came at him, it seemed, from everywhere, spread wide and past him, going

149

on cheerfully, maniacally, toward their next classes, their voices and the swing of their bodies hot and young, the boys' faces and the girls' blouses splendorously papuled.

He attempted to catch and follow separate faces coming and passing in the loud gangs. Do you know, young idiots? Do you see where we're taking it all? Ultimately bloodless, white-floured dancing. *Jesus.*

"Good morning, Mr. McCarron."

"Good morning, Mr. McCarron."

"Hi, Mr. Mac."

"Good morning, Mr. McCarron."

The wall at his back grew warmer. Good morning, good morning, goodmorning. Keep your sights low. Hear those voices, Grantham? The same ringing noise. That much you haven't touched yet. I know a scene I'd like to paint, young Jake Grantham. You happening like a peacock with all your goddamn brushes up your ass.

He felt better after that. You have to realize, if your team is going to win, that sometimes somebody will drop the ball. That not every time do you get through with no fouls, no fifteen-yard penalties. With no smart thinkers who believe they've found a way to improve the game.

After that, McCarron settled into a desk at the back of Angela Deek's class when the next bell sounded. He had hurried, first, back to his office for a pad of paper. This time, things would be done right. Make notes of things as you see them. Lower your sights, make a few notes, and you keep the upper hand.

He smiled sternly when she noticed him sitting there, and he bent to the pad and began writing. 1. Window shades uneven. Amnt, source, distrib. of lite import. 2. Blckbd clean. Check. 3. Appear. of bul. brd. cluttered. Visuals could be used to better advant. 4. Class quiet qkly. Check. 5. Appear.

of teacher— McCarron's thoughts had trailed away for a time after that.

Well, things were going. Another week got through. Another Friday night, another game.

He moved back to the window. So she's gone to bed for good, it looks like. Now if the others will, I can get some sleep.

He looked at his reflection in the glass. He straightened. Nothing wrong there, not for forty-three. He had kept himself in good shape around the stomach, he'd defy anyone to say he hadn't. That was the trouble with most ex-coaches. They let all that muscle turn to gut and flab and there wasn't anything that looked worse than an old coach gone in the stomach. That's what would happen to Dann in another five years if he didn't look out. Anybody built like that has got to keep with it all the time. And doing whatever it is he is doing down there in that house tonight won't help much. A coach ought to set an example. He'd tell Dann that. McCarron looked at himself again. He did wish he had some of Dann's hair to go with what he had left.

As he was standing there musing on his hair and wishing he could actually see his skin in the window, he saw a far-off familiar, brilliant light swing brighter and dimmer out of the desert far to his left on this side of the river. He watched the light wind and pick its way in and out of the sand hills. The Santa Fe El Capitan that would be, coming in late from Los Angeles. My old man, bringing it in for the zillionth, and for him, the last time. I should be down there mixed with the dozen old men and women who right now will be walking out onto the platform to watch him bring it in. Sixty-five. Well. This time when he climbs down out of the cab in his striped overalls, with his gloves and brown valise, he'll not look back at it. He'll walk away from it and won't see it again until in a month or six weeks he discovers he is retired and begins to walk down there one or two nights a week to watch it come in and go out with the other old men who look at trains. He'll walk away from it and the train-master will be there to shake his hand firmly, and then he will kiss Mother who will be standing a little to the front of the crowd—the dozen—with her black hat on. Then there will be loud jokes from the others. Then they will all go to the house and Mother will take the black pan of tag-lierini from the oven and serve it with homemade bread. They will drink Sanka and a little brandy.

I should be there. But I have my job, too. I have to watch.

McCarron turned from the window. From the far side of the room where they were stacked, he carried to the window four large pillows of the kind that belong to the seats or backs of sofas. He laid them out in a line on the floor. He turned off his desk light and felt his way to the pillows, guided by the blue night outside. He lowered himself down onto the pillows and took off his shoes. By stretching up he could see the light from the house down at the hill-bottom. He watched it. Then he lay back on the line of pillows and heard the El Capitan wail.

At about the time Angela was polishing her nails, Jake woke up from where he had been dozing, stretched on the floor. He sat up and yawned. He blinked at Bill who, so far as he could tell, had not moved in whatever time has passed, from his position against the wall, his shaggy forelock hanging down before his eyes as he watched his own fingers picking at the guitar strings.

"Christ sake, have I been asleep?"

Bill looked up. He did not answer until he finished the

fleeting cadence his fingers had been moving toward. "Yes," he said.

"They back?"

"Who?"

"Her and Baker."

"Oh." His head bent back toward the shiny guitar. "No," he said. He began another tune that dissolved after a few measures into other parts of tunes.

"Christ sake," Jake said. He stretched both arms straight up above his head. He hunched back down and looked at Bill again. "Drink?"

"I don't care."

But Jake did not get up and he could not reach the bottle and pitcher from where he sat. He continued to watch Bill's wide fingers move with delicacy over the strings. "Why don't you ever finish anything?" he asked.

Bill's head came up again. His eyes were distant and blind. "You mean the music?"

"Yes."

"Hell, I never thought about it." He shifted nervously, recrossing his ankles. "What time is it, you know?"

"No." Jake discovered then that by turning the other way 'round and stretching backward he could just reach the bottle. "Why?" he asked when he had retrieved it and sat back against the wall.

"No reason," Bill said. He began a flamenco beat on the guitar. He stopped. "When're they coming back?"

"Who?"

"Her and Baker."

"I don't know. Here." He handed the bottle to Bill who set it down beside his hip. "There's nothing to worry about there."

Bill looked at him again for four or five seconds. He

frowned. "No," he said. "I reckon not." His face when he was not laughing was a sad face, the big collage all seeming to point downward to the edge of his wide, square jaw, and farther, down the neck, thick, short, corrugated around with muscles and concave places.

"Why didn't Angela come out tonight?" Jake had found his glasses on the floor. He held them up to the night.

"Angela?" The guitar twinged and ran. "I don't know. Fuck 'er." He closed the subject by setting the guitar up against the wall and reaching for the water pitcher.

Closed to anyone but Jake. "Have you?" he asked and grinned.

The shagged head came up again. "Have I what? Oh. Yeah," he said. He looked into his glass. "A couple or three times."

Jake sat forward from the wall. He had his glasses on. He spoke as if he were wide awake. "Good?" he asked.

Bill shrugged.

"Well," Jake said and slumped again.

"She smells," Bill offered after a time.

"What do you mean, she smells?"

"She just does."

"I never noticed it."

"Well."

"Well, Christ sake," Jake mused. Then he said, "Could you—I mean, do you think—" he grinned. "You know, I've got to stop around here. That stomach and all." He grinned.

"Yeah," Bill said. He picked up the guitar again. He did not say anything else. After a while he looked over and saw that Jake had slid down from the wall and was asleep once more with his hand inside his pants. He finished playing the tune he was on all the way through. He moved then, and kneeling before the velvet-lined case laid his guitar away gently. He walked out onto the front porch and leaned himself and the case against a pillar. He lit a cigarette and waited.

Now and then he would lift his head and look first toward the hoop of light from the street lamp to his left, toward town, and then to the light at the end of the street, toward the desert. Once, when he lifted his head higher he saw a single light far up on the hill. From where he sat he could see the white moths dash in and out of the nearer light battering away their senses. Up in the unkempt tamaracks the limbs creaked now and then and an insect shrilled. He looked up into the trees that were only black forms that blotched the stars. He wondered what the locust—if that's what it was—thought he was doing rattling around in the middle of the night.

He saw her when she walked into the circle of light, her hands in her back pockets, walking slowly, her head down. He flipped away his cigarette and picked up the guitar case. He met her at the gate, or the place where the gate had hung when there had been a gate.

"Bill?" she said.

"Yes. I was just leaving." He stepped back to let her come through the opening. He could barely see her face. "Where's Baker?" he said although he did not care.

"He went off that way," she said, pointing vaguely. "To town, he said."

"Oh." He shifted the guitar case to his other hand. "Is Jakie up?"

"More or less. He's asleep in the front room. You have been crying," he said, and then wished he had not said it. It wasn't any of his business.

She laughed. "Don't worry, Bill," she said. She touched

his arm, lightly. She took her hand back when she felt his skin jerk.

He looked at the hand and then away toward the street light. His forelock wagged over his eyes. "I ain't worried," he said. "I don't have a goddamn thing to worry about."

"Thanks anyway," she said.

"For what?"

"For waiting."

"Yeah." He turned toward the car, parked as usual wrong-way to the curb. "You're welcome," he said.

Nine

Routine settles like dregs quickly in the town of Tigerstooth. There is something about this town, new people say for a time, and they work out shining plans for arresting it. Some would save it, some would serve it, some would make a playground of it and look upon their time there as the great gymnasium recess before serious life. They are every one of them wrong. What they don't know is that the desert burns the shine off plans as it does off mirages when they are approached. The product of those who would save it is another Young-marrieds Sunday School class that works its way from Genesis to Deuteronomy each year. The issue of those who would serve it is Job's Daughters, the idea being that through suffering nonsense, greater Eastern Stars are born. Those who would play with it devise more alluring spinners, more intricate square dances, more good seats on the fifty-yard line.

The others, the ones who have no shining plans at all, become their own routine.

It has been so in Tigerstooth since Tigerstooth has been. Since the days when the first clanking black engines could be expected at more or less the same time each week and

157

then each day and people began to watch their clocks by them the town was doomed to, or blessed with, routine. Habit is a warm thing.

"We've become a habit, I think," Anna Margaret said. It was Friday night again, the end of the fourth week. Now and then they could hear the sports announcer's voice from the Acropolis—snatches of sentences, a name, a number—and sometimes the frenzy of the spectators that at this distance sounded like locusts swarming.

"All the greater reason to come away with me to the city. More?"

"Yes." She held the glass while he poured from the bottle and then the water pitcher. When he finished she swirled the glass. The ice clinked. "We'll have to walk. Jake took the car."

They looked toward the glow of light down the street where the center of town was. They were sitting on the front steps of the house where they had moved to after dark, after the last of the game traffic had passed by and turned up the hill.

"It's not far," Baker said. "I manage to whirl down there and back every night, you know."

"How will you introduce me to your friends?" she said and laughed.

He stood and reached down his hand to help her up. "Simple. As my neighbor, the pregnant woman."

"Won't they wonder where you got me?" She set the bottle and glasses and pitcher behind one of the pillars.

"You must be thinking of some other town, my lovely. In the River Street Saloon you won't even be noticed."

"Thanks. I'll feel right at home."

As they neared the circle of light from the street lamp part way along the first block, he watched her face. "That lucky, stupid bastard," he said. She looked up briefly in the light and smiled. Her hands were in the big pockets of her maternity jacket. She did not answer.

"Are you going through with it, then?" he said.

"Let's just walk."

Tigerstooth, downtown, is not enough different on Friday night from other nights so that anyone would notice it. Except perhaps the absence, during the hours of the game— if there is a game—of the boys who lean beside the movie house in packs, watching for what to happen they haven't any idea. Once in a while a car will stop at the curb and they will break their pose to coagulate around it and shove their heads into it and touch it. Then the car will drive on, catching the marquee lights in its paint, and the boys will move back in clots against the building and hook their hands into the front pockets of their Levis.

In the River Street Saloon or the Kutkilya or the Hipa the routine goes uninterrupted by the routine of ball games on Friday or prayer meeting on Wednesday or Elks on Thursday night. Theirs is as much a fraternal order as any other with a ritual, too, but one that begins and ends with only a single order of business, all for the good of the cause. In any but a railroad town, it would be the cowboys, real or imaginary, who would hook their boot heels onto the rail beneath the River Street Saloon's mahogany bar (brought around the Cape by boat and overland from San Francisco by rail) and stare into their own faces beneath sweat-crowned hats. Brakemen and firemen do not stand at bars the same way cowboys do. They are heavier in the hips and across the shoulders. They have no boots for hooking, but stand flat-footed. They hunch nearer the bar and look into their drinking glass more than into the looking-glass.

But in either case the drinking done at the bar is a solitary affair no matter how many of one's brothers are attending, no matter how loudly the juke boxes play or the interlopers at the tables joke.

Baker held the painted glass door open for Anna Margaret. They stood just inside the door for a moment. "Fortitude, my lovely," he said. "It hits you all at once, doesn't it."

It was as if the long room were created in layers of peanut shells, people, smells, smoke, light, and near the ceiling, darkness, like a devil's parfait. Baker took her arm and led her between the backs of the men at the bar and the voices of the people at the tables.

"Professor!" someone shouted. The light was too dim to see who. There came raucous laughs. "Hey, Poet!" another voice called. "Do you know this one? 'There was a young man from Kent—'"

From somewhere else along the line of tables a woman's high laugh shrieked up and fell away in warbles.

Anna Margaret looked at Baker. His face was set and red. He looked down at her. One side of his mouth smiled. He shrugged. He stopped at a table. "The price of fame," he said.

A waitress stopped at their table. She licked her fingers and patted back a loose curl at her neck. "Yeah?" she said. She cracked her gum. The front seam of her turquoise Western pants separated and stretched the stitches down her belly before it disappeared between her legs. When she walked away the seam came into view again pulled first one way then the other.

"Tigerstooth Union graduate, circa 1955." He struck a match for her cigarette. "It's for their future we open McCarron's Miracle every day. Did you notice how much

160

farther over the table she could stick her turquoise twat for having studied French and Latin?"

"She looks content."

"Precisely. That's why it's all crap."

Anna Margaret frowned. She looked toward the waitress who now leaned against the bar counting bills from a roll of money, and toward the tables of men and women nearest. "There is better than this. Isn't that what you're for?"

"Do you mean there are better bars with better drinks, better music, more expensive smoke? With purple carpets instead of peanut shells?" He smiled. He reached across the table and touched her cheek with the backs of his fingers. "Lucky bastard," he said.

A man passing by their table thumped Baker's back. "Hey, William Snakeshit, when's the performance!" he shouted, and he laughed himself all the way the length of the bar.

The waitress brought their drinks then. "Here y'are, Steinhart," she said. "That's one-fifty." She rested her fist on her hip. She looked at Anna Margaret's long hair and at her maternity jacket. As she walked away she licked her fingers.

"I thought you said I wouldn't be noticed," Anna Margaret said.

"What?" He leaned toward her. The juke box had begun a new loud thumping record.

"Nothing." She drew herself up tighter to the table.

Imperceptibly, the noises in the room changed. The shouting voices dropped to another pitch. Baker nodded toward the juke box. "That's Old Salome," he said. "The B-girl."

Anna Margaret turned. There before the juke box, in the square of floor kept clear of tables and peanut shells for dancing, a gray-haired Mojave woman had begun to dance

161

all alone, lifting and planting her heavy feet in their oxfords in time to her private rhythm. When her hips swayed, the flowered dark dress lifted away from the back of her legs. Her stockings were rolled just above the lumps of her knees. She did not look up as she danced, but down at the floor or perhaps at her hands that flapped feebly sometimes in front, sometimes at her side. Her great bosom in its simple flowers rose and fell or swung to the side as she moved. Her face was lined deeply beneath the gray hair that hung down like oily tendrils along her cheeks and shoulders. The changing colored lights of the juke box spilled red or green or blue over her. She kept the grim lifting and planting of her feet despite the hysteria of the idiot-music. As if by some ancient-remembered signal she would turn half 'round and face another part of the room. She stamped nearer their table for a moment, then backed away. In that moment Anna Margaret had a clear sight of the old face, its mouth a tooth-less, humming line, its cheeks the only smooth places in the wrinkles, its eyes set deep back a thousand years, unfocused, unseeing, demented, drunk.

Anna Margaret turned. She touched Baker's hand. "Why?" she said.

He was looking at some spot among the peanut shells. He lifted and dropped his shoulders. "Who knows," he said.

She covered the sides of her face with her hands. "How pitiful."

Then the first tentative catcalls began. Take it off, Salome, a voice called, and Heap big dancing girl, and God would-jalooka that swingin' squaw, and Let's see them legs Salome, and the voices laughed. As she danced slowly by, a man reached out and with his fingertips lifted up one of her breasts and let it fall back again in its flowers. The other man and the two women at that table leaned their heads and laughed. The waitress in the Western pants paused behind the old woman and gave a turquoise bump and grind.

"Poor old thing," Anna Margaret said. Baker was finishing the last of his drink.

Then a man at another table had his cane up the back of the flimsy housedress lifting it until her brown lumpy legs showed above the stocking rolls clear up to the line of her buttocks. The woman with the man slapped at his hand and with her other hand hid her mouth and giggled. For her benefit he shoved the cane deeper so that it pointed the old woman's skirt in front. He wagged the cane back and forth.

It was then that Baker's chair scraped back and toppled onto the peanut shells and he moved the few steps to the other table. No one heard the slap, but most saw it and saw the man bring his hand to his own face in surprise, dropping the cane. At that moment the music stopped and everyone, except the solitary hunched trainmen at the bar who hear nothing, heard Baker shout—scream—at the man's face. "She's *human!*"

And then he turned and walked out, stumbling once against the mahogany bar, through the painted door.

The juke box clicked and shifted from red to blue. The robot hand inside it changed records.

She found him outside, not far from the saloon door, leaning sideways against the stucco wall. Again the sight of his back heaped in his shirt caught at her. From behind, his shoulders were very old. She touched his arm. With the side of his head still against the wall he looked at her a long moment. He smiled. "Well, my lovely," he said.

They walked along the rest of the block and crossed into the light at the corner and out of it again over to the park. When they came to the black cannon he stopped. He rubbed his hand along the muzzle. "Meet an old friend," he said. He patted it.

"Baker," Anna Margaret began.

"Feel how warm it is." He lifted her hand to the gun's barrel.

"Yes. Baker—"

He encircled the barrel with his arms and leaned his face on it. "Will you go on home?" he said.

"Home? Aren't you coming?"

"You'll be safe. It's not far."

She said, "I know. But, you?"

"You'll be home by the time Jake gets there. The game's over, now."

"Listen to me. I—"

"No." He dropped his arms from the cannon. "No. I will not listen. I'm going back down the street."

"Baker, you can't. That man will kill you."

He laughed. His arm in its white sleeve came up to her arm. "With his cane? No such luck, my beauty. Besides," he added, "there are other places."

"You must be drunk. Or crazy."

"Right on both counts. Old Salome and me, John the Baptist."

"Don't. You don't have to."

"Don't I?" he said. "Don't I?" He laughed again and turned back to face the lighted street where the four saloons stretched in a row. "At my age, Anna, one does not let a chance go by."

"For what?"

"For what?" he repeated. "Nobody knows that. That's the game, don't you see?"

She watched him until he crossed the street into the light and out of it. Then she walked along one of the paths that fanned from the black cannon to the other side of the park, to the street that led toward home. The after-game traffic came honking down into town to swirl around and around the central blocks. She could tell from the honking and the shouting and shrill whistles that Bill's team had won this time. At one point a car slipped along the curb beside her, its denizens leaning forward to see her face. She looked toward the car and dropped her hands from her pockets to her sides. A boy's voice said Jeez, she's already had it. The car squealed away. Anna Margaret smiled. How much difference five years make. Had it, Charlie Brown? You're right, Charlie Brown.

There were occasional couples walking back from the game who grew quiet and farther apart while they passed, and two or three times dateless small groups of girls moved by, intently giggling, flinging up their heads toward the street when cars with loud, youthful motors passed.

Anna Margaret had not noticed the lone boy at all until they came at the same time into one of the circles of light, he from the hill, and they met. She might not have marked him even so had he not moved farther from the center of the sidewalk than need be to let her pass, farther toward the dark edge. When she looked up he was watching her and circling away, agile and light-footed.

She stopped briefly, no longer than one lost step, caught by his wide eyes that carried over her and through her the same way they did the one other time when they had, by accident, come this near—the afternoon on the bleachers when he had chased after and caught up the football that had come spinning away from the field. She turned her head deliberately away and walked on out of the circle of light toward home, knowing he stood there watching, his eyes beautiful and warm and cold. That's Rudy, Bill had said that other day, and he will make the difference.

By the time she came near the house the traffic had ceased coming down the hill and only a few cars raced and cracked along the street, back and forth, looking for a sense of direction.

She stood at the gate and waited for a single car that came drifting down the hill. She watched it swing across the street, its lights blinding, and pull up wrong-way to the curb. The top was folded back.

"Hi," Bill said.

She walked to the car. "Hi. You won."

He grinned. He ran his fingers into his shaggy forelock. "We showed them bastards this time," he said.

"*Those* bastards," she said.

He laughed. "What about *um*," he said.

"Um?"

"Like in We showed um. What case is that?"

"You're hopeless," she said. Then she said, "Where is Jake?"

Bill turned to look at the house. "Isn't he home?"

"The car isn't. Wasn't he with you?"

Bill scowled. "Well, sure he *was*. But he took off the last half. I thought he came on home."

"Oh, he's probably painting up there in the art room, or something," she said.

"Yeah. He probably is."

"Or went downtown, maybe."

"Yes." He turned his head toward town as if the pink arc of lights from there would say.

"Bill, did he go to Angela's?"

He shrugged. He ran his thumb along the top of the steering wheel. "I don't know."

She waited.

"I think—I guess so," he finished.

"Well. It doesn't matter."

He looked up at her again. "No," he said. "I guess not."

"Are you coming in?"

He shook his head. "No." With one finger he reached tentatively toward the ring on her finger. Her hands were side by side over the edge of the door. He touched the ring and moved it sideways, back and forth, so that the light caught gently in its small diamonds. Then he held the ends of her fingers and laid his cheek suddenly on her hand.

"How warm you are," she said.

He lifted his head then and looked at her. He frowned. "I better get along," he said. He reached for the starter.

"Are you still going skiing tomorrow?" she said. "Angela said we could all use her boat, didn't she?"

"Sure," he said. "Sure. Only, you can't really ski like—like that, can you?"

"Don't worry. No, tomorrow will be a beautiful, beautiful day to ski."

Ten

AND it was. Depending on how a person has to view a day in Tigerstooth—whether he can escape to the green-edged river or whether he must sell drugs or drygoods or must switch engines in the railroad yards—all the days are either beautiful or hideous. Whatever happens begins to happen early. There is neither reason nor inclination to cower long in bed because the same sun that scorched over the day before is there again early, reaching a hundred degrees by eight-thirty or nine o'clock, even in late September. The sunlight can be kept out of bedrooms, but the heat cannot. The whirling blades of hundreds of evaporative coolers merely change their drone slightly and settle down to the unreasonable job of fanning wet air into the heat. By five-thirty on all but Sunday mornings the crash and clang of freight cars has begun in the Tigerstooth railroad yards, the cafés have been serving canned juice and dry cereal and coffee for an hour, the drugstore is opening, and the birds (even on Sundays) have begun their ribald pandemonium in the tamaracks, having forgotten from the day before the truth of the oppression to come in an hour or so.

By that hour, also, if one is a boy and the day Saturday or Sunday, he is already circling with his rifle in the humped, barren hills on the track of coyotes who have little to fret about from such quarters, or rabbits who have considerably more from both the coyotes and the rifle. In another hour or two he will have passed through his home to exchange the rifle for a fishing rod or for nothing at all. At any rate, long before noon whatever faded miscellany he had worn to begin the day will lie heaped in the sand close to an eddy or inlet of the river and the boy himself, like as not, will be a hundred yards up or down river chasing his dog or another boy or that other boy's dog.

Or if he is too old to chase dogs he may sit in a place where the willows come down to the water in a dark arch and fish. It does not matter whether anything is caught, but if something is—something edible—he may, when inclined, build a small, smudgy fire and roast the fish on a stick or under the coals if he has thought to bring a butter-greased wad of foil. Then he will probably sleep awhile. When he awakens he will fling himself into the cold water and swim or float down to the boat docks and look for someone who will buy for him or sell him a beer, or barring that, someone with his father's boat who will yank him pell mell up and down the river on skis. More probably, if he is that old, one ski will do.

Rudy Yhazi would have finished his sweeping and mopping late the night before, after the game, and be in the river swimming and then under the willows fishing long before the sun even began to drive the coyotes to their lairs or the citizens from theirs. He would be some farther up river from the other boys' festal places, nearer the Indian Neck groves where once the Mojave half of his ancestors lived, where now picnickers come on Sunday and where boys who have girls come to walk and swim or peer into one another's multicarburatored engines. Whatever he did he

169

accomplished with such insular silence that housewives only frowned at their own stupidity when they discovered ten sandwiches in the hamper when they believed—could have sworn—they packed a dozen; that men did swear that their best fish had escaped the stringer; that more than one girl gone off into the undergrowth looked up from her deliberations to discover him standing a dozen feet away with such splendor of manliness to make her gasp and such fullness of deep eyes to make her neglect to say anything at all to her puny swains when she returned to them.

In the Elite Inn, Mrs. Hampton watched from her desk Bill Dann, awakened by the heat, come down the stairs looking violent and pass by without speaking into the dining room. She rang for a maid to run up and change Mr. Dann's sheets.

In her bed Angela Deek lay coverless, viewing her face in a hand mirror.

The same sun brought Peter McCarron up suddenly on his sofa pillows, the sweat running from his temples and causing his shirt to stick to his back, to frown uncomprehendingly at the sun and then at the quiet houses at the bottom of the hill.

In his bedroom on the second story of his frail house, Baker Steinhart lay on his side and stared straight into the eye of the whirling blades of the cooler, wondering if indeed he would be castrated or decapitated by them should a bolt give way in the apparatus. He rolled his tongue over his teeth.

Anna Margaret awakened early but found that Jake was not beside her in the bed where he had come to her at two o'clock. She could tell from the way the covers were drawn up to his rumpled pillow that he was up for good, not just away temporarily in the bathroom. She luxuriated and stretched and touched her belly before rising. She put on the frivolous, laced, tucked, thin housecoat that he had loved to see her in (through) the first mornings of their marriage. Then she brushed her hair, pulling the strokes straight down from the crown.

In the kitchen she dumped out the leftover coffee that Jake had rewatered and reheated, and made fresh. She set the table in the dining room instead of in the kitchen with the silver his mother had given them, and two of the good plates and glasses. Then she went out into the back yard, and reaching through the fence she picked a dozen of the indelicate zinnias from a neighbor's flower bed. Before returning she stopped to look at Baker's house that resembled something a child would have made from a shoe box, painted, and stood on end. She flung a small rock at the house. It clacked once on the boards and fell with a small puff into the dust. In the kitchen again she clipped and trimmed the zinnias until they stood well in a glass.

She went to the door of the extra—the bare—bedroom and opened it. "Breakfast," she said and smiled. She leaned on the doorjamb.

Jake turned from the easel holding a brush in one hand, a coffee can of turpentine in the other. His hair was uncombed and young over his eyes. He had new blotches of paint down the front of his sweatshirt and Levis. He wore no shoes. "Okay," he said. Then he said, "Christ sake." He put down the brush and can and wiped his hands on his shirt. "Christ sake," he said.

"Good morning." She laughed and moved away from the door toward the kitchen. "You have to comb your hair today," she said. "And shave. Or no breakfast."

"Okay," he said and stared after her.

"What's the occasion?" he asked later at the table. "Hot-cakes and ham?"

She watched him pour syrup on the hotcakes and move the ham slices with his fork so that they oozed into the syrup too.

"Aren't you eating?" he said. He sliced the hotcakes and ham together.

"No. Just coffee and Pall Malls." She held one side of her hair back when she drank from the cup.

"Flowers?"

"Yes. From the Morrisons. Unbeknownst to them."

"Van Gogh would go wild over those."

"Do you have to paint today? All day, I mean."

He shrugged and speared another forkful of hotcakes and ham, swirling them together in the syrup. "No," he said. "What?"

"Let's go to the river. I'll fix a lunch. We can swim and sun and be nothing."

"Okay," he said. "Awful goddamn hot for you to be in the sun, isn't it?"

She put down her cup. A crease appeared above her eyes, then went away. "What did you say?" she said.

"I said the sun's too hot for you to be in it much, isn't it?"

"Why? Why is it too hot?" She was leading him the way a teacher leads a child to an answer.

"Well, don't look like you've just been goosed. You get any blacker and you'll begin to look like one of these Mojaves. Or Emil." He grinned. "In color, that is; I don't expect you to start growing a whanger." He grinned.

She sat back with her cup and saucer and finished her cigarette while he ate. She began clearing away the dishes.

"Are the others going?" Jake asked. "Bill and Angela and Baker?"

She stopped in the kitchen doorway. Her back was to him. He was watching the brown glow of her skin through the sheer stuff of her robe. She said, "Do you want them to go?"

"Sure," he said. "Hell, yes. The more the better." He finished his coffee and stretched.

She went on into the kitchen.

They sat on the edge of the sand down from the willows where a cove of the river swirled back on itself and lapped the sand and foamed a little over some twigs. With her legs wrapped in her arms and her chin forward on her knees, her long hair hung to hide her face. She wore one of Jake's old shirts with the sleeves ripped off at the shoulders over her bathing suit. Baker sat beside her completely clothed, his face shaded by an old hat and dark glasses and by the fuzzy thoughts of the previous night.

"Grouch," Anna Margaret said.

"God. It's enough to curdle your brains. I must have been a fool to let you talk me into this."

"You were drunk. Or hung over. This will boil it out."

"What are you, Carry Nation?"

"It's better than lying prostitute in bed all your life."

"No, this is a hell of a lot worse. And unless you're being funny, the word's prostrate."

She laughed. "Why don't you leap in the water and end it all?"

He looked at her and then back to the water. "Have you ever seen a blacksmith temper a red-hot horseshoe?"

"Yes."

"Well."

They watched as Angela's boat came blaring back down

the river, cutting blue and white back and forth across the water.

"He can ski, can't he," Baker said.

"Yes." They watched the boat swing in a wide arc toward shore. Behind it, transcribing a wider arc just outside the boat wake, Jake leaned back, slender and brown, atop the water, his ski sending out on one side white spray.

"Why don't you try it," Anna Margaret said. "It's easy."

"I can see it now. Dragged to death behind a goddamn boat going fifty miles an hour."

"Idiot. It's a good way to clear up your complexion, once and for all, but if you fall you're supposed to let go the rope."

"And then what?"

"Swim around until the boat comes back for you."

"That's just what I thought you'd say."

And they were quiet again, with separate thoughts, drowsed by the sun and the motorboats' drones on the river. Angela's boat turned back into the current.

"When will you tell him?" Baker said.

"You aren't supposed to care."

"No."

"Do I have the right to tell him?" she said.

"There you go again. It's for yourself that matters. Will you never see that? Christ sake—as Jake would say—I think you still believe in other people."

"No. Not *still*. It's a new thing. I had it all mixed up with something else. If I had cared, well—" Her hands lifted and dropped.

"Some natural tears they dropped but wiped them soon; the world was all before them, where to choose their place of rest. Paradise was lost a long time ago, my lovely."

The boat came close to shore. Jake let go the tow rope as

174

it swung by. He came nearly into the shore before stepping off the ski, sending it up onto the sand. He waded in.

"Okay?" he said.

"Yes," Anna Margaret answered.

Jake stood beside her and watched Bill nose the boat up to the sand. Angela, in the seat beside him, was laughing about something and running her fingers through her hair. Bill stepped from the boat. He lifted the picnic hamper out. "Ready for this?" he said. He brought it up to the sand and set it beside Anna Margaret. He stood looking down at her.

"Yes, but someone has to go down to the Landing and buy beer."

"I'll drive," Jake said and splashed through the shallow water to the boat where Angela sat adjusting the straps on her suit. "Come on, Baker. Christ sake, you can't just sit there all day." He flung himself over the edge of the boat.

Baker grumped, but he got up and brushed the sand from his rear and waded carefully into the water. "I may as well die by drowning as by broiling," he said. "At least I'll be cool."

Bill stood beside her and watched until Jake had backed the boat out into the river and then sent it roaring, nose up, downstream. In the back seat Baker was grasping the gunwale with one hand and his hat with the other. Bill laughed. His shadow fell over Anna Margaret's back and shoulders. When the boat's drone had settled in the air she turned up her face.

"Help," she said. He pulled her up to her feet. "I'm ready for some shade," she said. "Bring the basket."

He walked up the slope behind her to where the sand gave way to brittle grass and then to the shade of the over-bending willows a hundred feet up the river. When she turned she saw that his eyes were fixed where the backs of her legs had been. Rivulets of perspiration or water ran off his shoulders and hung midway down his chest. As she watched one of the beads broke through the thatched hairs and slid past one brown nipple and on down into the gnarled muscles of his stomach. When she looked at his eyes again they were watching hers belligerently from under his damp, shagged forelock of hair. His jaw hung a little loose in the collage-face and from his mouth the edge of his tongue flicked out and over his upper lip and then back. Both of his arms hung down his sides, the free one slightly forward of the one holding the basket. The fingers of that free hand clenched and opened, making the tendons of the forearm harden and disappear.

When the dragging willow branches moved, slits of sun-light flickered over his shoulders and onto her face. As if to brush away the rifts of light, his hand came up to the side of her face and then slid back under the long hair. With her cheek against the wet skin of his chest she said, "Put down the basket," and then waited to feel where the huge hand would find her body. Instead, it came to the other side of her face and together the hands tilted up her head. She saw that his eyes were bewildered and blue far back and deep. His two thumbs came forward over her cheeks to either side of her nose and then up and then away. "Please don't cry any more," he said and she could feel his hard ridge through his trunks and through her suit pressing into her swollen stomach.

All along the banks knots of willows plunged shafts of light into their own shade.

Out on the water the red and blue and white boats ripped and shattered the swift river.

On grassy banks boys lay down with their dogs to watch white smoke reel in and out of the branches.

A day's ride by car away, far up in the high meadows, beneath crowns of bronze, white birches stood straight down into the earth.

It was not until Bill had gone back down the shore to meet the incoming boat and she was standing, holding up the bathing suit by its straps to untangle them, that she saw through the V of the straps the brown, wide eyes and then the brown body of the boy. He stood silently inside the dome of the willows as if he had been there forever. For a long moment she stood with the suit against her chest and stared into his suppliant eyes. Then when her gaze moved down his body, darker but brown like her own, unmarred with strips of whitened skin, she saw that he, too, was naked and that he held, cupped from beneath in his hands, the greatness of his manhood.

"No!" she whispered. She heard her own voice hiss. Without being conscious of moving, her back touched the willow trunk. They faced each other through the six feet of space between them. Had anyone come upon them at that long moment he would have thought himself suddenly in an instant of prehistory to see the two still figures, one, the male one, standing with his head slightly tipped to the side, his body in barbarous gesture, the other with knees crouched, with flinted eyes, her lip drawn up from white teeth, her fingers crooked forward from her chest.

He did not move nearer. Only his eyes reflected his calculation and petition. Her own eyes softened, involuntarily, like her voice as she said again, "No," and like the curve of her hands as she covered herself. Finally his hands swung back to his sides, clenched into fists. He turned half-away from her. The way his black hair hung straight on his forehead was young, despite the pride of his stance.

Watching him still, she stepped into the bathing suit and jerked it up over her stomach and breasts. She moved to the picnic basket that lay on the ground behind him. She knelt there and folded back the cover. When she stood again, she reached toward his arm as if to turn him, as if to speak, but before her fingers touched his skin he turned his head toward the hand and they each saw the slit of sunlight that moved along it, onto his arm, joining for an instant the two shades of brown.

As his eyes lifted, she recognized, this close, the black, impenetrable stare she had known in the high meadows, had always known in mirrors.

She turned away and ran clumsily from the willows toward the beaching boat.

Quickly the boy stepped to the picnic hamper. His beggar's hands dipped in and out and he faded back into the willows.

She stopped at the water's edge and watched Bill pull the nose of the boat onto the sand. With his legs spread and feet dug into the sand he leaned back and dragged the bow up to himself. He hung there a moment and looked at her. Then he stepped into the water to take the case of beer Jake handed him. When he came back onto the sand he did not look at her. Baker stepped from one side of the boat, Jake from the other, and then he turned to help Angela.

"Wait," Anna Margaret said. She waded to the edge of the boat opposite Jake. "Wait. I haven't even had a ride in your boat, Angela." Jake was watching her from the other side of the boat, across Angela's legs. "You men can set up the picnic." She pulled herself into the boat. "Or have a beer. We'll be right back." She settled onto the leather seat beside Angela.

"Okay," said Angela. "Good idea." She laughed and slapped Jake lightly on the hand. "Well, shove us off."

Jake pushed the bow of the boat back into the water. Angela pressed the electric starter and the motor began its shrill roar. Blue exhaust puffed up and hung on the water and then went away. Just before the boat turned into the current, Anna Margaret looked back and saw the three of them. Jake stood in the water to his knees and behind him Bill stood cradling the beer case, his legs spread wide, and beside him Baker stood, thin, stooped and old-looking in his faded clothes under the flop-brimmed hat.

She signaled up river to Angela and then closed her eyes and let the wind above the river blow her hair back and cool her face.

She shouted over the motor's drone. "This is far enough. Stop."

Angela looked at her curiously from under her wild, gold curls, but she pulled the gear lever back to neutral and let the boat idle. Immediately its bow began to swing around to go with the current.

"What are you doing?" Angela asked.

"I'm going to ski." She lifted the ski from the back seat. She flung the tow rope back over the motor into the water.

Angela touched her arm. Her eyes were wide and excited. "But, you can't," she said. "You can't."

Anna Margaret let herself off the side into the water and then slipped the ski over the gunwhale. She kicked back from the boat. "Oh yes I can," she said, her breath shortened from the cold. She treaded water, waiting for the boat to pass in the current and bring the rope to her. "It's a beautiful day to ski, Angela!"

Eleven

THE Colorado, the colored river, cuts in intaglio fleet and deep and cold down from its terrible geneses through five life zones to the floor of the lower Sonoran silting with it two billion years of crusty history, the geologists say. And the petrographers nod in assent. Two hundred and forty-six thousand square miles drain into it, they say, when there is anything to drain, carried in the blue and gray jagged, fierce gorges of fifty small rivers and by creeklets more myriad than the pale veins of old leaves. After a thousand slashing miles it slices out onto the sand like the fragrance of the desert lily and, sometimes, with the carcass of a bloated corpse. Or it did. It did when de Alarcón sailed it four hundred and twenty-four years ago. And it did when Garcés cooled his Franciscan feet in it and remarked its Hakatai-shale red and could not have imagined hydroelectric might.

Twelve

McCARRON was there when they brought her in. Later, in a lucid time, he believed it was an act of preordination that set him precisely there in that awning-striped chair overlooking the river that had begun to take on green with the sun some to the west, behind him. He hadn't been down here in a long time, anyway. Someone at the Lions lunch Thursday, maybe it was Teddy Miller himself, had said McCarronyouoldfucker, how's come we never see you at the Landing and he had said Jesusteddy (or whoever) I don't know, and so he had remembered that this morning when he saw the river shine from his cell and decided it wouldn't do him any harm. He had come down about eleven o'clock and had a sandwich and a hard-boiled egg with Teddy Miller and a couple of other Lions. He had had a bottle of beer, too, and would have relished another except the high school boys had begun to pad in then, shifting on their skinny legs and eyeing him and clacking the bowling machine. So he had ordered a Coke, despite Miller, and eventually drifted out onto the sun deck and sat in a striped chair and crossed his ankles on the second from the top wooden rail. It was a good thing he had worn his fishing hat for it was hot as hell in the sun and the shade of the building wouldn't creep out that far for another hour or two.

It was a good view. The Landing stood part way up a steep bank from the river so from up here he could watch the boats backed off their trailers into the water, and see them get gassed up and iced, and see the fishermen coming in with some pretty good-looking bass, and see the skiers slicing the water like dorsal fins. He made two other observations, also, which went to underscore his decision to lower his sights this year. One, the high school girls would be stark naked if they wore anything less than they were wearing right now. Two, it's a wonder we won the game last night; there's the first-string quarterback and half the goddamn line down there oozing around those girls like maggots on a dead horse, and every one of them with a can of beer. *Jesus.* Dann ought to be here. He ought to see *this,* then he'd understand, maybe, that building a team that's out to win includes more than a couple of hours' practice every night. And smoking. Jesus, two or three of them smoking.

So he was there when they brought her in. He saw the white boat when it first came around the bend running wide-open right down the middle of the river. As it came he saw the other boats veering to right and left and skiers fighting to take up slack behind their tows in order not to swing out in the path of the white boat. Fool. Hit a loose ski going like that, he'll snap a pin and float for two miles there in the current before he can fix it. When the boat was almost opposite the Landing it turned and headed in, still running open, slipping sideways. Decelerate, fool. He saw someone stand up and lean forward to bring the bow back down into the water. Then it was slapping across the river pointing directly at the cutaway where boats were backed off trailers. McCarron saw that others had now turned from whatever they were doing to watch the white boat. The high school kids faded back from the shore. It was as if there was something particular, something crucial about the sound of the white boat that even now had not slacked its speed. Then McCarron saw who was driving it. No wonder. Even from here he could recognize the metallic gold hair and see, or thought he could see, the faintly wild eyes of Angela Deek.

But the boat stopped in time. A few yards out she cut the motor and the bow crunched lightly on the gravel of the landing space. Before it touched, McCarron saw Jake Grantham vault (Beautiful. That kind of body.) out of it and give it a pull from the front that locked it up on the land.

And then Dann was running up the wooden steps with her toward the building and people were fading back from him and then closing after him and then opening again for Jake and gaping at Baker puking over the side of the boat and at Angela's gold curls above the hands that hid her face there in the boat. And then McCarron was at the top of the steps staring down into the dreadful face of Bill Dann about to say, Here, what happened? until he saw his eyes and her white face and the limp arm and its hand swinging against Dann's bloody thigh, and he heard or thought he heard a low growl so he stepped back as Dann brushed past still running, with the thin lines of red lacing his thigh and calf and ankle like exposed veins, and leaving on the boards faint half-soles of red all the way to the glass door that Teddy Miller held open, his heavy belly hanging in his T-shirt. McCarron's eyes were caught by the red footprints until he was jarred from behind and had to catch himself on the railing and saw the narrow hips of Jake Grantham above the brown legs running across the sun deck and through the door and beyond until they faded. God what happened?

the voices were saying and God did you see the blood? and God the others answered.

McCarron was already down on his knees spitting on the browning spots and scrubbing at them with his hat before anyone noticed him. Even then it was a long minute before the voices started again God what is he doing? before he saw dimly the first pair of brown feet and felt the first hands under his arms and heard the first quiet voices close to his face and smelling faintly like beer saying Come inside Mr. McCarron, let's get out of the sun Mr. McCarron, come, and then he seemed to float into the sweat of Teddy Miller's giant T-shirt, and saw before the ceiling appeared above his eyes her lying on one of the leather benches with that arm hanging down to the floor and Bill Dann turning away from her toward the others like a cornered wounded animal.

The Santa Fe Hospital in Tigerstooth, like the other yellowing stucco buildings of any size, was erected in a busier time when railroad equipment was less predictable, before Safety had become a goal that when achieved promised not only health but reward in time off, when a certain number of cases of severed leg or shattered head were expected weekly from among the Indian crews who, apparently mesmerized by the swing of their hammers or the pumping of their hand cars or the heat, neglected to respect the black might of steam engines roaring down upon them. The single-story building lay at the edge of the green park, close to the depot. Over the front entrance, incongruously supported by two granite columns, balanced a neo-Doric entablature with what could have been a disturbing dictum if it had not been carved in Latin: *SIC TRANSIT GLORIA MUNDI,* it said, and *MCMXXVI.*

Inside, starched nurses swished on rubber soles and the

rubber wheels of hurried carts sucked at the linoleum of halls and passageways connecting unexpected wings added from time to time by some Santa Fe Daedalus.

Doctor James Paler who superintended the hospital had never been recommended for his charm or temperament. He had been refining it to a vitriolic edge for thirty years, almost from the time he came to Tigerstooth as the Santa Fe doctor, fresh out of school, with the fresh valuable knowledge that the best asset a doctor can develop to over-leap the gaps in learning is a thoroughly unpleasant nature. That, and the knowledge of where to fly cases he knows he cannot treat. Besides such professional acumen, Dr. Paler was fortunate in that his full hair grayed smartly from the temples which offset horn-rimmed glasses and his pink face.

He stood in the waiting room, just inside the portaled doors that gradually ceased swinging and stopped with a knock. He snapped his rubber gloves from his fingers and handed them to a nurse, and then he completed the button-ing of his fresh white coat. He looked from one to the other to the other of the three men just rising from the plastic and aluminum chairs.

"Which is the fool who let her get up on skis in that con-dition?" he said and his eyes flicked over them. Assuming the question to be rhetorical, no one answered. He watched, grimly, the three faces turn white.

Bill said, "How—" before he was cut off.

"Are you the husband?" Not are you *her* husband, but *the,* as if he were talking about sires and dams.

"No," Jake said. "I—"

The doctor shifted. "You're the husband? What kind of an idiot are you?" The doctor's voice sweetened but not his face. "Or didn't you know she was pregnant?"

185

"Was—" Baker began, standing a little away, leaning one hand against the wall.

"Who are you?" Doctor Paler clipped. But that question also was rhetorical. Back to Jake, *"Was* pregnant is precisely correct. Or it will be in a few hours. What did you expect?" His gaze flicked again, down Jake's bare legs and back to his face. "It's fortunate that you pulled her out quickly." He was grinning. "And that I was available. Another minute or two—" He let his voice end in mid-air and shook his head.

"Doctor," Bill began again, "goddamnit, tell us how—"

"Shut up!" the doctor said. His eyes followed an instant behind his voice and then he wished he had not said that. The look he got in return was deadly. "I beg pardon," he said and brought the fingers of one hand up to his temple. "She has lost much blood, of course," he said. To Jake he said, "But she will live." He laid his hand on Jake's shoulder and shook his full grayed head again. "You are fortunate, young man," he said. "You may see her, if you wish, in the morning," and then he turned and was gone.

"Bastard!" Bill said to the clacking doors. They stood there watching the doors, the one thick and heavy, his feet planted wide below knotted, hairy legs, the blood on his chest and arms and one leg now dried and flaking, the other taller, thinner, hip-shot. Baker leaned against the wall and watched their backs.

"But she is a good skier," Jake said. "I've never seen her fall. Never." He turned to Bill. "She should not have fallen."

"How many times you going to say that? For God's sake, she did. She did."

Jake sat abruptly on the front edge of a chair. "How could Angela have let her? She should never have—"

186

"Don't blame Angela," Bill said. "Christ, don't blame Angela." Then he said, "Poor, crazy bitch." He unclenched his fists. He looked up from under his shagged hair toward the red and green flowered curtains in the windows and toward the slow-whirling fan near the ceiling. "I'm getting out of here."

Yeah, poor crazy bitch. Poor crazy dumb screwed-up bitches, all of them. Every goddamn one of them, sooner or later, and I'm the one can really roll back the stones. Caroline and her brown tits. Angela and her stink. Anna Margaret and her knocked-up belly. Was. *Was,* that's the clue, when you get down to bare knuckles. It's always was. I was, she was, he was, you was.

Reba Hampton watched him come across the street and jerk upon one of the glass and wood-carved doors and stand for a moment shifting on his feet, cooling them. He glared at the two or three senile men who, ruminating like old buffaloes, pulled their heads forward on ropy necks from their leather chair backs to blink at this wide-legged silhouette that let in the heat and light. She intercepted him at the bottom of the stairs as he came across the lobby, intending at first to hear what news of the accident, but changing her mind when she saw his face and the flaky blood. She backed away a step or two. Her hand went to her neck in the old gesture.

It was sometime far in the night when Anna Margaret awoke to see Baker standing weedy and stooped near the foot of her bed looking out the window over the park. In the light from the moon or street lamp his face was long and shadow-creased. The light pronounced his nose and forehead and the concavity of chest in yellow and dark bands through Venetian blinds. Even in her dreariness of mind she knew he was not looking at anything and that he had been there a long time, that probably she had half-wakened once or twice earlier and seen him there. He was swaying a bit like some fall stalk. For a time she could neither think of anything to say, as if all words and thought had been flushed away in the green water with what had been her child, nor could she seem to remember how to go about working the muscles that make words, but she knew she was not surprised to see him. After a while he moved from the window and came to the side of her bed. He looked down at her.

"Well, my lovely."

She smiled. Or meant to, although she did not feel the muscles working. She could not see his face in actuality in the near dark, but she knew the expression it held. It would be a long expression beginning on his high forehead, running down through his cynical eyes, along his sad nose. One corner of his mouth would be tilted up, the other down. She felt his fingers move briefly, lightly, along her forearm covered by the sheet, the way you pet a sleeping kitten, tentatively, not enough to wake it, more to reassure yourself than it. Then he moved back to the window and with a quick backward set of one foot, balanced himself. He put his hands in his pockets again. He wore the same pants he had worn at the river. He began the rocking motion.

"Drunk?" she said.

He looked toward her for a moment, then back to the window. "Yes," he said. But not so drunk as he had been two or three hours ago when the bartender of the River Street Saloon closed its doors against his entreaties. Not so drunk as he had been when crossing the street toward the park and toward the hospital, he had fallen on his hands and knees at the curb, amid his own curses. It had taken what seemed to him a long time to calculate the direction his will must take to get up. He had stood a long time, then, in the park looking at the few lights of the hospital.

Anna Margaret chuckled. "How did you get in here?"

"In this condition, you learn to be sneaky," he said.

She drifted back into sleep, for how long, she didn't know, but when she awoke next, the direction of the late moon had changed Baker's half-figure.

"You have a cigarette?" she said.

"Yes." He came to the side of her bed and lighted one for her. She began to draw her elbows back to push herself up. She winced.

"Don't," he said. He held the cigarette for her.

"Where is Jake?" she asked.

Baker shrugged. He sat on the edge of the bed. "I don't know." He smoked from the same cigarette. "He'll be here in the morning. The doctor said he could—"

"Never mind," she said. She moved her hand under the cover down to her stomach. "Well," she said. "That's that."

"Yes."

When they finished the cigarette he ground the butt on the side of the metal wastebasket. Back at the window again he asked, "How did you have the nerve?"

She waited. Then she said, "For what?"

He came to lean over the foot rail, his hands curled on the bar. "How did you have the nerve?" he asked again. "Tell me. Tell me what it was like. What did you think? What did you tell yourself when—when the water?" He jerked back from the bed as if the metal were hot. "Goddamnit, tell me!"

"No. I don't know." She moved her head from side to side on the pillow. She made a sound like a mirthless laugh. "Anyway, I'm not the one to ask. I'm a sloppy teacher."

He turned toward her and clutched the bed rail again. "No, that's not what matters. Your mistake was in method. You just naturally handle yourself too well in water. You can't help it. And too many people to see. I don't mean that. What I want to know is, what did you do to yourself to get ready? What does one have to do to himself to finally reach the point where he can bring it off?"

He sat on the edge of the bed and took the point of her chin in his hand. He spoke more quietly. "Don't wag your head at me, my lovely." Her head stopped moving on the pillow. "There. Now will you tell me?" She did not say anything.

"Well," he said. "No matter." He traced the outline of her shoulder with his long white fingers. "Someday I'll find out." He laughed. "Ironically, the successful ones can't tell me either, so I can't blame you, my bungling beauty."

He heaved himself off the bed. Back at the window he spoke harshly. "You know you don't have any right, don't you?"

"Does anybody?"

"Yes, goddamnit. Yes. I have, for one. But not you." The light in the room was beginning to gray into shapes of the chair and night stand, the white screen folded in the corner.

"Because you're loved," he went on. "That's the whole difference. That's why you don't have the right. Don't snort. You may think not, but you are."

"Jake, for instance?"

Baker shrugged. "Mark that off. He's not the world. And you don't love him anyway, as if I were telling you something you don't know."

"But I wanted to love him."

"Okay. It's worth killing for. It's worth being a whore

for, if it comes to that. But it won't work, not for people like you and me. What a pair we'd make," he laughed. "The original half-people. Because that's what we are, only you're too damned young to know it. Half-people. And for our kinds of halves there never are maching halves."

She did not answer. She watched him, his hands in his pockets under the rumpled shirt tail, rocking on the balls of his feet. His face was gray in the gray light, haggard, deep-lined, unshaven. She saw that his pants were gashed at the knee and that he wore no socks.

"Open the window," she said. "The air should be lovely this morning."

He turned to her and smiled. He raised the Venetian blinds and the window. He leaned forward on the sill and looked toward the park. "Well," he said, "I see the sun will be back again."

It was then that the door opened with an efficient click and a nurse swooped in, all starch and silence. Whatever her mission, it was abandoned at the sight of Baker just turning from the window. "Oh!" she said. Her eyes took in his squalid face and clothes. She sidled toward Anna Margaret's bed, and after glancing at her, took up a position between them.

Baker started, "Don't panic—"

"Who are you?" the nurse said. "No one is supposed to be in here. The patient is not allowed visitors. Certainly not until ten." Her eyes were wide with indignation and fright.

Baker moved a step toward her. She backed against the edge of the bed. "It's all right," he said. Then he whispered, "I'm her lover!" He laughed. He raised his hand toward Anna Margaret. "Good-by, my lovely."

Baker found his way through the main halls of the hospital carelessly, slapping by in his loose loafers the nurses' stations that he had circumvented with such grim cunning four hours ago in the kind of intrepid clarity that comes sometimes in drunkenness. The sight of him materializing suddenly around corners at such an hour, with his shirt tail and arms and torn pants all a-flap was sufficient to muddle the change of guard at more than one station and to bedevil momentarily four Indian aides exchanging giggleries and aprons outside a linen room. When the four recovered, they began again the giggle-language that makes the spines of white people itch.

Another who was startled to see Baker pass was Mc-Carron who had that hour given up, finally, the thought of more sleep and had propped his door open and had rolled up the head of his hospital bed in order to occupy himself with the goings-on in the hall. The sight caused his stomach to begin aching again. McCarron had not had a happy or very sleepful night, despite the cautiously administered soporifics prescribed by Doctor Paler who found the case interesting enough to sit up rather late himself, poring over textbooks and journals on paranoia, schizophrenia, and dementia.

McCarron had not wanted to come to the hospital at all, had told them out at the Landing that he didn't need to, that he would be all right in an hour, but they wouldn't listen and brought him on anyway. Once soothed into the cool sheets, however, he had slept soundly until dark when he awoke sweaty and babbly to find his mother sitting by the bed watching over him. The sight of her sitting with prim hands clasped in her lap and the wrinkled, familiar touch of those hands was comforting at first. Then she began to talk, saying again that he should live at home where he could get a better diet, where he'd be welcome, where he and his father could maybe now and then enjoy a game of chess or go out in the boat and do a little cat fishing. Well, he had tried that. Ten years ago when he first came back to Tigerstooth, he had tried that. It wouldn't work.

Then she said, "You ought to forget about Karen, dear. You just worry yourself."

"Karen?" he said. "Why do you bring her up?"

His mother looked down at her hands in her lap. "I thought you had gotten over that," she said.

McCarron pushed himself up on one elbow. "Goddamnit, Mother, what you talking about?"

She brushed the lap of her dress. "It is not necessary to take the Lord's name," she said.

He flopped back on the bed. "All right. Now. What about Karen?" he asked, although he knew without her answering that he had been talking, or more likely, shouting, about Karen just before he awakened. That was a good reason for not living at home or with anyone else. His kinds of nights were his own, and not the sort that made other people comfortable or very tolerant.

And every time he was about to drift off to sleep during this night in the hospital his mind jerked back to Karen. It was the blood that did it. That was why he had had to give up hunting—fish don't bleed much—and rare steaks. There was a time for a year or two there when even the sight of a sudden nosebleed running on the upper lip of a football or basketball player was enough to set his stomach and head on end.

Once during the night he had tried playing the head-and-body game but the faces and torsos got all mixed up and out of control again, and the game ended in disaster with him vomiting in the hospital bed. He got the impression from the nurse who changed his linen that if he had been anyone less than the principal, he would have lain in his mess until morning when there are aides more specifically trained in such matters. And once the station wagon full of nuns returned to whirl around his bed. They were almost a comforting sight at first, laughing, their black and white cowls snapping in the air of the open window. It was not until he realized that they all had Karen's face behind their rimless glasses—all except the driver who had no head—that he shook himself up out of the vertigo and sat up, sweating, in bed.

Karen had had no head, either, the last time he saw her, the day the great sheet of glass came screaming down like a guillotine with her screams and his scream and left her body lying, as under shattered ice, on the carpet.

Lovely, delicate Karen who seemed to float into his life and arms like some sweet-scented, laughing vision almost before he had time to clear his head of the war, who seemed to be everything opposite to real life, whom he followed from surprise to surprise during the whole summer honeymoon in New York. That was her idea, too, so they drove slowly across the country from San Francisco and spent the two months in daily foraging from their sublet apartment. He remembered the way her hair blew back from her ears on the Staten Island Ferry, the way she held her head to one side when she didn't like a painting in a Greenwich Village window, the way she would sit quietly for long periods of time before a Turner or Rousseau in the Metropolitan. He'd leave her there and wander down to the armor and sarcophagi and statues where she would join him again, and they would laugh in whispers together at the funny-shaped peckers on the statues, or she would taunt him when they passed Bourdelle's giant gold archer on the mezzanine. She was always sad, though, when they came to a mutilated statue. She said she bet the castrated parts were kept in a forgotten box in some dusty storeroom of the museum. He bet they weren't, but the thought of the amputation made his groin ache, the same as it had once—and he never told her this—when in a laughing, vulgar gang of soldiers in Italy he had watched a Texas corporal chop off the penis of a statue with his tent tool and button it into his fly.

She would take him back again and again to the Metropolitan or the Frick and patiently talk and explain. He did not mind because the scent of her hair and the sound of her voice and the sight of her ankles boarding the Fifth Avenue bus seemed, then, to be enough.

He remembered the way she sat huddled in her scarves and sweaters in the grandstand when they were back in California and he was coaching his first high school teams. When the game was going badly, he knew that by turning around he would find her there, in the first or second row, directly behind the bench.

And they had built the small house up in the hills where they could just barely see the bay through the tall glass windows that made one entire wall of the living room. He had not liked the floor-to-ceiling glass, but as always, he came to like whatever she liked. She filled, in their seven years, the walls with drawings and paintings gleaned from antique shops in the city and artists' studios in Carmel, letting the light from those tall windows flow in to bathe them. On the patio, beyond the windows, stood the long, naked statue of Paris that he bought for her, not liking it much himself, saying it was too slender, modern, provocative. He had built a roof over the patio to protect it from the rain because it was of polished wood standing on a slender wooden pedestal. Karen loved it. It had become the favorite of all her joys because he had given it to her.

He would come upon her often, standing before the sheer glass wall, or seated on a stool, watching the lithe figure— or the red sunset beyond it, it was difficult to say.

The patio roof did not stop the wind that came one day, however. Neither could he who had built that roof and the house it sprang from stop her the day the wind came in sudden fury up the hills to throw down the statue from its perch. They were sitting there that morning, listening to the whistling wind. They both saw the slender figure rock sideways and back, once, then begin to lean again. When she cried out and began to run toward it with outstretched hands like a mother ready to snatch her child from death, he screamed but could not stop the splintering, hacking, slicing down-shatter of glass. When, still screaming, he bent down to her he drew back in horror. Facing him, near her outstretched fingertips, sat the leering head of Paris, the seducer, and there, almost between her hands, the sweet-scented hair tousled up from her head in the wind.

That was more than ten years ago, when the world he had gradually built on under Karen's patient gentleness disappeared from under him and threw him back down into the comfortless morass of the ordinary, where work became again work, a thing to pass the time, where once again boy-games took the place of full life, where in the searing desert to which he returned the petty became the real.

So now Peter McCarron, aged forty-three, balding, sat on the edge of his hospital bed pressing his gone-bad stomach with his palms, repeating to himself all the obscenities he knew in order to clear Karen and the nuns from his mind, wishing he were up on the Acropolis in his cell where he could look down upon the rising town and see the sun glint, beyond, on the river.

196

The sight of Baker Steinhart scuffing along the hall, while disturbing in a sense, was in another sense a pleasure to McCarron. He rang for a nurse. "Is Mrs. Grantham here?" he asked.

"Yes," the nurse said. "She can't have any visitors, though. What did you want?" She inspected his water pitcher.

"Just that, thank you," he said.

The nurse looked indignant for a moment, as if she were about to remind him that hospitals are very busy places, but evidently remembering the peculiar notations Doctor Paler had jotted about this case, she subsided from the room with a starched swish, drawing the door closed after her. McCarron had to get up to reopen it, bending down carefully to set the little rubber stop under it.

Outside, from the steps of the hospital, not knowing the effect of his passing on McCarron, not even knowing McCarron was there, Baker felt the heat of the early sun working into the park, lifting away the coolness that comes in that desert only in the two hours before dawn. The grass and the shade of trees on the grass still looked cool, but they were not. Already tiny white butterflies rose up from the grass, warmed by the morning, and flew about and bobbed in dizzy nonsense. Up in the trees, like mad winged instruments, the cicadas vibrated. On mornings like this, the Mojaves say, if you listen to the shriek of the cicadas you will be met by devilmen before the next moon-rising. A few sparrows, already voiceless, flew up from their feeding to the trees. Across the park, the drugstore doors stood open. Above them a three-bladed fan dropped puffs of warm air down on the heads of people passing under it. Three or four old men came down from their faded rooms, picked at the rack of Sunday newspapers on the sidewalk. A brakeman crossed the park diagonally from the depot and disappeared into the drugstore, idly slapping his gloves against his thigh. In the desert itself the coyotes and rodents had long ago settled under rocks and into burrows in the ravine bottoms. Here and there a swift roadrunner might be snatching a lizard or rattler from a stone where it lay too long sunning. At the river the younger boys, the ones too young to have been parked there in cars late the night before, began to gather in shouting clans.

Baker walked down the three steps and crossed the street into the park. He did not relish the half-mile walk up the shadeless street to his house where from lace-hung front windows Tigerstooth ladies would see him pass and then rush to back fences calling one another, Did you see, Goodness did you see? He felt dirty, now that it was bright day, with his unshaven face that seemed big and noticeable. His hair, worn long, uncombed since the day before, thatched over his eyes and came down in strands above his ears. His knees showed red and scabbed through the torn places. His hairless ankles appeared like white socks between his cuffs and shoes. When the path on which he walked came to the cannon, as they all did at last, he passed carefully behind it noticing that it still aimed, determinedly awry, at the top floor of the hotel.

As he walked around the cannon block, he found the half-Indian boy, Rudy Yhazi, sitting there looking at him with his solemn eyes as if he had been waiting for just this encounter, letting that same enigmatic smile spread that from his childhood had perplexed the few adults who had seen it, a smile both inviting and cold at once. He was dressed in Levis and a white T-shirt too tight for him except at the neck where it hung loose and frayed. Baker stopped. He watched his own hand, and the boy watched it, move involuntarily forward toward the boy's shoulder. When it touched it seemed for a moment that the white butterflies held their winged poses. Then the boy's black-lashed eyes rose, beginning at the fingertips, along the hand, and the arm, up to Baker's shoulder and then, above, to his face. Baker dropped his hand. He hurried on. He was too tired, too late, it had all been too long ago and required the peak of an agile mind.

He passed on out of the park and aimed toward home, clearing his mind with the problem of whether or not there was enough vodka left for one drink before sleep. He wished, remembering a sidewalk juice bar somewhere, for a glass of ice-cold coconut milk.

Jake Grantham saw him pass by the window on his way to the little house in back, but he did not rap on the window or shout to him. The painting was going well, after a night spent in false starts when every color seemed to turn to mud. He sat down in his chair and contemplated the canvas. More than half finished now, probably. Another hour or two will do it. He might send this one to the Tucson gallery the next time they have a show. Better get off a letter. According to *Art in America* this was what was being done in the East, it should cause some notice. The yellow was really great, but the green—the not-green of the desert—hadn't worked yet. But it would. A little sleep, say until noon, and then it would come. He bent forward to rub his tired feet. He brought one foot up onto the edge of the chair and picked out a black patch from under a toenail. Reaching a paint knife from the table he wiped it on a cloth and dug it under his toenails, working from one to another on that foot and then on the other foot. He tossed the knife back on the table and stretched.

In the bathroom he stood beside the bowl to urinate so

199

that by leaning his head back he could inspect his face in the mirror. Probably he should do a self-portrait. Twenty-five years from now he would wish he had, but they really weren't being done much any more. A three-quarter would be best to bring out the straightness of nose. He shook himself meditatively and lifted one foot to wipe away a wet drop from the instep against the calf of the opposite leg. A full-length, life-size might be interesting.

He opened the refrigerator door in the kitchen, then closed it again. He wasn't hungry. All those cigarettes and coffee. He should probably cut down.

He wandered into the bedroom and switched on the window cooler and stood before it a minute lifting first one then the other arm, letting the air blow onto his shirt to cool it and dry the sweat. He sat on the edge of the bed and ran his tongue over his teeth, wondering how bad his mouth would taste when he woke up if he didn't brush his teeth now. He lay back on the pillow. Then he sat up abruptly. Jesus Christ: Anna. He reached across the bed to the night stand to pick up his watch. Six-thirty only. Well shit, they wouldn't let him in now, anyway. She'd be asleep, what with all the drugs they give now. She was okay. They would have phoned otherwise. He replaced the watch on the stand and stretched out in the center of the bed. That painting might be worth three, three-fifty if the gallery hung it first.

Thirteen

As the tolling bells of the Catholic church set up their dissonance against the electric chimes of the Baptists' "Leaning on the Everlasting Arms," at eleven o'clock, Mc-Carron crossed the park hurriedly to Tigerstooth's single taxi, parked still at that time of the day on the west side. Later, after twelve, it would be found on the east side, the driver Tom Yellowhair having devised a system for keeping the cab in the shade except for the hour when the sun was exactly overhead so that nothing cast a shadow. McCarron let himself into the taxi, then looked back toward the hospital half expecting to see nurses, like frantic white sylphs, flowing over the grass toward him. He shook Tom awake and settled back into the oven heat. McCarron did not know where his own car was. Probably it was still at the Landing. Well, he could get it tonight.

Ten minutes later he unlocked the door and let himself into his cell. He immediately felt better in the familiar little room. It was cooler there, for one thing, being on the north side of the original old adobe and stucco building. And for another, there were his things as he had left them a long time ago. A long time? He smiled. A day isn't so long, except when everything is rushing in on you and past you and things you hadn't counted on sweep you up, a day can seem like half a life. There was the battered wooden desk with its narrow center drawer and its three side drawers saved from destruction by himself nearly ten years ago—snatched from the junk pile when the new steel furniture replaced it. The old swivel chair with the comfortable seat, missing its casters. The hot plate, still enough coffee in the glass pot for today, the sofa pillows, the small clutter of things on his desk. McCarron touched the desk.

He first thought he might cross to the gym and shower—he must stink, after a day and night of sweating in sun and nightmare. He imagined what it would be like to turn on all seven of the showers in a splashing row and run from one to another of them. But that would mean walking clear across the asphalt in the sun to the gym. And then back. Instead, he approached the window and was soothed to see, below him, the green- or brown-roofed yellow houses and out there between the bands of green, the glassy river. All of it, the town, the river, the hills, dazzled in the heat.

McCarron laughed. Old Paler will ruff up his feathers like a mad rooster when they tell him. They're phoning him right now, but they won't get him. Nobody has ever seen him on Sunday afternoon. I was his prize catch there for a while. *Jesus.* All that mumbo-jumbo this morning. I'm studying your case, Peter. Emotional tension, Peter. Neurasthenia, Peter. Long rest, Peter. Paler, I have shit—shat?—on your plans.

McCarron sat at his desk happily. Might as well compose tomorrow's bulletin and save the secretary some time. Besides, she just lists the announcements—no snap to it, no style. He drew a wire basket to him from which he sorted out the scraps of paper with notes on them written by himself, the vice-principal (fool!) or the teachers. A good, clear set of announcements, especially on Monday, dittoed and read over the p.a. system, made things run smoother the whole week. That was something else they'd neglected to point out in education college. He arranged the scraps in order of importance before he began to write. That was critical. You get their attention at the first, maybe, but it doesn't last long. He had tried to get the teachers to co-operate, to *make* the kids listen when announcements were read, but you just can't convince everybody.

1. The pep assembly scheduled for nine-thirty Friday has been changed to ten o'clock. We will follow Assembly Schedule D (teachers see Handbook, p. 8-9). Pep Squad, Cheerleaders, Song Leaders, Band, and Team are to be excused at nine forty-five in order to change. Immediately following the assembly, we will move to the parking area and send our Tiger's off to victory!

2. Any student, other than Pep Squad, Cheerleaders, Song Leaders and Band, who plans to drive their own cars to Barstow for the game is required to bring a written note from home in order to be excused at one o'clock. Remember, you are going as representatives of Tigerstooth Union High School and are expected to act accordingly. Your cooperation will be appreciated.

3. Football practice will begin at 3:30 this week instead of 4:30 for varsity and jv team's.

McCarron slipped that one in. Dann can stuff it. They're going to have to practice a hell of a lot harder if they intend to beat Barstow.

4. Students who drive cars or other motorized vehicles onto the school grounds are reminded that they

must be registered with the vice-principal. Please do not park on the south side of Calle de Jardin. Our neighbors there have complained again that their driveways are often blocked by student vehicles. If we are to continue having fine community-school relations, we must respect private property of others. We know you will want to cooperate in this.

5. Junior Red Cross members will begin collecting donations Friday. The class that gives most will win a placque for their room. All rooms with a hundred percent will be given a sticker for their doors. At times like this, it behooves us to search our hearts—and our pockets!—deeply, in order that we may share with those less fortunate than us. Our winning motto for the Drive this year was submitted by Rose Hume. It's a good one: Think High, Dip Deep, That Others May Warmly Sleep. Congratulations, Rose.

6. It has been brought to our attention that smoking is going on in the restrooms. You are reminded that in this state it is against the law, and Board policy, for minors to possess cigarettes or to smoke them on school property. Offenders will be dealt with severely.

7. Juniors may vote any day this week for their choice of class rings. The rings, and prices, are on display in the trophy case across from the nurse's office. The ring having the highest number of votes will be chosen.

8. Any senior interested in scholarships for next year should see the counselor. Also he has information about other matters of interest.

9. The biology field trip to the Desert Museum, scheduled for Friday, has been postponed, due to the game.

10. Menu for today:

Potatoes with Meat Gravy

Jello Salad

Mixed Garden Vegetables

Bread & Butter
Choice of Milk or Iced Tea
Fruit Delight
and
Peanut Butter Cookie

There. McCarron sat back from his writing. A good, clean set of announcements. Let the theorists theorize. What kept a school going right down the tracks wasn't fancy talk and experiment. It was a clear voice coming down, through proper channels, from the administration. A lot of administrators never paid any attention to details, that was their trouble. They didn't show up at extracurricular events, for instance, where the real pulse of a school throbs. Or else they provided hardly any extracurricular activities at all, which is really asking for it, especially in a town like Tigerstooth where there isn't anything for the kids to do at night but go down to the river and flop around under the willows. Happy kids make a happy school. It keeps the dropout problem down. Then, when they're eighteen and graduated, they can go to work for the railroad and raise hell all up and down the line—that's somebody else's problem.

McCarron began the second section of announcements, those to the teachers. But he did not get far.

1. Cafeteria supervisors for this week are: Mr. Jonah, Mr. Dobbs, Mrs. Deek,—

Mrs. Deek. Angela Morton Deek. Shit. McCarron sat back in his chair and threw his pencil down on the papers. He hadn't thought about any of them since early morning. He felt suddenly heavy about the stomach, and despite himself, the five faces spread across his mind like the pictures in one of those old multiphotograph velvet frames, the kind

205

his mother kept on the piano runner. Well, that knocks it. When things are going smooth, it's funny how some god-damn random thought jumps in to foul up the works.

He scraped back his chair and went to the window. There it was, her house, sitting down there like some toadstool in the forest. The little house, the only white one in a cluster of yellow, with its one window on either side of the door, looked benign and animated in the heat shimmers. Staring at it from this distance, one could almost imagine a Walt Disney face, The Little House That Could.

There was no sign of anything moving in the town, so far as McCarron could tell. The ragged tamaracks drooped in back yards. No automobiles moved on the parts of streets he could see. Over in the railroad yards not even any cars were being switched. The people who had gone to church were home, the women padding about in their slips and stockings trying to get together a cold lunch, the men sitting in their shorts reading football scores in the Sunday paper (not *The Tigerstooth Voice,* that came out on Thursday; *The Los Angeles Times* or *The Phoenix Republic*). The rest were all at the river drinking beer at the Landing or on picnic blankets, watching the endless blatant boats smack up and down on the water pulling their burdens of skiers. Under certain of the willows, doubtless, boys and girls attempted romance through clammy bathing suits.

There is nothing more completely, starkly alone than a desert town in the heat of a Sunday afternoon. It is then that it looks at once most outrageous and most cowed. It is then above all times that the desert looks most ravished and diseased as if this, the town, has burst up like a putrescent sore without life of its own but fed, nevertheless, by internal pods that open soundlessly. McCarron drew a deep breath. He felt very alone, too, as if he and the town, like the last two half-alive remnants of a civilization lost from the trail, had suddenly come face to face, neither recognizing the other, each too exhausted to fight.

He looked again at the white house. This time he saw someone in the back yard, briefly, at the clothes line. He smiled. It was like a signal, the brief sight of someone moving, the red thing left on the clothes line.

By the time he had reached his desk again, he had the shirt off, holding it up for inspection. Pretty bad. Dirt on the collar and cuff ends. Yellow circles under the arms. He ran his hand over his face. Still holding the shirt in one hand he dug into his desk drawer and pulled out a plastic shaving kit. Without closing the cell door behind him, he passed through his public office and out the side door, then headed across the asphalt to the gymnasium.

First he washed the shirt in the coach's lavatory, and dragging a chair behind him, he went outside and hung the shirt on the chair back in the sun. It would be dry before he was through with his shower. He took a sensible shower, using only one of the seven, after he had shaved. He luxuriated in the soap and the good physical smells of the locker room. He held his belly in and worked up enough lather in the hairs of his chest to send a whole rolling sheet of it all the way down to his feet. Then he turned around and faced the spray and let it sting and wash away all the soap. Gradually he used more and more cold water until he couldn't stand it. He tiptoed out of the shower stall and across the locker room in the ridiculous knee-bent fashion of dripping athletes in search of a towel. He unclocked the linen closet and took out two towels with TUH lettered on them in blue. By the time he was dry he was humming a little to himself. In the supply room he stood naked, searching the shelves until he found the boxes of athletic supporters. He took one from its box and stepped into it, feeling with pleasure the snap of the wide elastic on his stomach and back. He sat on a bench to put on his shoes and socks. Should have thought to wash these socks, too.

When he was finished he brought the shirt and chair back inside. The shirt looked better, he thought. He slapped Old Spice on his face from a bottle in the coach's room and combed his hair, being careful to rake the front part down some before sweeping it to the side. He locked the gymnasium and walked back across the campus holding his arms out from his body to keep the perspiration from forming.

In his cell again McCarron put away his shaving kit and hummed a bit louder. He did not go back to the window. He wished he had his car, but he supposed the walk wouldn't hurt him any, all downhill, if he could just keep from sweating up too much.

He walked slowly, deliberately trying to find the correct pace that would set a balance between perspiration and evaporation. He hadn't thought of what he'd say. Probably he ought to have a bottle of wine or something, but there isn't any place between here and there to buy one. The principal ought to call on his teachers—faculty—more often. God, it's been five or six years since I stepped foot in one of their houses.

McCarron knocked. He practiced two or three smile versions trying to picture in a mental mirror which would be most youthful and engaging under the circumstances. Karen had always said he had a nice smile when he looked at her, but he wasn't at all certain he could find that one any more. He knew what she would say when she opened the door; Why, Mr. McCarron, she would say.

The door opened. "Why, Mr. McCarron!" Angela said. She stepped back and held open the door. "Come in," she said and laughed, running her fingertips into her blond hair over the temples. "What a surprise."

He closed the door after him. The room was almost dark. Blinded by the sun he could see nothing for several moments. He laughed nervously. "Just passing by," he said. "This looked like a good place to get in out of the sun. God, it's hot, isn't it?" He waited for his eyes to become accustomed to the change. "Can't hardly see a damn thing," he said. He laughed.

"Oh. Oh, here." She took his wrist and led him to a chair. "Here."

"Thanks."

"I like it dark, don't you?"

"Well, yes—"

"It keeps out some of the heat, I think. It's hot, isn't it. I mean, when does it start to cool off around here? Oh. Wait. You want something cold to drink? Wait. Just a minute." She rushed out of the room, her full skirt brushing his knees as she passed.

As he waited for her, McCarron began to see the objects in the room come clear. He found himself staring into the face of a tin Mexican mask on the wall opposite. It was a long and narrow face beneath an elaborate headdress. Around the round eye holes the tin had been cut in strips and curled back like eyelashes. It had a pyramid nose and a small mouth hole with thick, curled lips. From each ear hung a long loop, longer than the face itself.

She came back, butting the kitchen door with her hip. She carried a tray. "These are margaritas," she said. "They don't cool you off much but they make you forget about it." She pushed away some magazines from the table nearest him.

He wished he had a tall highball with ice cubes.

"You drink them right over the salt, see? There." She handed him the glass, holding it near the top so he could get at the stem. "Do you like guacamole?" He looked into the bowl of green mash she offered. "I happened to have this in the fridge. And crackers?" She held up another bowl. "Guacamole and margaritas do wonders," she said and laughed.

He dipped a cracker into the bowl. "Thanks. You didn't—"

"Here's to us," she said. She clicked her glass against his causing him to spill a few drops on his lap. He was concentrating on the cracker, turning it to keep the green stuff from oozing off. He tasted the drink. The salt and the tequila made his mouth pucker.

"Isn't it good?" she said. "I think they're marvelous. At home, my husband—he's Doctor Fred—Frederick—Deek, of Nashville, you know—and I always drink one margarita every evening before dinner. And in this heat they're better for you than martinis, don't you think? All that salt." She settled down at his feet with her wide skirt spread in a circle on the floor. Despite himself, his eyes followed the quick, flitted movement of her fingertips along the top of her peasant blouse. From his position above her he could just see the beginning of the cleavage when her hand went away.

"Come on," she laughed. "You have to get the first one down so you can enjoy the second." She reached up to his hand and tipped his glass so that he had to gulp quickly to keep the drink from sloshing down his shirt. "There. That's better."

She sank lower into her splayed skirt. She held her glass in both hands and sipped over the edge, her eyes on him. McCarron was trying to think of something to say. In this dark room her shoulders looked smooth and brown.

"Oh," she said suddenly. "Are you all right now?"

"What?"

"I mean yesterday."

"Oh, that." He grinned. "Sure, I'm all right. It was just a temporary—"

"Poor Anna. Wasn't that just awful? I mean, losing her baby and all that." She shuddered. "It was just awful. I couldn't help it, you know. She just decided to get out of the boat and ski. I couldn't help it." She dug the fingers of one hand into her curls.

"No, of course not," McCarron said.

"I just turned around and there she was, crashing down in the water. I got back to her as fast as I could." She was looking up at him with wide eyes.

This was making him nervous. "Now, now," he said. He was beginning to feel like a principal.

"But I couldn't get her up. I was yanking and yanking. What was I to do?" There were tears in her eyes.

He found himself patting her arm, not the bare shoulder, but at the place where the puffed sleeve was. "There, there," he said foolishly.

"Well," she said. "It's a good thing that boy got there when he did."

"Grantham?"

"Jake? No, I mean the Indian boy—you know—"

"Oh."

"He got there first. I guess he'd been watching. He got there long before Bill and Jake." She took a long sip from her glass. "You're not drinking your margarita," she said and shoved his hand again. She lifted the edge of her skirt and wiped at each eye once. She looked at the damp spots. She dropped the skirt.

McCarron drank while he thought of something to answer. "That boy's a good athlete," he said.

"Yes."

"I've seen him swim. He can go like the dickens, can't he."

"Yes." She stared at the floor. "Did you know I have a son?"

"No. Do you?"

"Yes. Like that. He's eighteen now." She frowned. "No. He'd be nineteen."

"Well. I didn't know that."

"Yes. He's beautiful. You know, strong, and his eyes—" Her voice drifted away.

McCarron sat back in his chair. He held up the glass and closing one eye, squinted through it. "So she lost the baby."

"That's what Bill—that's what I heard."

"I suppose she'll be all right?"

"Yes. I suppose so." Angela sighed. She rose up on her knees. "Guacamole?" she said and proffered the bowl.

He took the bowl from her and watched her rise, bending forward enough that the front edge of her blouse, heavy with embroidered red and orange flowers, swung away from her chest. She took his empty glass. She hobbled a bit when she walked toward the kitchen. McCarron continued to hold the bowl. God, how long's it been? He wondered if he could still go about it. He didn't know if he any longer had the mental agility to work things around right. He didn't want to make a fool of himself. It would be so easy if you could just come out and say it. *Jesus.* Forty-year-old people ought not have to court. There wasn't time. He dipped a cracker in the guacamole and left it standing there, one brown corner showing out of the green. He imagined what she would look like undressed. He saw a white-pink painting— Rubens? Titian? Jesus, I used to have those straight, mem-

orizing for hours so Karen . . . well, no matter. Giorgione?
—of a sweet-faced fat woman bathing one foot in a spring,
gazing directly out of the picture at him.

Angela bumped the kitchen door again and returned with
fresh drinks. "Now. This one will be easy." She sat on the
floor, seeming to telescope herself under the skirt. "Here,"
she said. "Why don't you sit down here?"

He laughed. "So I won't have so far to fall?" Pretty
feeble. He scooted himself off the front of his chair with
a show of agility, balancing the glass by its stem.

She giggled. Please, McCarron thought. Please. There's
nothing that turns it off so fast as giggling. "I have records,"
she said. "Would you like music?"

He touched her glass with his. He knew his face would
be sore if he didn't stop grinning. "No. Never mind."

"Mostly dance records," she went on. "I used to dance
a lot," she said.

"I was never too good."

"I used to dance a lot." She traced her finger along the
upper rim of her blouse. "Do you know Nashville?" she
asked.

"No. I've never—"

"I used to dance a lot in Nashville. Once I even danced
at Cheekwood. That's this gorgeous home up on a hill."

"Oh."

"Formal gardens. The most beautiful place in the world
to dance, in the back, where the porch looks out to this
fountain. It's a museum now, or something," she said. "All
the furry ladies go up there now for bridge luncheons." She
smiled. Then she looked back at him and saw him staring
at her chest.

"You don't want any more guacamole, do you?" she said.

213

When Anna Margaret awoke and saw Baker standing there again, his hands in his pockets, looking out the window from her hospital room, she thought for a moment that he hadn't really gone at all, that it was still early morning and she had only drifted back into sleep. Then she felt the heat of the room and saw the brilliant strips of sun in the Venetian blinds. She stretched cautiously.

"What time is it?"

Baker turned. "Hello, my lovely," he said. He looked better now. His blue shirt was clean, his brown pants whole. He had shaved.

"You look better, now," she said.

"So do you." He came to the edge of the bed. He touched the side of her face with the backs of his fingers and pulled away a strand of hair from her cheek. "Except you're hot. Want a drink?" He peered into the water pitcher and shook it to hear if there were ice cubes. On the outside of the plastic pitcher there were rivulets of moisture.

"No," she said. "What time is it?"

He set the pitcher down. "I don't know. Three o'clock about."

"Oh." She turned her head away from him toward the window. "It looks vicious out there."

"Yes."

"Does it ever stop?"

"The sun?"

"Yes."

He shrugged. He poured himself water from the pitcher into one of the scratched plastic glasses.

"I feel like a rat that's been driven into a corner," she said.

"Yes."

"Do you know what I mean? And he can't go in any direction because the heat has got him cornered."

214

"That's a good metaphor for this desert. The rat trap." Baker laughed. It was a short laugh, without mirth. He watched the bubbles rise in his glass of stale water.

"It's got him cornered and now the walls are going to move in and squash him. There isn't any place he can go. He has to just sit there and watch them come."

"Sounds like Edgar Allan Poe." Baker poured another glass of water. "Here. Have some of this awful water. No. Wait." He stood from the bedside. "I have a surprise for you. For us."

"Who else but you." She watched him as he poured most of each glass of water back into the pitcher and then unscrewed the flask cap and poured whisky into the glasses. "But it's not silver," she said.

"Sorry," he said. "Here." He handed her a glass.

"Medicinal?"

"Strictly."

They touched glasses, the plastic making a dull whack. The drink was warm.

Baker walked to the window. He lifted one of the slats and looked out. "You're overlooking the alternative," he said.

"What?"

"I said, Poe gave a choice."

"Oh. Yes." When she bent her head forward to drink, her long hair hung down on either side of her face. She sloshed the liquid in her glass. "How drunk do you suppose we can get on that—however much that is?"

"A half-pint. Not very."

"Pity. It would do wonders for this hospital." She swirled the whisky and water in the glass. "What do you see from the window?"

"Nothing."

"A penny?" she said.

"Not for these thoughts," he said. No, not for these. Not a million pennies. Not for these, the last of my treasures. How alike they look. And how like the day. Whenever I looked from my window he seemed to be watching, his brown face turned up with the blue, still water behind his head, his brown body on the white sand, toying with the wilting scarlet hibiscus blossom snatched from the banks of them bursting from the old hotel walls like rubies. That was a younger time, much younger, when I could bear rejection or its opposite, harder to bear, when five long nights and as many idyllic days lead toward, one knows, the sixth, the day the beach lies empty but for drifts of wood and a waddling pelican and all the rubies fail to burst. How like the day.

Baker did not hear her move until she stood beside him. The fingers of one hand touched his arm. Her other arm stretched, like his, to the window and lifted another of the slats. He did not move. He felt a tinge of anger come and pass over him like a hot movement of air. Then it went away. One does not keep for himself that which is no longer his.

"Is that Rudy? How long has he been out there?"

Baker shrugged. "Forever." Then he smiled, the lopsided, unhumorous smile. "I don't know. All day. All night."

"Who's he waiting for, you or me?" she said.

He did not answer, but he seemed to straighten a little, and to lift his chin. Anna Margaret watched him, curious. With his chin held up and in the diffused light, his face looked tighter and younger. The gray along the sides of his hair faded into the natural color. She let go the window blind and leaned both hands on his arm. "Help me back to bed."

He turned, startled. "My God, what are you doing out of bed?" With one arm around her waist he guided her.

When she was settled he looked toward the window once more through which no sun streamed now that all the slats were in place. "Should I go out there?" he said.

"No."

"Do you understand? About me, I mean?"

"Yes," she said.

He sat on the bed, near her feet, and faced her. "Then why shouldn't I?"

She told him, briefly, hurriedly, of the encounter in the willows—the later scene, the one with the boy. There was no need to tell of the first one. As she talked she saw the youthful tightness of his face sag. When she finished he did not say anything. He stepped to the night stand and slowly poured more whisky into each of their glasses. He handed her one. He held his own up in salute.

"*Félicitations. A la gagnante.*"

"Don't."

"Sorry."

"Do you remember you once told me that we can never mean as much to anyone else as we do to ourselves?"

"Yes," he said. "And you said that was a sad thing."

"I don't know if that's right or not. But Baker," she touched his hand, "leave the boy alone. This time listen to yourself."

"None of it ever works, does it, when it's put to test."

"It will be a sad thing."

"Do you care?" he said.

"Yes."

"We all have our private suicides." He smiled. "And our private abortions. Drink your drink. Any moment now, I suppose, one of those starched Amazons will barge in here to throw one of us out." He stood looking down at her. He held his glass in one hand, with the other he smoothed a corner of the sheet. "It's really too bad, you know," he said.

"I agree, but what is? And will you crank that gadget some? There. At the foot."

He bent to examine the crank. He began to turn it. "It's too bad. We could play Frederic Henry and Catherine Barkley. Our own farewell to arms."

"That's enough, thanks."

He folded down the handle. "It's the perfect chance. In reverse, of course. In transvestite, I suppose you could say."

"Would you row us up the Colorado until your hands bled? The way Frederic did for Catherine? Or would I have to do that?"

Baker laughed. "You're always so beautiful." He looked toward the window. He drank from the glass and sighed. He walked to the window.

"You're going to wear a path in the floor."

"You know, the Mojaves had the right idea in the first place. The simplest solution. When a boy showed signs, they just whomped out a ceremony, made him a dress, gave him a metate instead of a bow and arrows, and set him to grinding mesquite beans with the women. *Alyha,* they called him."

"Don't, Baker."

"The Yumas had a better word for it, though. *Kwerhame.* That comes close, doesn't it."

"Let it alone," she said.

"Lucky for gambling, the Mojaves said, and short of life. Idyllic." Baker turned toward her and smiled the cynical, lopsided smile. "And whores were called *kamaluik,* my beauty. But nobody cared. Have at it any way you like it, the Mojaves said."

"You make it all sound so sweet and clean—like a bath in acid. Couldn't we have another drink?"

He came back to take her glass. "This is the last of it and a good thing. You'd be swacked by supper time. Which, come to think of it, might improve the meal. What do they feed you, taglierini?"

"That's t-a-silent g, and so on? Yes."

He laughed. He handed her the glass and let his hand touch a moment against hers. He walked back to the window. "I wish he would leave."

"Why? I told you why he's there."

"It's not now I'm worried about. It's later. Knowing he is there when—as doubtless, the local ladies say—I come staggering out of the last bar at midnight." He pulled a cord. The Venetian blinds spread. The sun was beginning to slant deeper, losing some of its heat.

He turned back to her again. "And I might as well get started." He came to her bed. He touched her cheek and said, *"Zum letzenmal letz' es mich heut' mit des Lebewohles letzten Kuss."*

"Whatever that means."

"See you later, Kamaluik. It could have been lovely."

She smiled. "So long, Alyha."

When McCarron got the door unlocked he almost fell against his cell desk. He leaned there panting, his face red and bursting in sweat, with one hand over his breast. He thought in panic of heart failure. It happens to younger men. His throat was parched, but he couldn't close his mouth to swallow because of the gasps—and the grin that seemed to have locked itself onto his face. *Whoosh.* I shouldn't have run all the way up the hill in this heat, but Jesus. He flopped down in his chair and waited for his eyes to focus out of the black and red spots. *Whoosh.* Where are you going Peter? she had said, Stay and we'll have dinner, and they had laughed when he got his leg tangled in that damned little table and couldn't get his pants on, Would you like another drink now? she had offered, and he had got his shoes on the wrong feet. She wouldn't ever understand, there wasn't any sense in trying to explain, but, Jesus. But, Jesus. How long had it been, thank God for nature, and he'd got confused because she hadn't made any attempt to cover up those marvels and it wasn't until then he discovered he'd left the jockstrap on the floor kicked out of the way next to the guacamole but he couldn't undress again and start all over then. There was the cell to reach, she wouldn't understand, you can't hold your breath under water forever, can you? and you can't hold your thoughts forever either. McCarron leaned back in his chair and grinned. *Whoosh.* He thought of a ballet he'd seen somewhere where the guy in his black-cased legs kept jumping up and whacking his heels together, a silly thing to do, he'd thought then, but he thought now he understood. If he had his breath, he'd try it.

When the spots were gone from his eyes, and his breathing had settled, McCarron stood up from his chair, and holding the edge of his desk, bent his knees tentatively. Still grinning, he walked around the tiny room running his fingertips over the walls, the bookcase, the desk.

McCarron was long asleep on the sofa pillows when the sun blazed red, which meant the weather might break, and went away beyond the undulating sand hills, leaving for a few minutes orange strokes in the jagged mountains that rose like tigers' teeth to the east, beyond the river where now men wiped at their boat motors with oily rags and women buttoned terry wrappers over their fat thighs and gathered checkered cloths into picnic hampers, where sun-burned boys, their eyes maniacally blue against their skin, drifted from one another, hunting, remembering suddenly that a night must not go by untested, that despite school tomorrow, there might indeed be a willing girl to huddle with, at least until the coyotes begin their lamentations in the very dark.

McCarron smiled often in his sleep that night, even when, near morning, the nuns whirled round in their station wagon like a multiple dervish, angry this time, scowling at him through rimless glasses, wagging their forefingers, shaking their veils.

Fourteen

T HEY found his body the next morning. It was a
brakeman, cutting across the park to the depot along one
of the fanning walks, who saw him and knew because of the
slits and red-blotched tears in the shirt that he was dead and
ran back across the park to the drugstore to tell it, first to
Mr. Fannin, just setting out the newspaper rack, and then
over the phone to the police. The brakeman hadn't been the
first to see the body, but he never knew that. A half-hour
before, when the sun first glazed the park, it struck the faces
of two young Indian men and awoke them from where they
had been overcome by the seductive lawn during the night
when, having traveled this far toward home from their shift
at the ice plant in company with a half-gallon of wine, they
sat here to rest and drink and, as they imagined would
happen, to sleep. As the sun woke them they turned puff-
rimmed black eyes on one another and sat up. One scratched
a bite on his heavy, powdered-chocolate arm, watching the
second inspect the empty bottle. They yawned, and without
speaking rose by getting first on all fours, then straighten-
ing. At the base of the cannon they kicked at the white man
to move him. One of the men had already begun to urinate

on the cannon wheel before, looking back at the body, he realized that by turning it over as they kicked it, they had exposed a whole expanse of hacked, jagged wounds, that what at first they took to be dirt and mud was in fact clotted, dry blood. Blue flies do not swarm on mud.

Despite their wined senses, those parts of their minds that sense self-preservation—inherited through millenniums of fighting culture and a hundred years of white man's cunning—locked into place for the time it took to kick the body over again and to walk out of the park and cut over the tracks toward the village. Nor would the day be an easy one even then, spent on the river bank where it would be quick to slip into the great marsh bed of tules that clogged the inlet for a quarter of a mile—should police or sheriff cars come dusting along the fence and in through the village gates. They had been told in school, but had no reason to believe, the old one about guilt and innocence.

So it was the brakeman who got to tell it, who shouted it into the phone in a rush and then was able, by running, to get back across the street and nearly to the cannon before the druggist. And it was they together who, by waving and calling to the old men come out for their papers and the trainmen going to work, got enough of a crowd together before the police arrived for the brakeman to tell it two or three times more. "I come around this corner, right here, see? right along here, I don't know what made me do it I don't never come this way and there 'e was layin' there just like that, I never touched him—that's the first thing they tell you, never touch nothing—and I could tell 'e was dead, anybody could see that, so I run over to Fannin's and called and then got back here didn't I Mister Fannin—and I tell you I nearly shit when I come around that edge and seen him layin' there. I seen him first, I guess."

And the others, You done the right thing, that's for sure, and Who the hell is he? and Look at the fuckin' blood, and Christ, somebody sure must've had it in for him, and How long agoja find him, Joey?

When the two police cars got there and the four of them ran into the center of the park, their round paunches swung below wide tooled-leather belts, the first action they took was to grab the body by one arm and fling it over, face up. The small crowd moved in, then fell back. One side of the ripped shirt stuck to the ground so that when they turned over the body the whole front was bare. The brakeman, preparing to tell his story again to official ears, turned pale. One of the old men, grown with the railroad when no accident was too hideous to expect, was the first to speak. "Looky there. Them's his fuckin' guts. His entrails, them blue-like things," and he touched them with the toe of his shoe. The brakeman was sick, suddenly, on the other side of the cannon. When the policeman dropped his arm, the body rolled half over again, on its side, and seemed to sink into itself and become skinny and gaunt, one hip pointing up sharply, the legs a little bent at the knees.

In her room in the hospital, Anna Margaret had been lying awake before she began to hear the dim shouts. When the sirens came she went to the window. In the center of the park, by the cannon, she saw the crowd, a dozen or two dozen—being constantly filled at its edges by running boys and men—and without knowing why they gathered, her stomach turned. She rang for a nurse, jabbing the button by her bed again and again. Then she saw that the nurses were gathered on the front steps of the hospital watching an orderly run over the grass toward the crowd, his white pants flicking like shears. When he came back, he held out his hands to the nurses and shrugged. He shook his head.

224

He stopped at the bottom of the three steps, in front of the women, and turned, as they were, to face the park.

Anna Margaret yanked at the cord of the blinds until they rattled up out of the way. She opened the window and called. Finally the nurses turned and located her in the window. One of them broke from the bunch and ran into the building. Anna Margaret was waiting for her when, after what seemed a long time, she rushed into the room scolding.

"You! What are you doing out of bed? You mustn't be up yet."

"Who is it?"

"What?"

"I said who is it? Out there." She held to the foot rail of the bed.

"Never mind, now. You have no business out of bed. Come." She took her arm. "Doctor will be angry. Don't you know you can cause complications—"

Anna Margaret threw off the nurse's hands. "Tell me who that is out there—what has happened!"

"Now listen, young lady—"

"Tell me." Her voice was quiet and when coupled with the look in her eyes it was enough to make the nurse answer.

"A man's been killed," she said. "That's all I know. Now come." She held out her hand to guide Anna Margaret.

"A man?"

"Yes. That's what the orderly said."

"Didn't he say who it was?" She moved to the side of her bed and sat on it.

"No. He didn't know. There, that's better." The nurse pushed her down onto the pillow and spread up the top sheet. "Rest now. It will soon be breakfast."

"Will you find out for me? Please?"

225

"You're a patient, you know. You shouldn't get upset." She fluffed the pillow and inspected the pitcher. "But I'll find out for you."

The nurse went to the window to close it and adjust the blinds. She stopped to watch the activity. "They're bringing him across in the stretcher now to the hearse."

Anna Margaret sat up. "Can you see him? What's he like?"

"Well, hard to tell from here." She leaned forward, her hands on the sill. "Wearing a blue shirt and brown pants. About all I can tell. Looks tall and thin. Middle-aged. There. They're putting him in now. Wonder how it happened, don't you?" She finished closing the window and let down the blinds. "You still want me to find out?"

"No. Never mind, now," she said.

"Okay, honey. You lie quiet." The nurse went out.

So. He had come back into the little park the way he feared he would, drawn into the deadly center of the web at last to be mutilated and butchered like the butterfly who, insane at the sight of a flower, traps himself in the garden spider's intricate tracery.

Reba Hampton had seen the men running and had watched the crowd tighten down there in the park, but it was too far away for her to see much, the hotel being a full block away. She wished she knew at least something because there wasn't much sense in phoning otherwise. There wasn't anyone in the lobby to send—no one at all, in fact, until she saw Bill Dann coming down the stairs, dressed, ready for his breakfast. She clutched at her throat and intercepted him.

So it was Bill Dann who first said "His name's Baker Steinhart" to the policemen, but they only eyed him briefly and said they knew that, Yeah, the others said, everybody knows that, I seen him just last night at the River Street or was it the Kutkilya? Bastard drunk, anyhow, I know that, and everyone laughed a little and felt well enough to ask the question that they knew there wasn't any answer for yet, Who done it, d'ya think?

And so it was Bill Dann reporting that gave Reba Hampton her sense of direction and caused her first to phone McCarron's home, then his office.

When the phone began ringing in the outer office Mc-Carron had been lying on the sofa pillows, his hands behind his head, softly watching the sun moats stream above him and spread on the desk. He had carefully kept himself half asleep so that the pleasing thoughts that had accompanied him through a long, good night continued to drift and re-appear. He could not imagine that the day—the days—would be otherwise than perfect. He was young again and virile. She was good, no denying that, she knew how to do it, and who wouldn't be a little nutty? God knew he could understand that. That would be part of the good thing about it, it would shape them both up. He wondered if he could keep from grinning like a sap all day and what he would say to her, and she to him, when they met today in the halls or the office or the cafeteria.

He heard the phone ring twice or three times before he turned his head toward the door, expecting to hear the secretary's voice. Even when he remembered it was too early for the secretary to be there, he let it ring on until it rang the tenth or eleventh time. He rolled off the pillows and caught finally by the persistence of it, ran into the outer office reaching for it before it could ring again.

He recognized Reba Hampton's voice but had no time past Hello before the sweep of her first telling of it raked his ear and mind. Killed in the park, Last night, Terrible, terrible, One of our teachers, Peter, how could it have happened? Will there be school? Can I help? and on and on until he believed he would scream if she did not stop but he was no longer hearing words; instead, he saw and heard the soundless crash of a glittering gold castle that disintegrated as he watched himself watch, leaving clouds of yellow dust puffing like fog where it had stood.

He sat at the smooth metal desk holding his head in one hand, the phone in the other, waiting for the sound to stop. Then he said, "I understand, Reba. Yes, yes, terrible. Will you call the radio station? No, there can't be school today."

He was sitting there still, a half-hour later, with his head in his hands, trying to will away the pain from his stomach, when someone from the police department called. Did he know where Steinhart came from? Whom should they notify? No, no permanent address in his file. There were names of some schools where he formerly taught, they could try those. And Yale. He went to Yale fifteen, twenty years ago. They could try that. They would. Was that in New York or where?

As the morning grew in the park, so did the crowd. The brakeman, disappointed that he had not been subpoenaed from his job, waved solemnly from atop his caboose as the freight train pulled away, stretching his neck to see over into the park and to be seen. No one waved back. The druggist had returned to his counters across the street and phoned for more ice cream and for the girl who helped on Saturdays to come in as soon as she could. The telling was left at first to the old men until no one listened and they drifted over for coffee arguing among themselves about which of them had been first to know and about which way the body had faced, north or south, before the hearse came

228

to take it away. Women left the breakfast dishes soaking
in soapy water to gather in hushed groups at the edge of the
park, now and then walking in twos to the cannon and back.
Someone from the depot had thought to send over a janitor
with a bucket of disinfectant water and a stiff broom to get
rid of the flies that glistened like moving jewels on spots in
the grass and buzzed at the urine on the cannon wheel. Atop
the cannon two boys sat in their fourth-graders' overalls,
one pointing out the place to those his age or older who
came late, the other straddling the barrel trying to peer
into its mouth for hidden clues. The men who on an ordinary Monday would by now be counting change into cash
drawers or cleaning glass counters or setting velvet cards
of rings and watches into windows were gathered with their
arms folded across their white shirt fronts in a semicircle,
talking some, looking down at the place in the grass. Teen-
age boys moved in and out of the bright clots of girls
restlessly, touching them sometimes, testing. The girls, for
their part, wished they had known earlier, early enough to
have dressed in shorts. Here and there at the edges of the
paths and on either side of the drugstore doors, silent, heavy
Mojave women appeared with beaded belts and purses and
necklaces to spread out on newspapers. They sat with their
legs out before them, crossed at the ankles. They did not
lift their eyes from their working fingers except now and
again when the fingers reached to brush back a strand of
straight gray hair into the mass that hung down the back
of their flowered shawls.

Those who did not watch the place by the cannon watched
the front entrance of the City Hall, opposite the depot,
where the police department was and where right now they
and the coroner and Judge Tobin must be finding out why it
was done and who did it. Part way up the steps, to the side,

229

Bill Dann sat with his chin propped in his hands watching Jake Grantham, a step lower, sketching in expert charcoal strokes the scene before them.

So it was that likely no one saw Angela Morton Deek hurrying along the edge of the hospital and into it. Not that it would have mattered if they had. The two or three nurses taking their break at the front steps moved aside for her to pass but could not have said a minute later that she had. The receptionist had to think a moment and then turn to her file even to remember the room number when Angela asked for it.

Anna Margaret was seated in a chair by the window when she came in. Angela stood beside her for a minute, not speaking, bending down to see under the uplifted blind, bunching the cloth of her skirt in one hand.

"Oh, Anna," she said, her voice a rushed whisper, "isn't it awful?"

Anna Margaret turned to her then and was caught by the frantic blue look in the other woman's eyes, the wild gold curls, the deep pores of her skin shadowed like scars by the strong light. "Yes," she said. She looked again at the crowds in the little park. "Yes," she said. From the corner of her eye she saw the twisting hand.

Angela walked to the bed and touched the rail. She came back to the window. "Have you heard—do they know who —you know—who killed him?"

"No. I don't know. Calm down, Angie."

"Oh, I'm all right. Upset. Naturally, I'm upset."

"Sit on the bed, if you like."

Angela looked at the bed. She said, "No. Who do you think killed him, Anna?"

She answered quietly, "He did it himself."

Angela's fingers stopped twisting the skirt. They went

230

up to the top of her blouse. "Himself? But I thought—but I thought—I heard he was all— But how could he?"

"Oh, never mind, Angie. I don't mean that. I don't mean it that way."

Angela looked out the window again, over Anna Margaret's shoulder. "You could have seen it from this window. Didn't you see anything? Or hear anything? Did you?"

Anna Margaret turned. "What's the matter with you?"

"Nothing. Nothing." She walked to the bed. "You didn't see anything?"

"God, Angela. No, I didn't see it or hear it." She got up from the chair. "But I know who did it."

"How do you know?"

"I just do. I think I do."

Angela came close to her. Her voice was quieter but with an edge as hard as metal. "Who was it?" she said.

"Angela, what does it matter? He's dead. He's out of it."

"Tell me."

"Besides, maybe I'm wrong. And it wouldn't matter. It wouldn't make any difference."

"God *damn* you. Tell me!" Angela ran her fingers through the gold curls. Then she sat on the bed and bunched and smoothed the red and yellow skirt. "All right," she said. "All right, I'm sorry." She breathed calmly. "All right. But I have to know."

"Why, Angela? If they find out, well, they find out. Otherwise, what I think won't help Baker."

Angela faced her. Her blue eyes were calmer. "Do you think it was Rudy Yhazi?" She said it simply.

Anna Margaret frowned. Then she said, "Yes."

"I thought you might—somehow—have figured that. He said you—"

"He? He, Angela? What do you mean?"

231

"Are you going to tell?" Angela watched the other woman's eyes.

"How do you know this? What do you mean *he?*"

"Are you going to tell!"

Anna Margaret walked to the window. She turned back to face Angela. "I don't know."

"Because if you are, let me tell you something—some things. Anna Margaret, you can't, you must not. What good would it do? You say that yourself, what would it matter now, to Baker—but it will matter to you and—to me."

"I don't understand you, Angela. Why are you crying? And, my God, how could it make any difference to us?"

"Just listen, then, and I'll tell you. He said you might know—might have figured it out—"

"*He* again? Do you mean Rudy? Have you seen him?"

"Yes. Yes!" Angela stood from the bed. "Yes, goddamn you, yes! Yes yes yes yes!"

"Don't scream."

"Yes, I've seen him! He is at my house now. He's been there since—since, oh, I don't know. Since midnight."

"Instead of coming here why didn't you go to the police? Angela, what is the matter?"

"Shut up. Just shut up. I'm trying to tell you. I came here to find out if you knew—because, if you did, I had to make you understand, you cannot tell."

"All right, I'm listening. Tell me."

"He said if you knew and I did not make you be quiet he would tell everything." Angela shrugged. "First about—about—well, him and me."

"My God."

"Is that a surprise? Well, that's just the beginning. He knows about you, too. About you and Bill—the other day when—the day at the river."

"Yes. I'm not afraid of that."

"I didn't think so. Anna, Anna. Well, there's more. Do you know where I came from? Right before here, I mean? Before Tigerstooth?"

"No, of course not."

"He knows. I told him that, too, one night. Don't you see? I have a son like that, those beautiful eyes— Well. They don't know where I am," she laughed. "And they're not going to find out. Not unless he tells them—not unless you tell."

"Angela, be calm. I don't understand."

"See if you understand this, then. You ought to. You're as much a whore as the rest of us. I was in a place—an institution, you could say. And you know why, Miss Anna?" She laughed and ran the tips of her fingers into her hair. "Can you guess why?"

Anna Margaret shook her head. "Do you mean—your son?"

"Yes! My own son." She laughed. "How do you like that? How the hell do you like that!"

Anna Margaret turned back to the window. She leaned her hands on the sill and watched the people milling in the park, getting restless now in the heat, now that nothing new had happened, that no word had come down the white steps from the police. In their center the black cannon still pointed awry, shed now of its riders who had moved out into the crowd in search of someone who would give them a nickel or a dime to spend for ice cream in Fannin's drugstore. She listened until Angela's crying quieted. Then she said, "You'd better go. Here come Jake and Bill."

By three o'clock that afternoon there was no one left of the crowd in the park, the last of them having drifted away

233

to the drugstore or home or to work, quietly cursing the inefficiency of the police; In any other goddamn place they'd've caught him by now, and Yeah, and They oughta let us know if we're in danger, Jesus, I got a wife and kids. The Mojave women moved their wares around to the north side of the depot, the side in the shade where the four o'clock train from Los Angeles stopped, sometimes long enough for people to get off and stretch their legs in the park or take pictures or buy beaded purses.

McCarron's stomach hurt badly. He sat at his desk staring out his window seeing and not seeing the far jagged hills floating gray beyond the green-edged river. The school would be closed another day, until after the funeral, and maybe by then he could be ready for it. There were things he could be doing now, there was a substitute to be found for Steinhart, and his personal things to be cleared out of his room and sent where no one knew yet, there had been no luck tracing a family.

McCarron had not left his cell that day at all except to phone once and once for twenty minutes to walk down the hill and back. He had called and she would not talk, he had gone down there but she would not let him in. He did not understand that. He did not understand why after yesterday she refused him or why after yesterday's beauty, today's pain. It was not fair, he knew that; there should be rules a person could depend on and follow.

Well, I might have known. Those were the two from the beginning I knew would give me trouble. What else could I have done? Those were what they sent me but, *Jesus,* I've been at this long enough to know.

Fifteen

The interment of Baker Steinhart was accomplished the following morning. The decision was announced by radio late the night of the first telling and repeatedly early next morning—a decision reached by the officials who held that in their opinion nothing further could be gained by keeping the body, confirmed by the mortician who pointed out the additional expense the county stood to spare by quick disposal making embalming unnecessary—and the law could be stretched by six or eight hours—especially considering the amount of delicate work needed before the steps of embalming could proceed, and considering, further, that the wooden casket furnished in the county package, when used for an embalmed case, was something like setting an emerald in brass.

There was no church service. It hardly seemed reasonable under the violent and perplexing circumstances. Besides, Steinhart was a Jewish name wasn't it? and it would be like taking a needless chance, it seemed, running the risk of confusing the entrance of his soul into Heaven, or wherever—Valhalla, Mrs. Marspack thought it was. At any rate, the Catholic priest certainly wasn't interested, nor the Baptist

235

preacher, who pointed out that he would have to lay off a day from the railroad in order to do it. The job of the graveside words fell at last to the Methodist minister, the same small gray man who had a few weeks ago welcomed Tigerstooth's new teachers to their first plates of taglierini.

The Tigerstooth cemetery lies atop a sand rise, East Mesa it—the hill—is called, beside the road that leads away from the town to the east, the road that in a while crosses high over the river on the silver bridge. Rio Vista, the cemetery itself is called in black wrought iron letters over the gate. And it is. From there can be seen the river bending wide and lovely and flat, spreading out in myriad inlets and coves that catch blue sometimes in the light, made more blue because of the deep banks of green reeds. It is from here that in parked cars at night the yellow lanterns of catfishermen can be seen down there among the coves like fireflies. On the other side of town, up river, a mile or two beyond Miller's Landing, another mesa rises over an equally breathless view. There the town's garbage is burned.

At ten, then, when the black hearse came and stopped and glistened at the gate of the cemetery, and the volunteer pall bearers—three off-duty trainmen, a deputy sheriff, a policeman, a young man from the mortuary—had slid the casket out on the chrome rollers, the people followed it in through the gate and over to the far side where brown heaps of clay and caliche marked the new place. Back a way, under the feeble shade of a mesquite, two Mojave grave diggers sat watching, their shovels resting out from their laps like oars. The people were not many, of course. Burials are not very interesting matters.

Anna Margaret walked between Jake and Bill, leaning on Bill's arm. He watched her as they walked down and across the rows. Now and then he looked over her head

236

toward Jake who carried the canvas chair and was squinting at the brown-green weeds and the white markers. Doctor Paler had tried earlier to make him listen to the reason she would have none of, when he came in the black-lacquered car to get her. In a final rage the doctor brushed the tips of his fingers over his gray temples and said, "You are a fool and an idiot. I wash my hands" and he held them up, palms inward, as if ready for the gloves "of all responsibility in this case." "Maybe you should have stayed," Jake said while he watched her dress at home. "You don't look good." "Don't I?" she answered.

When the casket was in place, resting, rocking a little on the apparatus that would in a while let it down into the grave with a tiny clicking, the minister stepped to the head of it and the others, the dozen, gathered nearer. A small clod of dirt toppled down the sloped earth and rolled against Anna Margaret's shoe. In the high lush meadows poppies and blue lupin covered, in a season, any scar of ground untended. No one had thought to send flowers.

> Remember now thy Creator in the days of thy youth, while the evil days come not, nor the years draw nigh, when thou shalt say, I have no pleasure in them;

From the other side of the grave, Angela's eyes watched hers; still, frantic eyes beneath the gold curls held down this day by a black mantilla.

> While the sun, or the light, or the moon, or the stars, be not darkened, nor the clouds return after the rain:

Eyes that held in their look defiance and deep pleading. Her hands twisted gently in the lace that came together over her breasts.

> And the doors shall be shut in the streets, when

the sound of the grinding is low, and he shall rise
up at the voice of the bird, and all the daughters
of musick shall be brought low;

Near Angela, to the side, a little back, the wide black-edged eyes of the half-Indian boy watched also across the gray casket. Such beautiful eyes. Warm and cold and brown. And the faint, pleasant smile that called you to corners.

And the almond tree shall flourish, and the grass-hopper shall be a burden, and desire shall fail: because man goeth to his long home, and the mourners go about the streets:

McCarron stood secreted in his own thoughts at another point along the grave, shivering in the sun and the remnant visits of a long night. From time to time his lifted eyes connected in the jacob's ladder of glances.

Or ever the silver cord be loosed, or the golden bowl be broken, or the pitcher be broken at the fountain, or the wheel broken at the cistern.

Bill Dann did not look up at all. From where he stood huge behind her, he looked down at Anna Margaret sitting in the canvas chair in his shadow and felt the sweat circling under his arms and desire rise.

Then shall the dust return to the earth as it was: and the spirit shall return unto God who gave it.

At the cemetery gate, when they had returned to it, Jake was the first to speak. "You and Bill wait a minute, okay? I want to sketch this while it's fresh." He dug from the collection of papers and books in the back seat a sketch pad. He stood for a minute flipping over pages. "Yes," he said. He turned back toward the gate.

They sat in the car waiting. Bill cracked the knuckles of his huge hands. He stared ahead at some spot down where the river was, or perhaps on the window glass. "Poor bastard," he said finally. "I'd like to get my hands on the guy that done that." He cracked his knuckles.

She turned to him. "Would you? Would you really if you knew?"

He blinked. "Well, hell yes. Jesus, somebody oughta have to pay. You can't just kill people."

"No. But if you knew—I mean really knew—what would you do?"

He looked at her. "Well Jesus, Anna."

"What would you do?"

"I'd sure as hell turn him in."

"No matter who it was?"

He smiled. "Not my own grandmother, maybe. Hell yes, I would." He lifted his shoulders then let them drop. "You can't just kill people."

"What if, when you do it, you screw up three or four other people? Yourself, for instance, and everybody else?"

Bill shook his head. The forelock of shaggy hair slid down over his eyes. "I don't know what you're talking about." He glanced over her shoulder toward the cemetery where, besides Jake, the two men from the mortuary still stood near the grave watching the apparatus. He let his glance slide back along Anna Margaret's hair and face. He looked again toward the river. "Did these other people have anything to do with the killing?"

"No. But the telling will blow up their lives. Who should decide that?"

"I don't know. Nobody should have to decide that." He frowned down at his big hands. "But you can't just kill people. Somebody has to pay."

"Yes."

"And it's not so great living with yourself any time. Ever."

"No," she said. "No, it isn't."

He took her hand from where it lay in her lap and covered it with his own on the seat between them. He seemed surprised that his so completely hid hers. "Anyway," he said, as if the word lifted away prior thoughts to make room for new ones.

She laughed. "Are you going to say, Anyway, tomorrow is another day?"

When he looked at her his eyes were blue, far back, like sightless eyes. "Yes," he said. "Something like it."

"Well," she said, "that much is certain." He frowned when she laughed. And then Jake came back to the car, springing on his toes the way he did when excited, fingering with his left hand the gold fraternity badge on his chest. She moved to the side to make room for him on the seat.

Jake flung the pad onto the rear seat. "Christ sake, it's hot, isn't it?" he said.

At about the moment the car moved away outside the low adobe wall that fronted the cemetery, the Mojave men drove the points of their shovels into the fresh soil and leaned on the handles. They watched until the mortician jerked on the brown cord that let the lid of the outer box down over the casket. One of the grave diggers tossed in the first shovelful of crumbly dirt. They both leaned over a little to watch it fall on the pine lid and spurt, rattling, dry, over the boards. Then together they settled into a rhythmic scooping that would, in a half-hour, end in a smooth mound that by noon would have dried in the sun enough to be unnoticeable in color from the other ground. By spring the sand would be settled by the wind, and the rain if it came, and the weeds that come up, grow, and repeat themselves without ever having been green. Perhaps, if it rains much,

240

the place will lie lower for a season than it had until the sand fills in. Perhaps the edges will be laced with small fissures. If the fissures slit deep, a coyote will some night run sniffing along those cracks. His howl will carry the misery of timeless famine.

Sixteen

TIGERSTOOTH is a railroad town. There are, it is true, three roads that lead from it besides the railroad and the river. But you know when you leave it by train that the town is a train town and that so it has always been. The passenger embarking is funneled into the arch of the great yellow giantess along one of the fanning walkways that lead first to, and circle, the black cannon and become one walkway into the arch—the center arch, the biggest one, the one that rises up above you as you enter under it until you have to look down. Your shoes ring on the Mexican tiles and the softest voice throws back so that you whisper and walk fast through it. On the other side the sun shows yellow in matching arches and slices blue along the tracks until the diesel engines come wailing with their silver-sided cars and cover the tracks.

On Thursdays, as on all other days, the earlier train stops in the late afternoon coming from the Coast for the few minutes it takes to change crews and sometimes to let off or take on one or two or three passengers. Those who get off still stand for a moment beyond the porter's reach, shocked by the wall of heat between them and the depot, just as their predecessors were in the old days.

This Thursday, Anna Margaret Grantham was one of the half-dozen to board the train at Tigerstooth. The Negro porter who had done this for so long that he could calculate the weight of an arm on his was surprised that she leaned so heavily for one so slight. Perhaps it was the way her hair hung straight beside her face, and her eyes, that stopped him from saying, "You all right?"

Through the window she could look directly out at the yellow station. By one of the arches, seated on the pavement with their legs out before them, two Mojave women slowly gathered into paper bags their displays of beaded belts and purses. Seated facing them, her long hair full and black down her back like theirs, a little girl watched. In the shadow of the center arch, Bill Dann stood with his hands in his pockets staring belligerently at her or the train, she did not know which.

Jake stood out in the sun looking up at her, his face perplexed still as it had been since last night when she told him she was leaving. Now and then he reached up to the nose piece of his glasses, then touched the fraternity badge. As he breathed, the sun glittered infinitesimally in the four chip diamonds at each corner of the badge.

He had not been angry—anger dissipates the senses—when she told him, but he had tried to sound so, and he had been, still was, perplexed.

"Christ sake, Anna," he had said. "You haven't even given this place a chance yet. It'll be fine in another month when it cools off some."

"It's not the heat, Jake," she answered. "That's not it at all."

"Well, what then? You said you never wanted to go back there, so why are you going?"

She did not answer that.

243

"Christ sake, I don't know. I don't know. What am I going to do with all this goddamn house?"

She had smiled then. "Bill can move in. That should be a blast."

He had thought about that a moment before answering. "That's a good idea," he said. "But, look. If it's the baby, well, okay. Fine. We'll start another one as soon as you can." He had grinned. "I'm ready whenever you are." He had bunched the front of his trousers in his hand.

"No," she said. "Oh, Jake, let's drop it." She had gone back to the packing of a suitcase.

"Well, frankly, if you want to know what I think, I think it's cowardly—going off like this just because I've had to start in this town." He sat on the bed and watched her pack.

She had stopped for a moment then. "Yes, cowardly is probably right. You don't know how right you may be."

He shook his head. "Jesus, you don't have anything to be afraid of."

"Don't I?"

"Is it because of Baker's getting killed? Christ sake, Anna. We all feel terrible about that, but my God. You're not afraid of our getting killed or something, too, are you?" He laughed. "You know how Baker was."

"Yes."

"Always running around town drunk. Insulting people. Look, I liked Baker, too. But, Christ sake, you know what he was looking for, running around at night, don't you? I mean, you're sophisticated enough to know that."

"He wasn't looking for anything more than the rest of us."

Jake had shook his head at that. His look was desolate. He had gone off, then, to the other bedroom—the studio—and left her to the packing.

244

Her night had been a sleepless one but for snatches on sofa or chair or flung over the bed, each time ending in jerk and abrupt waking. Once during the night, late, the wet oppression of the heat led her to the cool cement pillars of the front porch. The sky swung heavy, the glittered stars mostly blackened by the first gathering of clouds, the first of the false starts of autumn that would burn away by sunrise leaving no track of their coming. Up on the hill she saw the single, wan light in a window. She turned back into the house and through its rooms as a hundred times before during this night. The old house snapped and groaned. She pushed open the door to Jake's studio, and leaning against the jamb, watched him sleep stretched flat on his back on the floor, one arm crooked over his eyes, the other hand cupped loosely in his pants.

The painting—the one he would call "The Killing"—stood above him on its big easel, its half-achieved colors sadly bright and wet.

As she walked up the hill, turning as the street turned, she felt the weakness in her thighs and the nausea return that had skirted her for the past days. She did not see McCarron until she was herself nearly to the ragged darkness under the tamaracks that rose, misplaced and awkward, opposite Angela's little house just beginning to lighten with the sky. He stood there, not against the trees but in their darkness, slouched into himself. He faced across the street toward the house, but, Anna Margaret knew, he had known her coming. He did not shy back from her as she thought he might if ever he had to face her alone. He moved away a step but it was more as if he were making room for her under the branches.

"I did not expect to find anyone," she said lightly. Lightly, because the man's shoulders, whole body, hung heavy and

245

deep inside his clothes. And because, finding him there, a new strange weight hovered.

A tiny wind scudded under the tamaracks, rattling their dry fallen needles, and lifted his sparse hair and the tips of her long hair and passed, leaving a greater stillness.

Then he said, "Why?" and the word carried in it all question and fact and anguish. The word hung, and gradually, from among all its voices, she felt the new weight settle on her. She turned to him, startled, "Do you mean—Angela? You and Angela—" but he went on, then, as if she were overhearing a dream. "We would have been good. It would have helped," he said.

"Do you know?" she said. "Do you know who is over there?"

"Yes." He seemed to shudder, softly. "The boy." The boy, as if it were understood. She heard him shift his feet in the dry tamarack droppings. "It will be a bad time," he said.

"What will you do?"

She saw the heavy shoulders of his white shirt straighten. He said, "I will stop it." He turned to her then, for the first time, his face gray but softened like the light. "I can, you know. I am still in charge."

"Yes."

With the coming day behind them the jagged east mountains stood fiercely black on the other side of the river which would itself begin soon to catch light.

"I can stop it," he repeated. "This is not allowed, you know. That boy must be taught."

"No. I will end it," she said. "Give me until night. But be ready. She will need help then. God knows, we will all need help then."

He faced Angela's house again. "Will she?" he asked.

His voice lifted. "Will she? That's good," he said simply. "This time I'll be ready."

When the Santa Fe leaves Tigerstooth going east you can see River Street, or part of it—the upper stories of it —above the yellow, tin-roofed sheds that are outgrowths of the old depot. You can see the opened windows of the second floors where listless plissé curtains hang or stir sometimes when there is cause. Below those windows, down a flight, although they cannot be seen for the sheds, the neon signs above the four saloons have been on since noon. As the sun goes down the lights will grow surer.

If you look back part way and up you can see on the other side the town's highest dun hill, flattened on top, and the white Mexican-arched building that stands there. If the sun is right you will see it catch and flash on the windows of that building as the train moves.

And then in a few minutes, through the windows on the opposite side, you can see the cluster of green-topped white cottages of the Mojaves coming up in rows nearly to the tracks. From the grassless spaces between the rows a few children and maybe a dog will look toward the passing train. Beside one or two of the cottages you may see the dismantled husks of old cars.

Anna Margaret saw one of the Indian children wave. She unfolded the newspaper bought at the depot: *The Tigerstooth Voice* it read at the top in Old English letters. The headlines were thick. Over all the town the people would be paused in their work reading the first printed telling of it. Along the drugstore counter and the polished bar tops owners of papers would be reading aloud to clusters of others who held their coffee cups or glasses carefully and twisted their necks to see the paper. Reba Hampton would be read-

247

ing it over the telephone, the paper spread out flat before her on her desk.

When he came to the empty place beside her and sidled into it, she folded the paper and rested her head back against the seat. As she turned to face him she saw him, sitting straight, boyish, curious, looking at the other passengers, the conductor, the scenes sliding outside the windows, and she knew that of the thousands of trains he had seen and heard, he had never before entered one.

When he caught her watching him, he relaxed. His secret, faint smile spread and his black-lashed eyes were beautiful and deep and cold. His brown hand touched her wrist.

"Shh," she said. "It's a long ride."

It is almost a full night's ride after crossing over the green river before the tracks of the Santa Fe lift up to the plateaus of lush meadows where in another turn of seasons lupine and orange poppies will lie together so bright it will blind the eye.